One

FIRST OF ALL, LET ME JUST SAY: I AM NOT A WITCH. I KNOW there are a lot of rumors about me floating around, and trust me, I get it. People fear what they don't know, but people are also freaking idiots who refuse to even try looking beyond themselves. I'm sure if you actually stopped to talk to me instead of giving me the side-eye to which I've become accustomed, you'd quickly realize that I don't bathe in the blood of virgins or sacrifice goats on a pentagram-painted basement floor. I don't even have a basement.

No, I don't own a cauldron or a pointy black hat. I've never taken a ride on a household sweeping device. One time I did have a wart, but it was on my foot and I'm pretty sure the result of ill-fitting shoes.

Not that any of these points would get me off the hook. They are just ridiculous stereotypes: commercialized visualizations meant to trivialize a misunderstood source of ancient power. Truth is, I'd love to be a witch. It would make my life so much easier. If I were a witch, I'd have access to so much more magic than I do now. I'd conjure up spells to make me snacks, do my homework, or get me out of gym class. What I do now is nothing compared to the realm of true sorcery.

I am reminded of this every day; there's nothing like working in your family-owned magic shop to constantly bring to mind your very non-magicalness. In the right hands, the collections of chickens' feet, amethysts, and silkweed I am tasked with keeping presentable could do some serious damage, but in my possession, they'd make up the world's weirdest charm bracelet, and I'm not really into accessories.

"Amber, can you please start bringing out the pillows?" Mom calls from behind the display of natural perfumes in tiny crystal vials. "I don't want there to be another fiasco like last week."

"Oh yes, because Gods forbid a Wicca butt touch a manmade material like linoleum," I reply.

Mom pokes her head around the corner with her less-thanamused face. "Not now, okay? Just get the pillows."

She's stressed; I know it. My picking at the scab doesn't help. Any minute now, her coven will be here for their weekly meet-up, and for the past several weeks, things have been . . .

To those who fight for love

off. Not being an official witch myself, I wouldn't fully know what it's like to be part of a magical group that's "on," but even as a humble outsider, I can sense something's different.

They meet every Tuesday to try out new spells and discuss mystical occurrences as well as any other pressing witchy business. It's kind of like a book club, only with less boozy housewives and more loopy Wiccans. Coven of the Dawning Day has never been super hard-core about sticking to strict pagan teachings; for as long as I can remember, the group has always been more of a social thing. I've known most of them since I was an infant, and though this circle has been home to many generations of Sands, I will never be an actual member.

It's 9:01, meaning Windy City Magic is officially closed to the non-supernatural. Mom pulls down the silver security gate at the entrance just as our retail neighbors do the same, only our safeguarding efforts are much different. The pattern in the metal links has been enchanted to let certain individuals enter ghost-style. All they have to do is mutter the password *"factum"* and they can walk on through. Mind you, it's not just about knowing the right thing to say; if I tried this trick, I'd have diamond-shaped gate marks imprinted on my forehead.

I've barely finished pulling out the pillows from the back room when I hear the password being uttered. Wendy Pumple, the oldest witch of the bunch, is always the first to arrive. She was best friends with my grandmother Edith Sand, who used to be high priestess of this coven back in the day. Hierarchy-wise,

Wendy should have taken over the position when my grandma passed, but she didn't have much taste for magical politics. In fact, she decided years ago that Dawning Day should be a democracy, without a presiding witch. It's been that way ever since, but with how things have been going lately, I'm not sure it will stay that way for long.

"Amber, dear, would you mind pulling out that nice wing-back chair your mother has in the back?" Wendy asks me in her honey-laced elderly voice. Truly, if you looked up "adorable old person" online, you'd find a picture of this sweet witch. "My bones can't handle sitting on floor pillows these days."

"Sure thing. I'll grab it," I say with a smile. I don't often respond to requests with such pleasantness, but it's hard to deny my grandma's BFF. I set down the pile of pillows and pull back the red velvet curtain to Mom's private den. This is where the real magic lies—not that our shop's offerings don't live up to their promises (my mom's a witch, not a crook), but back here, Mom casts spells for clientele of her choosing. I can't even tell you about some of the out-of-this-world stuff that has happened in this tiny, candlelit room. If you've never been invited behind the curtain, well, it probably means she doesn't like you very much.

I drag the chair out and finish setting up the pillows—ten in all—in a circle in the center of the store. The rest of the coven is thankfully less prompt than Wendy, so the scene is properly set before anyone else arrives. I'm not allowed to handle any of the other staging (Gods forbid a non-member touch the ceremonial candle), so now I can just blend into the background like a decorative plant (although really, plants have the power to turn sunlight into food, a pretty amazing spell if you think about it. If I could do that, I'd never go indoors).

"So, dearie," Wendy starts in, "how's your love life?" Her eyes twinkle with her own perceived cleverness.

"Oh, you know, same as last week—nothing to report," I say, my smile a bit less genuine this time. We seem to go through this same routine every Tuesday. I'm not going to say it's dementia, but . . .

Wendy answers with a cute little laugh. "I think what you do is so . . ." She searches for a positive adjective. ". . . neat. It must be nice to be so in touch with such a delightful subject."

"Thank you, Mrs. Pumple," I say. I know she's trying to extend a mystical olive branch, but really, it's not necessary. There was a time, yes, when I wasn't as thrilled with what the Fates had dealt me. But I'm a big girl now, and I've come to terms with my place in the world.

You would think magic would run in our bloodline, and you'd be right; the Sand family has a long, proud history of witches and sorcerers. But sometimes magic skips a generation or takes a transmuted form. Mom may not have passed her bewitching genes down to me, but I did get one highly specific mystical talent that still gets me a check in the paranormal column. While I may not have the swagger or power of your everyday witch, I've come to realize that what I can do is still pretty badass: I can see true love.

I don't mean the chocolate-covered, mushy-gushy *signs* of love, but real, destined-to-happen happy endings. All I need is five seconds of eye contact, and I'll envision anyone's soul mate.

I'm a matchmaker.

The rest of the coven is starting to trickle in, and rather than answer more questions about my love life (or lack thereof), I decide to head out. I wave to my mom, who's already in full hostess mode, to come let me out through the gate. She weaves through the huddle of long skirts and Birkenstock sandals and meets me at the front.

"Have a good meeting. Be witchy and stuff."

Mom nods. "I'll see you at home." She lays her hand on the enchanted section of gate and peels it open, like turning a page in a book. I slip through the metal, and it clangs shut behind me; from the outside, the shop looks vacant, with no visible light or people. Another one of Mom's magic tricks.

I step outside and feel the cool lakefront air on my cheeks. Chicago's city lights glitter against Lake Michigan's dark waters. Our shop is nestled within the insanity that is Navy Pier: part carnival, part convention center, 100 percent overpriced tackiness. Among the kiosks hawking everything from shot glasses to backpacks emblazoned with "Sweet Home Chicago," and cheap jewelry that falls apart the moment your feet leave the pier, rests our humble storefront filled with actual, quality products intended to improve someone's life and not just clutter it with junk. I hate pretty much everything about Navy Pier, from its garish neon lights to its constant churro stench, but I certainly don't hate this view. Being the most eastward point of the city means you get to take in the entire skyline in its glory.

But my serenity doesn't last long, because as soon as I pass the docked tour boats, a group of sophomore girls has spotted me. In no way will this lead to anything good, and I consider jumping in the lake, knowing full well my insides would turn to icicles the moment I hit the water. Still, history has proven that would be preferable to what will happen next.

I met one of them—I don't remember her name—at school the other day, when she begged me to reveal whether or not her current beau was THE ONE. Normally, I avoid match-making at school because the results are never pleasant. And yet, this girl has chosen to follow me like a psychotic shadow, and after three days of her whining at my heels, I guess she decided to corner me at my place of business. Why a Chicago resident would freely visit this tourist trap is beyond me, but whatever.

"Amber!" she coos, waving like we share matching friendship bracelets. Her entourage circles around me. "Please talk to me. I know this won't take long; can't you help me out?"

I grit my teeth, wishing I could use her body to pole-vault

over to the bus stop. Dammit, I guess we're doing this now. "Is this really what you want?"

"Of course! Why wouldn't I? Tristian and I have been dating for, like, ever, and I just KNOW he is the one!" Her friends nod in agreement.

"Then why do you need my confirmation?"

"Because!" She smiles brightly. "It would solidify my love even more."

Ugh. That is not what I wanted to hear. But okay. Here we go. I look into her eyes, and after a few seconds, a montage of scenes play in my head: this girl—whatever her name is—and some boy, doing a bunch of coupley things. Skiing down a hillside, shopping for bedding. Scooping mounds of wedding cake into each other's mouths. Only the boy is not Tristian Michaels, the loser who pushes freshmen into trash cans. I have no choice but to reveal the absolute shocker that no, her hormonally charged, high school lunkhead of a boyfriend is not her lifelong match.

"Well, I have news. Whether you categorize it as 'good' or 'bad' is up to you. Personally, I think it's a win," I start, though I know the long-term benefit of being moron-free will be lost on this audience. "You have a match and he seems swell, but it's just not Tristian." The words have barely left my lips when her claws instantly unfurl. (Not actual claws, mind you. Any being sporting that kind of hardware would not be so careless as to flash them in public.)

"You're wrong!" She points an accusatory finger. "What the hell do you know? You're just a bully!"

"A bully?" I feign insult, clutching imaginary pearls. I have to fake some sort of reaction, as this kind of allegation happens more regularly than I'd like. "You're the one who's been stalking me."

She huffs again, pulling up her scarf to hide her reddening cheeks. A single tear slides down her face, and I resist the urge to roll my eyes. You would think she'd be relieved, seeing as how her boyfriend is such a dud. Shouldn't it be a blessing to know there's someone better out there? Someone who doesn't belch randomly during study hall? Haven't I provided a service? I never understand this reaction.

"So, that's it? How can I believe anything you say?" she asks. "You didn't even do anything . . . magical."

"What did you expect? A puff of smoke? A rabbit out of my hat? That's not really how magic works."

"Ugh. You and your 'witchcraft.'" She throws in air quotes, trying to regain herself. The girls all giggle.

I'm really tired and definitely over this unnecessary encounter. She's not going to leave me alone until she's exacted some verbal revenge, so I'd better set her up so I can get home to my sweatpants. "I'm actually in the business of l-o-v-e, but I understand this misconception."

"You're in the business of heartbreak!" she spits. Tears start piling up, and her friends rub her shoulders in support.

9

"Maybe you're not a witch, but you're definitely a bitch."

Remind me to get that on my tombstone. Satisfied, they all storm off, and I'm left to catch the bus in peace. You know that saying "Don't shoot the messenger"? I really should invest in a bulletproof vest.

Two

"**MOM, DO YOU THINK THE HUMAN HEART HAS A LOVE LIMIT?**"
I ask out of the blue, during a particularly slow afternoon at
Windy City Magic. (Don't you just love the name of our shop?
We don't. Unfortunately, it's practically written into Navy Pier's
lease agreement that your store must have a cliché name and
equally cheesy logo. Ours is an impossibly cutesy, black-hatted
witch perkily perched atop a broomstick, with an undeter-
mined source of wind in her wake. She's blond and bubbly and
completely sickening. We couldn't pick anything classy or even
remotely culturally appropriate, as that might scare off the candy-
chomping tourists who wouldn't know a magic spell if it hit
them in the fanny pack.)

Mom stops straightening the bottles of anti-cellulite potion and turns to me. Her long black-and-gray-flecked braid falls down her back.

"Why do you ask?" she says in a noncommittal tone. Mom constantly gets approached by people looking for answers they're too embarrassed to find. An open-ended question about how things grow usually is a thinly veiled foray into how to go up a cup size. Mom knows that words usually hold more meaning behind them.

"Just curious," I say casually. It's something I think about a lot, especially in relation to myself. I spend a ton of time channeling love stories but have yet to start a single sentence of my own.

"With all these top-notch love connections I've made, I just hope I'm not wearing out the Fates' patience for romance in my general direction."

Mom sighs. "The Fates? Amber, really." She returns to her straightening. "You know better than that."

And I do, of course. I just want to hear her say it. The Fates really don't have time for an individual's drama; they are more "big picture" sorts. You can believe that one person can make a difference and we all hold the power to change the world, blah, blah, but the powers that be are generally uninterested in the day-to-day events of the common man, not even the magical ones.

I am just about to comment on that very fact when a customer walks in, a dripping raincoat hood covering his face.

"Welcome to Windy City Magic, where the mystical becomes reality." My delivery is monotone. It's my "I can't believe I have to say this spiel" voice. "Can I interest you in an aura cleansing with Madame Sand?"

"No, thank you, Amber, but I do need to talk to your mother." The man pulls off his hood, revealing a very familiar face. It is John "The Blitz" Blitzman, former Chicago Bears quarterback and current city mayor. Not only is he the youngest QB to win a Super Bowl with the Bears (not that I follow such things, but it's been repeated so many times it's kind of impossible not to know), he also boosted tourism for the city by implementing a lot of smart changes to the Loop. He's pretty much a supercelebrity.

He's also my mom's oldest friend and (not-officially-confirmed-but-c'mon-it-just-has-to-be) high school sweetheart. They are not soul mates (my talents have made that clear) but have remained close through adulthood. They were there for each other when John's wife died and my dad left. I usually only see the mayor in passing (he's a very busy man, after all), but I know he and my mom talk often.

"Oh, sorry, I didn't see you under there, Mr. Blitzman. I think she just ducked in the back. I'll get her for you."

"Amber, I've known you since you were born. You can call me John," he says warmly.

"Okay, Mr. Blitzman." Like I'm going to call our mayor by his first name.

I pull back the thick velvet curtains to Mom's private meeting room. It's equipped with all the expected accessories: tarot cards, crystal ball, incense. Most of them are just for show; a real witch doesn't rely on gimmicks. But when people pay for a witch's services, they expect to see a certain level of "mystical properties." The real magic—talismans, herbs, stones—are only brought out for very select patrons. Patrons like John.

"Mom, John's here. Wants to see you."

Her expression darkens. "Yes, send him in."

It is rare to see her so grim. Being a witch means being able to channel the energy around you; usually she makes a conscious effort to let positivity in and filter negativity out. I can't feel it, being so low on the magical totem pole, but there must be something wicked in the air.

"Is everything okay?" I ask.

"Amber, we'll talk about this later." Which means no. I hurry back to John, who is pacing between the displays of soothing sleep tea and skin-calming balm, and escort him back.

"Lucy, I—" he starts, once behind the curtain, but Mom nods sharply, indicating he say no more. I don't know if this is to keep potential secrets from me or from any lurking Navy Pier patrons, but either way it's annoying. Clearly something is going on, and it's the most action the shop has seen all afternoon. I want in.

But I'm most rudely shut out. Mom promptly pulls the curtain closed, and after two audible finger snaps, all sound from the other side is dampened. A soundproofing spell. Dammit.

I slump back to my post. Although I'm technically responsible for the entire shop while I'm on duty, I usually stick by my matchmaking table. Mom set it up for me when she felt my skills were ready to go pro. It's just a square folding table covered with a pink crushed-velvet cloth, but many a wandering soul has been set on the path toward love after sitting here with me. Above the table hangs a sign:

FIND TRUE LOVE! CONSULT A MATCHMAKER!

I even added the glitter-encrusted hearts myself. I'm so crafty.

I no sooner sit down than am greeted by a good-looking guy with nicely defined biceps straining against the confines of his rain-flecked T-shirt.

"Hey, are you available?" he asks.

I blush. Maybe I won't mind being on this side of the curtain after all. He shifts uncomfortably, waiting for me to make the next move, which is when I realize he isn't asking if I, Amber Sand, am available, but if I, random possessor of matchmaking abilities, can help him out. Of course. No one is ever looking for just me.

"Yes. Please sit," I say, feeling embarrassed and stupid for ogling. While checking out extremely attractive people is essentially harmless, it's also frustratingly pointless in my case. Sure, I can take in any attractive view, but the moment my eyes meet theirs, all I see is their soul mate, and not once has that person ever been me. Talk about a mood killer. It's kind of hard to properly work up a full-blown crush when you know you'll never be the endgame. To be clear, I have dated, despite never locking eyes with my particular Romeo. I never let things go too far, but a girl gets lonely, okay?

Once he's seated, I notice his ear tips poking out from his shaggy haircut. Pointy. Yup. Definitely of elfin descent. It's a common misconception that all elves are short. Maybe back in the day of knights and dragons they were, but centuries of interspecies hookups have made elves almost indistinguishable from humans. Except for the ears: they seem to be self-conscious about those things for some reason, always trying to hide them under creative hairstyling.

"What brings you here today?" I say, trying to segue back into professional mode.

"Well, I'm pretty sure I already know who my true love is, but I just want to *know*, you know? She's pressuring me to propose, and I really want to, but . . . I heard you're the girl to see about these kind of things." Supernatural creatures are way more accepting of magic than your average human.

"You've heard right! This shouldn't take long." Making a confirmation of someone's match is the easiest (and most cost-effective) of my services. "Do you have a picture of her so I can confirm?"

"Oh yeah, tons." He pulls out his phone and starts smiling

as he scrolls through the pictures. Finally he settles on one of her laughing while mixing a bowl of something in a kitchen.

"She's lovely," I say, which she is, but I always say that regardless. It seems to help calm down those on the other side of the table before I peer into their souls. "Place your hands in mine." I lay my forearms on the table, palms facing up. I don't really need to hold someone's hands, but it seems to be more satisfying for the patron if there's a physical connection; it makes my conclusion feel more real. It's all about creating an experience. "Look into my eyes, and open your heart."

He takes my hands and goose bumps spring up at his touch. I can't help it; it's been a long time since I felt a boy's hands. I look deep into his brown eyes. Suddenly, there she is, the girl from his phone, surprising him with a steak dinner and picking up their pink-tutued daughter from ballet class.

He sits in suspense, waiting for my verdict. "Congratulations," I confirm. "You've found your match." I release the cute elf's hands, and he smiles with relief, thanking me profusely and paying my fee before bolting out of the shop, no doubt on his way to propose. Geez, so adorable. I like when people get excited; it makes me feel worthwhile, and I can't deny that sometimes a speck of hopeless romanticism worms its way into my crusty old heart. I'd be a pretty crappy matchmaker if I didn't still believe in love.

It's right before closing when John and Mom emerge from her room. His cheeks are splotchy, like he's been crying, and it's strange to see a face so regularly splattered on newspapers and football paraphernalia look so defeated. Mom speaks to him in hushed tones, patting his back as she walks him toward the door. I manage to hear a "don't worry, we'll find her," which gives him some comfort. The whole scene is screaming TOP SECRET EMOTIONAL TRAUMA, which makes me want to know what's happening even more.

As he is putting on his raincoat, the diamonds from his Super Bowl ring catch the light, spreading some sparkles over his grim expression. "Good night, Amber," he says through residual sniffles. "Have a good day at school tomorrow."

"Thanks, Mr. Blitzman." I want to say more, like, "Whatever is wrong, my mom will fix it," but decide to let it lie.

"I'll let Charlie know you say hello," he adds, before walking out.

My face falls. Dear Gods, please don't do anything of the sort.

Ugh. Not Charlie.

Three

I HAD TO TELL MY BEST FRIEND, AMANI, ABOUT IT THE NEXT day during a particularly awful period of gym class.

"The Blitz breezed through the shop last night," I say as we both do our best to look like we're participating in the designated gymnastics unit, which we, of course, are not.

"Reeeeeeally," Amani replies, throwing her hands up in the air to appear as if she just completed a cartwheel. "Did he come to finally sweep your mom off her broomstick?"

I make a face. "You know that's never happening. No, he came in and was very upset, very mysterious. I thought maybe you could dust off your crystal ball and fill us in on what's going on with him." This is a pointless request, yet I make it anyway. Amani is a precog: she can see the future. But while

I am plagued with this unavoidable urge to help people find their happy endings, Amani doesn't share my altruistic views. "It might distract us from the sea of terry-cloth shorts," I say, tugging mine down. I'm generally not a fan of exposing so much leg, especially for such an unworthy cause as tumbling.

"Why do we have to do this anyway? Who ever heard of gymnastics for teenagers? Isn't this better suited for toddlers?" she complains. Amani loves to complain.

"Agreed," I say, crouching in a ball as if about to perform a somersault. "So what do you say? Can we find out what's troubling our dear mayor?"

She gets down on the floor with me, making a half-assed attempt at the splits. I know that my question, while seemingly simple, is making her brain swirl in an unpleasant way. We made a pact back in middle school not to let our supernatural tendencies interfere with our friendship. In fact, she first approached me in sixth grade because she'd already seen we would become best friends. Usually, she can't have premonitions about her own life, so I think technically she was having one about mine. That seems to be a common magic drawback—your talent will not work on yourself. I guess the Fates decided that would make life too easy, tipping the scales unjustly. Bastards.

From my uncomfortably balled-up position, I notice her brown roots have recovered from her blond dye job. A few weeks ago, we both decided to color our hair together, just to mix things up right before senior pictures. Amani, who has always been infatuated with *Cinderella*, decided to finally go for it and commit to the blond tresses of her fairy-tale idol. She has said to me COUNTLESS TIMES how she wishes she could meet a prince and lead a life of wonderment. As if being a freaking fortune-teller was not amazing enough. But I digress. Once we started painting on the bleach, she had a change of heart, worrying Momma Sharma would be upset at seeing her only daughter as a blond beach babe. I know she would've rocked it had she gone through with it, but I helped her rinse out the bleach before it was too late.

I went for something a little more random; my hair is naturally black, making color changes kind of a pain, so instead, I added some jade-green and cobalt-blue streaks to the top, creating a cool peacock effect. I loved it, until some jackasses at school started calling me "peacock" with extra emphasis on the latter syllable because teenage boys are just so charming and worthless.

"Ugh. No one should ever have to be this flexible," Amani says, trying (and failing) to touch her toes.

"Amani!"

"What?"

"Are you listening to me?"

"Yes! Gods! But what do you want me to do? Read his palm and say 'great danger lies ahead'?"

"Yes, exactly that. I always get left out of the actual magic, and it sucks. I want to be part of an adventure and not just fast-forward to the ending." I try to conjure the saddest puppy-dog eyes ever, even though I already know she won't go down this path.

Amani is a superior human, but as a supernatural being, there are some struggles. If it seems like fun, having a fortune-telling friend who can save you from upcoming embarrassing mishaps and bad choices, in actuality, it's not. During the infant stages of our friendship, she'd tell me everything about my life before it happened; her visions came to her fast and furious, just like mine, so she couldn't help but tell me what I was going to get for my birthday, or how a movie we'd never seen would end. It got to the point where I felt like everything I did was old news, every adventure a repeat. So we agreed to keep our visions to ourselves, unless something legitimately life-threatening was around the bend. (Not that I'd ever see anything of that nature. I only see fairy-tale drives into the sunset and happily-ever-afters.) And in case this isn't already blatantly clear, yes, Amani is much more magical than me, a point she's been very gracious to never rub in. On the scale of magicality, it goes: witches > precogs > birthday-party magicians > matchmakers.

The suppression of her visions worsened after that; as her talent continued to grow, her parents were scared she was having some sort of psychotic break and immediately put her through intensive "deprogramming" therapy. Needless to say, it had a pretty rough effect. They are psychologists, which I guess is why they veered this way, especially since as far as we know, there's no magical lineage in her family. Amani's precognition seems to be a freak occurrence.

And it can be freaky: I've seen her deliver premonitions to others, though not for a while, and it's crazeballs. Back when she was fast and loose with her visions, they came to her without side effects, but now that she's spent so much time keeping them at bay, it's a real effort to make them happen. There's a wildness in her eyes, almost as if her visions were actually germinating from the eyeballs themselves. Her pupils start to dilate, and her gaze refuses to rest on any particular thing. There's been one or two times in the past few years where a vision managed to break through her vault of self-control, and we're convinced those precognitions only came through because nearby supernaturals used her like a magical conduit. Jerks. Mom says the more one willingly denies her talents, the more likely those talents will fade away completely. I've tried to tell Amani this, but she brushes it off. I don't always like that she's given up magic so completely, but she's my friend and I support her no matter what. If my gift came with a side helping of *Exorcist*, I probably wouldn't do it on command either.

She groans and swings around to sit cross-legged. "Amber, you are awesome and will therefore lead an awesome life, full of crazy awesome adventures. Your brand of magic is just as valid as anyone else's."

"There. Was that so hard?"

"Not as hard as it will be to get up off the floor now."

And simple as that, the subject is dropped.

Just then, an aggressively perky body flips and lands mere centimeters from where we sit. Amani and I jerk back so as not to be toppled on, but the girl sticks her landing perfectly.

"Watch it, freaks!" she shrieks, despite the fact that everything is fine and we had absolutely no effect on her trajectory. "You could have made me fall!"

I wish, with every beat of my heart, that Ivy Chamberlain was not such a stain on my existence, but sadly, life is full of unavoidable pests. Every school seems to have one: that insanely good-looking blonde who terrorizes the student body with her unattainable perfection. Head cheerleader, student council president, loved/hated by girls and guys alike . . . blah, blah, barf. It's sickening, right? Well, rest assured that no one is that flawless without some sort of black magic at play.

Ivy's a siren: a real-life femme fatale. Instead of calling out to weary sailors with hypnotic songs, she mesmerizes the school with simplistic cheerleading rhymes. Even her name embodies her ability to strangle living creatures into submission. Sirens are notoriously manipulative, probably because their gift comes with an expiration date. It is physically impossible to be so beautiful and powerful their entire lives, so they are forced to rely on a concentrated dose of influence. Ivy, being the one-woman brain trust that she is, decided to use up her power in high school; a poor choice if you ask me. Why be a world leader or cure cancer when you can spend your time standing on top of human pyramids and lying underneath idiotic football players? It's so cliché I almost feel bad for her. Except that she's a conniving, terrible wench, so I really don't.

"Good Gods, Ivy, you're the one who came barreling into us," Amani sneers.

"Not that 'Gods' talk again. Do you really believe there's more than one? You two decided you're not undesirable enough, so you keep throwing mystical garbage into the mix?" Ivy asks, twirling the end of her golden ponytail.

"Um, hello, it's called religious freedom. Welcome to America circa 1776," I say. While Amani and I are both technically pagans, we aren't exactly zealots. We're more like the Catholics who only show up to church on Easter. Still, even if I'm lapsed, I'll take any chance to pick a fight with the school's head wench.

"It's too bad your Salem ancestors never lived to see that day," Ivy says with a grin.

"Yeah, it's a shame. They were really good at sniffing out supernatural sea garbage on the Massachusetts coastline," I throw back. I take a few overdramatic whiffs of air. "In fact, I think I smell some now!"

She puts her hands on her hips and looks down at me, trying extra hard to think of a clever retort. Ivy knows I know she's a siren, just as she knows I'm a matchmaker. You know how dogs always sense other approaching canines? Well, supernatural beings can sniff each other out too. (Not literally, of course. That would be awkward.) For us, those facts are clear as day, even if our peers never take notice. It's like our own little game of covert affairs, except with the entire school under her spell, she's taken a gigantic lead. She doesn't have to hide her siren abilities; she doesn't need to. Even if she stood in the middle of campus and screamed, "I'm manipulating you all!" the response would be a series of cheers.

Finally, she comes up with something. "I'm glad I have no idea what you're talking about, just like no one else at this school does. You're just two little weirdos who will only ever have each other." And there it is. Even though I know Ivy is a siren and her sense of power is false and fleeting; even though I know she is a horrible creature whose presence should be disregarded at all costs, it still sucks ass to be verbally attacked when you're wearing unflattering green gym shorts.

Once Ivy leaves, Amani lies back on the gym floor, letting out a low guttural groan. "Uggggggh. She is the wooooooorst."

I nod. "Please tell me she gets eaten by sharks or sucked into a cosmic wormhole in the future."

"As satisfying as that would be, I don't even want to spend the energy trying to find out," she replies.

Mercifully, gym class finally comes to an end, and we shuffle into the locker room to change from one uniform to the next. Uniforms are a simple fact of private school, and Manchester Prep is no different: green plaid skirts for the girls, ties and coats for the guys. I think it's hilarious how school administrators think making kids dress alike for school will force them to view each other as equals. It is the furthest from the truth. Uniforms inspire students to be more creative, to really dig deep and search hard for character flaws and other irregularities worthy of potential abuse.

Anyway, we are walking down the wood-paneled hallways, when out of nowhere, I'm shoved into a locker by some meat-head man-beast who calls me a "witch bitch," which honestly is not very clever, and seriously, who pushes a girl?

Amani immediately jumps in, pushing back on my perpetrator. "What was that for?" she screams at Trent Simmons, who is a school football "star."

"I hear you tripped Ivy and almost made her break her ankle," he growls, a purple vein bulging from his neck. Gods, we've been out of gym for what—six seconds?—and Ivy already used her siren song to rally her troops.

"You must be Ivy's sucker of the week," I say, turning my head to avoid his breath. "Does she have you guys on a roster rotation or something?"

He pounds his fist on the locker for effect. "Don't talk about her that way!" Ol' Trent here has giant blood in his lineage, which is why he's so upset over something so trivial. Quick-tempered, disproportionate brain-to-muscle mass, easily manipulated? Classic giant traits. Natural prey for a siren. "Ivy's amazing, and you're just jealous, witch."

"Sure, and I bet she does amazing things for you," Amani says with a pointed look.

This sends Mr. Anger Issues into a blind rage, but luckily, Mr. Boger, the school guidance counselor, happens to be walking by at that very moment and puts a stop to the madness.

"Enough, Mr. Simmons," Mr. Boger says, easily pulling him off me. "Violence against women is not only a reprehensible moral crime, but cause for expulsion at Manchester. And we wouldn't want that, now, would we?"

"I would," Amani interjects, raising her hand. Mr. Boger shoots her a glare. "Just saying." She shrugs.

"You two, my office: now," Mr. Boger orders Amani and me. You might wonder why we are being sent to the office when we did nothing wrong, but ever since my ten-year-old self set Mr. Boger up with his husband, he's always looked out for me. And sometimes I do need extra protection, because just as Trent McGiantpants starts plodding down the hall, I can't stop from yelling, "It'll never last!" after him. This inspires the riled-up onlookers to start a chorus of "ooohs!" and Trent replies with a tidal wave of words a nice girl like myself doesn't use. Whatever. I've looked in Ivy's eyes, and trust me when I say Trent Simmons is not her destiny.

"Why do you have to do that?" Mr. Boger asks when we are nestled safely in his cherry-wood-lined office. "Why egg them on like that?"

"For sport?" I say. Amani snorts.

Mr. Boger sighs, running his hands through his salt-and-pepper hair. "Amber, I know firsthand how special you are." I notice a framed picture of him and his husband, Richard, on his desk. So cute, those two. I remember that day: I was at a farmers' market in Wicker Park with my mom, who was low on sage. I saw Mr. Boger also perusing the herbs, and we briefly made eye contact. Naturally, I instantly envisioned his future love, which didn't seem like anything noteworthy. I was constantly seeing strangers' destinies. But a minute or two later, who should I see but Richard purchasing a bundle of rhubarb. I couldn't believe it at first; I'd never crossed paths with someone's match so soon after having a vision. It was fate! I ran off and grabbed Richard's hand, dragging him over to Mr. Boger. If I had done that now, it would be creepy and weird, but since I was still young, it was charming and endearing. They've been together ever since.

Mr. Boger continues. "I understand that being special means being different, which can be hard. But sometimes I think you are actively trying to make people dislike you."

"I'm simply treating others the way I am treated," I say. I like Mr. Boger, but I'm not in the mood for psychoanalysis. Because you know what? It's fine. Sure, it's not the biggest self-esteem boost to be called a freak on a daily basis, but school is not forever. Someday I will get out of here and meet someone amazing and live happily ever after. Or not. In which case I'll move in with Amani and her future husband and force them to adopt me.

"Well, try to rise above. You've got a long school year ahead of you. I'd like to see you make the best of it."

"Who said we aren't? Seeing Trent go nuclear was the best part of my day," Amani jokes.

Mr. Boger's face melts into one of an exhausted parent, tired of having his words unheard. "Okay, be gone, you two."

As we exit his office, I decide not to tell my mom about getting in trouble yet again. Parents generally don't delight in getting that kind of news, and as you can imagine, Mom is extra sensitive about the mistreatment of magical folk. Sometimes I like to envision her going all dark after learning of my being bullied, transforming into a tornado of fury and turning all my schoolmates into warthogs. While that would be temporarily awesome, I don't want to go to school in a pigpen.

So I keep it in, like always, isolating myself yet again. It puts me in a weird mood, but I know what will make it better.

CHOCOLATE.

Four

BEFORE HEADING TO CRAZY PIER AFTER SCHOOL, I MAKE A quick stop at MarshmElla's, my absolute favorite place in the city. It's not just a bakery; it's a direct path to heaven. When you open the door, you are instantly enveloped by the warmth of the oven and sweet aroma of melt-in-your-mouth desserts and pastries. I myself once acquired a full sugar high just from smelling the eight-layer dark chocolate fudge cake fresh from the oven. It is sinful, in the best and most decadent way.

This place—the things they create—this is what I aspire to. Matchmaking will always be my bread and butter, but becoming a pastry chef is my dream. After all, baking is really not so different from magic. Both require a basic understanding of the craft; a willingness to experiment and manipulate an existing selection of variables and ingredients. Balance, patience, and creativity are needed from both witches and bakers, and isn't the perfect recipe just an edible spell? My mom mixes potions from her grimoire; I mix batter from a cookbook. She wears charms to ward off spirits; I wear aprons to ward off stains. Candles versus ovens, herbs versus sugars: it's all about using the tricks of your trade. So what if I'm the only woman in the Sand family who can't make objects levitate or disappear? Can they bake a dark chocolate cake with vanilla bean mousse and cherry sauce that literally takes people's breath away? The two trades are basically made for each other; you can't tell me that biting into a moist red velvet cake doesn't put a spell on you.

When I'm free from Manchester Prep, I hope to attend the Chicago Culinary Institute. I'd like to open my own bakery, and who knows? Maybe I'll create a one-stop "find your mate and order your wedding cake" shop. I mean, who wouldn't want to order up a soul mate with a side of buttercream frosting?

Only crazy people and Satan don't like frosting.

The silver bell above the doorframe jingles as I walk in, and Ella, the owner, looks up at me from behind the counter. This time of day marks the start of the evening rush, and she's stocking platters high with cupcakes for those wanting after-dinner desserts. The bakery's décor is composed of neutral tones, letting color pop from the pastries themselves, like a treasure chest of sugar sparkling behind glass. Ella gives me a warm smile, a splotch of vanilla frosting on her round cheek. She is a master of the culinary arts, though somehow she always ends up wearing a portion of her creations.

"Hi, Amber," she says, stacking cupcakes in a spiraling pyramid. "How was school?"

"Awful, as expected," I answer, scanning the chalkboard menu for today's victim.

"Well, that's the spirit," she replies. Ella may have lured me here years ago with her sweet tooth, but she's kept me coming with her sympathetic ear. She gets me, whereas most people do not.

"I need something extra scrumptious today, something that will make my blood sugar skyrocket."

"That kind of day, huh?" Ella stands, wiping her face but somehow still leaving the frosting intact.

"Yup, and I still have to go to the shop and spew love predictions. Give me something that will make me sweet."

Ella scrunches her face. "I don't think I have anything that powerful." I laugh. "But I do have this." She walks over to the cooler and pulls out a heaping cup of dirt and worms. While it may not sound like the most fancy or desirable of desserts, Ella's version is beyond compare: homemade devil's food pudding, mounds of hand-whipped heavy cream, a box full of crushed chocolate cookies, and soft, tangy gummy worms. I don't care if it's kid stuff; it's amazeballs.

"Yes, yes! Now, please!" I say, stretching my arms out like an impatient toddler. She hands me the cup, and I spoon up the pudding. Ah, there it is. Suddenly, everything is better. An interesting quirk of being supernatural is that regardless of parentage or pedigree, we all have highly sensitive tongues. I've never met a beastie who didn't lose it over a tasty morsel that would skew way too sweet or sour for a regular palate. Salty pretzels, bitter lemons: everyone has their weakness. I don't know why this is, but I certainly don't fight it. Amani carries Taco Bell hot sauce packets in her purse at all times to juice up her entrees. My particular poison is sugar, and I welcome its sweet hold on me every single day.

"I made it just for you. Somehow I knew you'd be by today," Ella says. "Maybe I'm becoming psychic."

"A psychic baker? Gods help us. I don't think the Fates would allow it," I gargle through whipped cream.

She pouts. "Too bad. I'd make a killing."

"I'd say you already are." I nod to a swarm of moms and excited kids who just came in. The young ones are positively vibrating at the anticipation of cake, and I don't blame them.

"Can I get you anything else?" Ella asks.

I lick a cookie crumb from my lips. "Yeah, can I get a lavender whoopie pie for my mom? I need to butter her up for information."

Ella smirks as she wraps up the treat. "Intriguing. Fill me in later?"

"I always do!" Happily, I take the bag and squirm my way

out of the crowd. I feel so much better than when I came in; that's the power of pastries.

I devour the rest of my dessert while waiting for a bus. I could take the "L" train, but sometimes the sway of the cars flips my stomach in an unhappy way. Coughing up dirt and worms is one surefire way to piss off weary commuters. Besides, the bus route will bring me much closer to the pier; it just takes longer.

As I'm scraping the last of my pudding from the cup, another person joins me at the stop. Only, I can sense immediately she isn't exactly a person. Long, wavy auburn hair; guitar case strapped to her back; clothes that look like they were sewn from a rose petal. Yup. Definitely part fairy. Something about that lineage always cloaks its descendants with that crunchy granola vibe. I'm surprised she isn't handing me a recycled-paper flyer about veganism or organic tea tree oil.

She looks up at me (fairies are generally pretty short, probably because their ancestors slept in pinecones), and I can see from the corner of my eye that she senses my supernaturalness too. Usually I avoid eye contact with strangers at all costs; matchmaking out in the wild can be dangerous and unpredictable. Two years ago, I was cornered at night by a vampire who was afraid he'd just drained the love of his life. Spoiler alert: he had. I remember the blood on his lips as he came at me, furious at my confirmation. Luckily, I had mace in my pocket, but from then on, I've tried to avoid random public premonitions. I try to refer them to Windy City Magic, where I can perform with the safety of a powerful witch at my side. But my pudding has me in a good mood and this little sprite looks harmless, so I turn and meet her gaze.

Instantly, I'm flooded with scenes of the fairy girl and her equally crunchy mate: growing herbs in a garden, riding bicycles along the lakefront, playing together in some sort of musical group. Hmm. I wonder if she's already met him.

"Hey," I say, trying to sound casual and not like a cheese-ball. "Are you in a band?"

"Yeah, well, we're trying to be a band. We've only been playing together a couple weeks, still gelling." Her voice sounds like a rainbow, if that's even possible.

"How's your lead singer? Any good?"

She gets a twisty smile on her face, the kind that tries to stay hidden but can't help itself. "He's all right."

Suuuurrre, you can't fool me, fairy. I see the bus rumbling up the street; better wrap this up fast. "Singers are so important for a band. I have a feeling he'll be pretty important to you too."

Her smile grows; she can't deny it now. With rosy cheeks, she says, "Thanks," before climbing up the bus steps. See? That's how it should always go; happy endings for all. I am a patron of love, people! Not a harbinger of death.

Sheesh.

Mom is initially delighted by my sugary offering, but after one bite, begins questioning its purpose. I watch her face morph from one of pleasure to one of suspicion.

"Why did you bring me this?" she asks.

"Because you are the best mommy ever and I wuv you beary much?" I bat my eyelashes innocently.

"Amber."

I sigh. "Fine. Because I want to know what you and John talked about last night." There's no point in lying to a witch.

She picks up a napkin and dramatically spits out the chewed cake.

"Mom! Gross! You are a respectable businesswoman and manipulator of magic; you can't just spit out food like a petulant toddler."

"If that's so, why am I being treated like this? You think the only way to get me to confide in you is through bribery?"

"Um . . . yes?" She never tells me about the high-priority spells. It's like there's some kind of security clearance for magic, and since I'm just a lowly matchmaker, I'm denied access. "I want to know what's going on so I can help."

She tilts her head, exhaling through her nose. She's softening to the idea. Maybe the whoopie pie was an obvious play, but Mom's true soft spot is my taking interest in the family business. Sometimes I think she feels bad I wasn't born a witch, so when I pursue magic even despite my lack of ability, it moves her.

"Amber, you know I would love to have your help. But your

gift, while very powerful, is also very specific, and I'm afraid will not apply in this situation," she says gently.

"But is everything okay with John? Is he in danger? Are radioactive vultures swooping in to take over his golden empire?"

Mom laughs, once again picking up her treat. "No, nothing like that."

"Then what?"

"He simply needs help finding someone."

"Oh, well, that's easy enough. Should I grab the ingredients for a locator spell?" I ask.

"No, I tried that already. This missing person is very skilled at remaining hidden," she says.

"Like, do they have an invisibility cloak or something? 'Cause that would be cool."

"Perhaps." She takes a bite, contemplating the possibilities as she chews. "I can't quite figure it out."

"Shouldn't John file a missing persons report?"

"He wants to avoid any public attention on this, if possible. You know how the media is." Oh, I do. A few years back, a local paper tried to make headlines by spinning some cracked-out idea that the occult was taking over Chicago. Windy City Magic, along with the trend of black nail polish and Ouija boards being sold at Urban Outfitters, were among the culprits. Because if anything is responsible for spreading knowledge of the paranormal, it's the trend-obsessed hipsters at Urban Outfitters.

"So what are our next steps, then?" I ask.

A soft gray strand of hair falls between her eyes. "*We* don't have next steps. I will be working on this alone."

"I want to help."

"Not this time."

"But I—"

Mom stands up, dismissing her dessert for a second time. "Amber, I don't want you involved here. Leave it." She storms off to the back of the store, forcefully pulling the curtains behind her. I don't bother following; I hear a series of clicks and know she's put up a barrier. Ugh. I wasn't trying to invade her magical space or something. I just want to know what's going on.

And if she won't tell me, I'll find out on my own.

Five

I SPEND MOST OF THE NEXT DAY AT SCHOOL DAYDREAMING about this mysterious missing person and why the mayor doesn't want their identity revealed. Maybe it's his long-lost aunt Mildred, whose centaur roots could ultimately discredit John's football records for using illegal superpowers. Or maybe it's an old college girlfriend, whose disappearance proves John's association in a Skull and Bones–type secret society that was planning to assassinate the president. Or maybe, just maybe, John has amassed such a fortune he actually acquired a unicorn for a pet, and it ran off on a rainbow or something. (Confession: I am obsessed with unicorns. Maybe it's that last sliver of childhood left in me, but the idea of a horse with magical powers just seems so freaking amazing. I've never seen one, but that doesn't mean they aren't real, right? If vampires and werewolves roam the city streets, why can't beautiful unicorns run free in pastoral Ireland or something? I don't know. It seems possible, and I don't want to hear otherwise.)

I'm envisioning myself riding bareback on a unicorn with flowers in its mane when someone calls out my name in the hallway.

"Amber Sand?"

I turn around, frustrated at the interruption from my pleasant daydream.

Oh good Gods, it's Charlie freaking Blitzman, a.k.a. Mr. Manchester Prep's Most Wanted, a.k.a. gag me.

"Yeah?" I ask, pressing my notebook against my chest like a shield. I can't remember the last time I talked to him; it had to have been at his mother's funeral when we were kids. You'd think our parents being besties would translate into at least a forced friendship between us, but somehow it never played out that way. Charlie exists in a different stratosphere; being the son of the most famous man in Chicago comes hand in hand with fame and money. Buttloads of money. And that alone means he's incredibly more desirable than your average teenage male, making the demands for his attention frequent and fervent. He always has a lot of people clamoring to be near him, yet I rarely see him roaming the halls with anyone, playing the role of dismissive loner instead. I guess we commoners are just too lowly and unwashed to mingle with his greatness. Which is fine by me. I don't have the patience to take on some brooding, poor-little-rich-boy companion.

He walks toward me in long, confident strides. His uniform is impeccable; while most guys here push the limits on acceptable dress code, Charlie looks like a walking brochure—no shirttail hanging out, no loosened tie. He's even wearing a tie clip with a tiny gold fox on it; I had no idea Manchester even sold tie clips engraved with the school mascot. His grooming is a little more relaxed but still carefully presented. Light brown hair cut shorter on the sides but longer on the top, slick black glasses with a bold orange stripe running through the frames, tucked behind silver-studded pierced ears.

I can't tell you how many girls have come up to me wanting confirmation that Charlie was their destiny. Don't get me wrong, it's not like he's some repulsive troll (coincidentally, trolls think humans are extremely unattractive, and I once had one tell me my looks were so offensive he might vomit in my presence—so there you go), but wanting someone based on something as trivial and fleeting as social standing is so empty and sad. Not surprisingly, I've yet to meet a shallow hopeful who's turned out to be his true love. But since he's blocking my path with no exit route in sight, I guess today will be the big reveal; I stare straight into his forest-green eyes and wait to see that lucky someone who will steal his heart one day.

And there she is: all porcelain skin and big, bright smiles. I'm treated to a quick highlight reel of their happiness, including an afternoon shopping spree on Michigan Avenue and a vacation in Tokyo. I have to say, Charlie's future leading lady is not exactly who I pictured him with. While this girl seems cute and fun in an eclectic, kawaii-style kind of way, I just assumed he'd end up with some vapid, gorgeous Barbie doll. Isn't that what all rich guys want—arm candy? Mind you, it's not like I sit around thinking about Charlie Blitzman's love life, but I've been approached by so many lovesick girls hoping he's their "one" that, yes, I have occasionally entertained the thought. His match is a stranger to me, meaning none of the Manchester harpies will ever get their claws in him. Ah, satisfaction.

I must have some slack-jawed look on my face because Charlie slowly waves a hand in front of my eyes. "Uh, hello? You okay?"

I wipe my face, trying to reset. I'm usually much better at zipping through the romance portion of my daily interactions. "What do you want?"

His eyebrows tense. "I'm sorry. Am I bothering you?"

Aaaaaand now I'm being rude. "No, sorry, my mind was just elsewhere. I'm present now. Fire away."

He clutches the strap of his leather messenger bag as if it were attached to a parachute. He seems to be regretting initiating this interaction, but hey, that's not my problem.

"I was just wondering if I could talk with you after school, in private somewhere," he says.

"Okay, about what?"

"I'd rather not say right now, hence the request for privacy." Charlie gives a quick look over his shoulder. I follow his glance to see a gaggle of giggling idiots drooling over him down the hall. They try to look casual, pretending not to see the object of their affection, but they may as well be lifting their shirts to get his attention.

"Wow, it's like your own paparazzi, only less subtle," I say, giving the girls a wave. They scowl back. Delightful.

"Yeah, it's the reason I get out of bed in the morning," he deadpans. "So where can I meet you?"

"I have to work after school, so I'll be at my mom's shop."

"Navy Pier, right?" he asks.

I nod.

"Yeah. That works. I'll see you there. Later," he says, heading off. The girls follow like lap dogs in his wake. As they pass by, one sizes me up, probably trying to assess why a jewel like Charlie would waste his breath on rubble like me. From the way she raises an eyebrow and smirk in tandem, I can tell she's classified me as a "non-threat" in the imaginary competition for Charlie's heart/money/whatever. I smile back, just as smug, feeling satisfied that this girl who hates me for no logical reason will ultimately fail in her quest. I could give two craps about who Charlie ends up with, but this girl does, and I take pleasure in knowing it won't be her.

I feel more eyes on me as I head toward second-period English. Curious whispers curl beside me, and I have to admit

I'm equally intrigued as to why Charlie came off his pedestal to talk to me. He usually moves through the halls like a ghost, his presence felt but never truly absorbed. Something important must be forcing him to come down from on high, and I can only assume it's a matter of the heart since he came to me.

"Oh my Gods." Amani bombards me the second I sit down. She is literally on the edge of her seat as she asks, "Did Charlie Blitzman just ask you out?"

"What? Who told you that?"

"Alison Bleeker."

"Seriously?" I'm surprised my fortune-telling friend could so easily become victim to rumors, even if she's let the well run dry. "You've lost your touch, Amani. Do you really see Charlie and I dating?"

She pulls at her knee socks. "No, but you told me not to poke around in your tomorrows anymore, so I don't see you dating anyone."

This is not surprising, though it does sting a little. On the flip side, I know almost everything about her future husband. The tidbits on him have been building over the years, and now I feel like I know him almost better than I know Amani. He's a vampire with a penchant for expensive custom suits and strong Italian coffee. I'm not sure if he does so now, but someday he will run a haute cuisine restaurant in the Gold Coast that will be known for booking elusive musicians and attracting an eclectic clientele. I even know his name—Vincent—a detail that only appears after spending significant time with someone. I rarely ever learn the names of my clients' matches because I don't have the patience or willpower to sit with someone that long.

Their union will work out nicely since Amani has a very young-looking face—she once got pulled over simply because a cop thought she was a child who had driven off in her mother's car. It will take a very long time for Amani's aging to catch up to his eternal youth. She comes from a family with six kids, and all that craziness led to her firm decision to never reproduce, which again is perfect since he will be physically and mystically unable to. She is also quite the night owl—you see where I'm going with this? They are meant to be. I don't know when or where they'll meet, but when they do: BOOM.

"Thanks, that's very reassuring." I try to say it lightly.

She slaps my arm. "Quit it! Did it happen or not?"

"No, of course not. He said he needs to talk about something," I say.

"When was the last time you even spoke to him? Middle school?"

I shrug. "I don't remember. Maybe? We've never really been tight or anything."

"Do you think it has to do with his dad's visit to your mom?" she asks.

"Maybe." Huh. I didn't even think about that. Duh, Amber.

"I've never talked to him before. What was he like?" she asks.

"I don't know . . . fancy?"

"Fancy? What does that mean?"

"He was wearing a tie clip."

She laughs, slouching back in her chair. "He seems like a jerk."

"Then why were you so worked up at the prospect of me dating him?" I say, raising my voice.

"Because!" she shouts back. "I don't want my best friend dating a jerk."

"Well, neither do I."

"So, I don't end up with a jerk for a husband?" she says, hoping I'll spill a secret.

Normally, I would, but I don't feel like it today. Over the years, she's tried to pry out details about her future beau, wanting little hints as to whether he plays an instrument or is a dog person. Of course, I never reveal anything specific, but because she's my best friend, I do reassure her that she'll live happily ever after.

That kind of reassurance has never been reciprocated. When I've asked her to share a scene from my future, she gets real quiet, and not just because she's trying to keep a secret. For me, her eyes stay still, with no buzz of excitement behind the sockets. And I'm pretty sure it's because she's taken a look at what lies ahead and has seen what I've feared for quite some time: that I will never fall in love.

I wave a finger. "Ah-ah, no poking in tomorrows." I laugh.

Besides, I need to focus on what's coming later today.

I'M KNEE DEEP IN A PROLONGED MATCHMAKING SESSION WHEN Bob, our part-time employee, starts doing his best impression of a boulder. This is a very inopportune time for him to mentally check out, seeing as how we have a paying client sitting with us.

"Is he okay?" the customer asks with an expression that is clearly questioning the validity of our operation.

I let go of her hands momentarily and wave some smelling salts under his nose. "Bob . . . Earth to Bob . . ."

He shakes his massive head, blinking his eyes at doubled speed. "Oh. Sorry. Did I space out again?"

"Yup. What were you thinking about this time?"

"Fire. Lots and lots of fire," he says, the tips of his mouth curling like a flame.

"Oh, that's nice, and not at all creepy," I say. I turn back to our horrified client. "Don't worry about him. He's brilliant at what he does; he's just . . . challenged at about everything else." She nods uncomfortably, and I take her hands again, even though I already have a clear picture of her future beau. For an additional fee, those looking for love can actually see it, thanks to Bob's sketches based on my descriptions of what I envision. Bob's what we in the community refer to as a "mending magus": someone who got a little too deep into the black arts and had to be pulled out before disappearing altogether. Basically, he's a recovering magic addict, and him working here is like being on parole. You can't really take away a wizard's source of power, but you can monitor it. While plopping him down in the middle of a magic shop may seem like dangling whiskey in front of an alcoholic, it's actually a safe space for him to channel his energies.

About two years ago, I discovered him producing some *Mona Lisa*–level drawings in the back room using old flower petal ink that never sold. Because I am brilliant, I decided to put him to work as my sometimes assistant, charging a premium to those wanting more than a simple physical description of their meant-to-be. I describe what I see, he sketches it on some archival parchment, and customers dig into their wallets. Win, win, win.

Bob adds the finishing touches to his drawing. Something about actually seeing a match always turns patrons to mush, making them forget any preconceived weirdnesses about magic.

It's funny how many a wandering soul will make their way into our shop, putting on an air of disbelief and self-righteousness that instantly dissolves the second they find what they've been searching for. The woman clings to the drawing, abandoning her discomfort, while tracing Bob's lines with her fingers, swirling atop the dark curly hair, and caressing the strong jawline. I'm happy for her, but I can't wait for her to leave, so I gently nudge the tip jar in her general direction.

"You seem twitchy today," Bob says, plodding back over to the register. Mom has been working with him for years, and he's gotten much better at controlling his urges. He even comes to coven meetings every now and then. Still, he can't seem to shake his lucky rabbit's foot, which is basically a furry blankie. "You didn't even give her your regular post-match spiel about turtledoves or whatever it is you say. What gives?"

"Nothing, sheesh. You've been off on a different astral plane for the past thirty minutes, and *I'm* the one acting weird?"

He chuckles. "Okay. If you say so." Bob's a good guy, despite his slightly disturbing daydreams. He's a big dude—I'm sure somewhere on his family tree there's an ogre or two—but while he'd happily demolish an evildoer in the most painful way, he's fiercely protective of the ones he cares about. He's like a gentle giant whose dark side you never want to awaken. Also, I'm pretty sure he killed the rabbit whose foot he's always rubbing.

And he's right—I'm definitely not myself. I keep my mouth busy with a too-dry vending machine cookie while my head spins. I feel weird about Charlie's impending visit. Besides Amani, it's very rare to have someone from school make a conscious effort to see me at work; if I do get approached for my talent, it's usually just a quick hallway or parking lot exchange. It's not a secret I work here; still, I feel strange sharing the space with an outsider. Opposite worlds colliding and all that jazz.

If Charlie is coming to talk about his mysterious daddy problem, I won't have much to say on the subject. He really should be talking to Mom, but maybe he assumes his dad already covered that angle. Or maybe he really is looking for some matchmaking assistance. Who knows? But for some reason, I'm jittery, and no amount of low-quality baked goods can help calm me down. I wander around the shop, looking for something to clean or organize while I wait for Charlie's arrival.

Navy Pier can either be the center of the universe or the edge of oblivion depending on the day. The peninsula hosts a rotating slew of special events, from car shows and holiday extravaganzas to lavish waterside weddings. The conventions and overpriced parties draw in spectators like a tractor beam, and all those extra bodies from the far-flung suburbs and neighboring states usually result in added sales for us. I mean, who wouldn't purchase something called "Nap in a Bottle" on a whim? (It's actually pretty awesome, like liquid narcolepsy. Can't fall asleep? This will knock you out before you can put the stopper back in. Mom doesn't like me "wasting" the magic she makes for purchase, but once I used a drop of it on Ivy to hilarious results.) But on those off times, the afternoons are painfully slow, and I wish my talent was not matchmaking but rather time travel so I could become my future pajamaed self.

I'm stacking a display of geodes to look like the Leaning Tower of Pisa when Charlie strolls in. He's still wearing his uniform, only he's lost the jacket and traded the oxfords for black Converse. I myself have changed into my work outfit, which Mom likes to classify as "magic light." No one would take us seriously if we walked around in black pointy hats, and yet, customers still crave that aura of mysticism when shopping for magical tokens and whatnot. So today I've layered up several pagan charm necklaces on top of a silver star-printed tee. Presto! Magic light.

"Welcome to Windy City Magic. What can I do for you?" I say. The words sound weird, even though I say them every day. This is my home turf, but mixing in a Manchester specimen makes me feel oddly out of place. I make sure to do a quick eye-lock with Charlie so I can speed through his happily ever after and get down to business. Yup, there's his dream girl; they're madly in love, yadda, yadda, yadda, and scene.

"Is your mom here?" Charlie asks.

"No, she's out. Were you hoping to talk to her?" Maybe I won't have to deal with him at all.

"No, I just wanted to know if she was here, if she'd be listening. I don't know how it works with . . . witches." He says it carefully, like he's afraid he might offend me. With his stature, I'm sure he's spent time doing media training and learning the importance of political correctness.

I cross my arms. "We prefer the term 'magically inclined,'" I say.

He winces, eyes panicked. "Oh, really?"

"No." I laugh, relaxing my stance. "That'd be obnoxious." Charlie breathes a small sigh. "But seriously, why are you here?"

He gives me a look I don't know how to interpret before answering, "It's about my soon-to-be stepmom. She's missing."

Aha! Jackpot!

"Right, right, your dad was in here the other day. My mom's working on it."

"Yeah, I figured as much. Has she made any progress?"

"Don't know." I shrug. Looks like this will be a quick visit after all. "I'm not exactly on the case."

"Oh," he says, disappointed. He sticks his hands in his pockets, looking around the room. It seems like he wants to say something else, but instead he just stands there.

"So I know this is a magic shop, but I'm not exactly a mind reader. If there's something you want, Charlie, you're gonna have to spill," I say.

"It's just that . . . there are people who like you for you, and people who like you for what you've got. My dad, for all his smarts, is kind of stupid when it comes to this. He's always looking for the diamond in the rough when most people are just plain coal. I know he's worried about Cassandra, but honestly, her disappearance is for the best. I'm kind of hoping you'll help me keep her gone."

Whoa. Wasn't expecting that. "Because . . . ?"

"Because she only wants him for his money. It's so obvious I'm kind of embarrassed for him."

"Ooh, a wicked stepmother. How very Brothers Grimm."

"Yeah, and I guess that makes me Cinderella," he says wearily.

"If the slipper fits."

Charlie turns his back to me and faces a display of porcelain dragon figurines. "These are . . . really something," he observes. He picks one up: a sparkly teal monstrosity with outstretched wings. The damned thing looks like it would sooner burst into song than flames.

"Yeah, I think Navy Pier requires all merchants to stock a certain percentage of tacky useless crap," I say.

He gives me a sideway glance, dark-green eyes peering out-side the field of his lenses. I can tell he doesn't know what to make of me; the feeling is mutual. What kind of person actively tries to keep a loved one away from someone they love? Match-makers are approached to bring people together, not tear them apart.

"So are you going to help me or not?" he asks, replacing the dragon next to a statue of a pixie playing a flute.

"Well, this kind of request is new for me, and it comes with a disclaimer: if Cassandra is your dad's match, there's not much I can do about it."

"What do you mean?" He turns to face me. He's taller than me but not by much. I look directly at his downturned mouth. "Can't I just pay you to do a spell or something?"

"Despite what you may have heard, I'm not actually a witch. My magical inclination is targeted to one specific organ." I poke my finger at his chest. "I'm a matchmaker."

He looks down at the spot where I touched him. Whoops, that was probably too much. I know he has desperate girls invading his personal space all the time. I don't want him getting the wrong idea. All this uncharted territory is making me even more twitchy.

"A matchmaker?" he questions. "Like in *Fiddler on the Roof*?"

"Well, I see the Blitzmans have their Broadway In Chicago season pass up to date." I smirk.

"But seriously, folks."

"Yes, like in *Fiddler*. Think of me as an honest-to-goodness Yente. Although"—I tap my chin dreamily—"I do wish my matchmaking sessions came with the completely unhinged bonus of ex-wives rising from the grave, like hers do. That would definitely give my reputation some edge."

To this, he says nothing, which means he either thinks my reputation is bad enough as it is, or that I'm a complete nutjob.

I give him a few seconds to decide which, but when I can't stand him just staring blankly at me anymore, I blurt out, "Look,

I have a whole display of medicinal herbs that won't alphabetize themselves, so . . ."

"Sorry." He shakes his head. "I've heard kids at school call you a matchmaker, but I tend not to believe anything I hear in those hallways."

"That's probably a best practice," I say.

"I guess I didn't realize matchmaking was an actual thing."

"So you accept witchcraft as reality, but you draw the line at matchmaking?"

"No, I just . . . I guess I never thought about it before."

"Well, don't worry about it. Real-life matchmaking hasn't exactly reached the cultural zeitgeist. I won't hold it against you."

His face goes back to a more normal, less confused expression. "Okay, well, can you tell me if Cassandra is my dad's match?"

"That I can do," I say. "Though take it from me, people don't like to hear that the person they're hooking up with is a waste of time."

"I'll worry about breaking the news," he says. "I just want to know for sure."

"Okay then, step into my office." I gesture to my overly pink matchmaking station.

We sit across from each other. "So, how does this work?" he asks.

I don't usually divulge the tricks of my trade, but since this is an unconventional matchmaking scenario, I guess I'll have to give some hints. "Usually I just need to be around a person and I automatically visualize his match."

Charlie's eyebrows rise in surprise. "Really? That seems kind of invasive."

"Oh, it totally is," I say. "But it's not like I lie awake at night replaying other people's tender moments."

"Well, that's good, I guess," he says with a small smile.

"Anyway, I've known your dad long enough to have a clear vision of his match. Do you have a picture of Cassandra so I can confirm?"

He frowns, pulling out his phone. "I don't think so, but I'll check."

"You know, if she's such a parasite like you say, I'm surprised I haven't seen her pictures in the press. Fame mongering usually goes hand in hand with gold digging," I say.

He's scrolling through his phone. "You'd think so, but she's kind of weird about being photographed. I thought they were just keeping their relationship quiet until the engagement was official, but she won't even let Dad take pictures at home." He sets down his phone in defeat. "I got nothing."

"Well, if you want my help, you'll need to find a picture."

"All right, I'll work on it."

"I'd do it soon, because once Mom starts conjuring stuff it's kind of hard to make her stop," I advise.

"Noted." We sit, business concluded, and I don't know what to do next. Usually, I process payment and offer some sort of poetic love quote or something, but I can't charge Charlie because nothing's happened yet. This whole situation has really got me thrown.

"So . . ." I start.

"So I'll see you around, then. Thanks for your help, Amber."

And with that concludes the most civil interaction I've ever had with one of my peers.

Seven

AMANI'S FACE IS GROWING A FUNGUS. WE'RE ON MY COUCH, cheeks slathered with a highly pungent avocado-and-grape-seed-oil face mask she swears will brighten our complexions in thirty short minutes. (As if Amani has a problem with her skin. She is so youthful-looking I sometimes wonder if her mom drank from the Fountain of Youth when she was in the womb.) The mask smells like day-old guacamole, and not in a "wow, I could really go for tacos" kind of way. More like an "I forgot to take out the garbage and now rats are flocking to my doorstep" way. The concoction has started to harden, meaning we can't open our mouths wide enough to eat the dark chocolate pretzel bars I spent two hours making. Still, she loves this kind of girly thing, so I continue watching the clock because that's what best friends do.

"How many more minutes?" she asks with limited lip movement.

"Nine," I say, feeling a spot on my chin crack.

We're watching some reality show where women compete to win their dream wedding dress. For a program whose central theme should be romance, there sure is a lot of screaming going on.

"Wait, why is the brunette girl crying?" I ask.

"Because the curly-haired girl won the beading challenge, and now the brunette is in last place," Amani replies.

"So now she won't get to walk down the aisle of dreams?"

"Right. Her life is basically over."

"Clearly."

I'm glad I don't have to deal with this relationship stage with my clients. I come in way before the wedding and am usually forgotten about by the time "I dos" are exchanged. Which is for the best, since I know next to nothing about tulle, letterpressing, or what the different colors of roses represent. Amani, though, has already planned her entire wedding and is just waiting for Mr. Right to make his grand entrance.

"These girls have such gaudy taste anyway," she says dismissively. "My dress is going to be simple, elegant. Like something Audrey Hepburn would've worn."

"I can see that."

"With a little blusher veil off to the side. Very fifties chic, very classy."

I nod (I have no idea what a blusher is). "Sounds very *Leave It to Beaver.*"

"Well, I'll have a flask tucked into my garter, duh."

I snort, and a chunk of moldy green falls into my lap.

"Don't laugh! Only a few more minutes till perfect skin!" she scolds.

"Praise the Gods!" I say, raising my hands to the heavens.

This time Amani laughs, making her forehead crackle. She taps it carefully back into place, ensuring none of the mask falls on her pink dress. The two of us could not be more different on the outside; Amani is always dressed like a "lady," in something that would respond appropriately if she twirled. I like to rotate a collection of T-shirts and jeans, and if I'm feeling particularly wild, I might mix in leggings or a hoodie. We may not sync as shopping buddies, but we're pretty much identical on most other points of the friendship checklist.

The women on the screen have been challenged to a pie-eating contest, only with wedding cake. Most of them are holding back (trying to maintain their wedding-day figures, I'm sure), but the curly-haired girl is going to town. That one is in it to win it.

"So how was your meeting with Charlie?" Amani asks once she's reassembled her face.

"Informative," I say. "Turns out it's his future stepmom who's missing."

"Ooh, intriguing. Think the Blitz blitzed her?"

I shake my head. "Doubtful. Charlie says he's crazy for her. Besides, John's a total softie."

"So why'd Charlie come to you?"

I peer into the kitchen, where Mom is mixing up some stress-relieving elixir. Her supernatural genes didn't give her extra-sensitive hearing or anything, but who knows if she's using a sound amplification charm to listen in on our conversation. Charlie was right to be wary; it's definitely possible. Usually I wouldn't mind—I'm pretty open with my mom, even if she isn't always so open with me—but I don't want her knowing about Charlie's concerns until I verify John's match. I turn back to Amani and use sign language to continue talking. (One of her little brothers had serious hearing problems when he was little; he eventually went deaf. The whole family learned to sign, and I did too, mostly to support my friend but also because sign language is pretty much the coolest.)

I tell her everything Charlie told me, though I struggle signing "gold digger." That one's not in my vocabulary.

Amani signs back, *Sounds mysterious*, and then adds, *How was it talking to him?*

I hesitate, not because I don't know the signs, but because I don't know how to describe talking to Charlie. "Unnerving" seems too severe, but "nice" is too affectionate. I settle on "fine."

"As in, *he's so fine?*" she says aloud, in a sassy voice that mimics the bridal contestants.

The timer on my phone goes off, and I bolt to the bathroom

to scrub my algae-ridden face. Amani is close behind.

"Amber Sand," she says, our faces dunking in the sink. "Do you think Charlie Blitzman is cute?"

"What makes you say that?" I ask, picking green from my eyebrow.

"You sure did run away from my question."

"I've been inhaling this toxic scent for a half hour. The sooner I can breathe, the better."

"Mm-hm," she replies. Even underwater, her eyes are rolling.

"Yeah. Besides, even if I did, which I am not admitting, there's no point."

"Why, because he's not your match?" she says in a frustrated tone. Amani has heard me rationalize cute boys away before. And sure, maybe it's something I've done on occasion. But you try daydreaming about a boy when all you see is his future wife.

"Ding, ding, ding," I say.

"Please tell me it's not someone we know."

"Nope, a total stranger."

Amani pats her face dry. Her skin does look brighter; mine just looks not green. "Well, that's good," she says.

"Yeah, I thought so too."

"Because you like him?" She smirks.

"No, because I am a terrible person who takes pleasure in other people's pain."

"Ah yes, I forgot about that."

"Also because I am doomed to roam the earth alone,

remember?" I throw her this line, seeing if she'll take the bait. Amani likes to talk about boys and likes to tease me about liking boys, but whenever I try to "get real" with her, she just changes the subject. I know we have our pact and everything, but I've toed the line, feeding her curiosity with inconsequential attributes about her future husband. She seems to view the pact as an iron-clad, legally binding agreement that would incur some kind of mortal peril if breached. It's not like we made a crazy blood oath; we were just two kids trying to figure out our magical selves. When you're young, your magic comes pouring out of you, and you have little ability to reel it in. But we're way past that now. I wouldn't mind if she let a detail slip every now and then, because every time she glosses over my half-joking self-pity, my poor little heart goes deeper into preparations for solitude. I mean, it's not like Amani has ever said, "Amber, you are destined to be a cat lady." But she doesn't have to: her body language says so much more.

We watch the rest of the dream-dress show and eat the treats I made (I put cayenne powder in Amani's to give them that extra spicy kick she craves). The curly-haired girl advances to the next round and delivers a monologue about how wonderful it is to have one special day to celebrate love.

"Life is hard," she says, "and it is not only our right but our responsibility as people to appreciate the good things. Sure, weddings can be lavish and excessive, but isn't that what makes them good? Isn't doing something so over the top in the name of love a beautiful reason to be alive? If we don't celebrate the good things, we've missed an opportunity to live life to its fullest. At least, that's what I believe."

Amani goes home to finish her calculus homework, and I sit in my room, thinking about the curly-haired girl as I polish off my pretzel bars. For having just consumed a three-tiered wedding cake, that girl sure did speak eloquently about love. Maybe her words were spoken on a ridiculous TV show, but that doesn't mean they're invalid. Love *is* a powerful thing, and while I am making matches constantly, it doesn't mean it's a given or easy to find. I know love is real—I KNOW IT—but that doesn't keep it from being an evasive little bastard that works in mind-boggling ways. I see it every day: people who should be together don't always find each other, and some attach themselves to others when they should keep looking.

If you are lucky enough to find love, you should celebrate it. You should shout it from the rooftops, or sing it in a song, or compete in a reality show to make your dream comes true. You shouldn't let love pass by unnoticed, especially because there are many who will never experience it. Like this girl right here. I have no clue what's in the cards for me. I'm hoping there's passion and friendship at the end of my rainbow, but all the magic in the world cannot guarantee such a thing.

I mean, c'mon . . . a matchmaker without a match?

Talk about irony.

Eight

WITH MY HEAD A CONSTANT SWIRL OF RELENTLESS ROMANCE
and lemon Bundt cake recipes, you'd think there wouldn't be
any room up there for schoolwork. Actually, while I know quadratic equations and dissected frog entrails will never apply to
my chosen professions, I get a certain satisfaction from excelling
at school. (If I were a full-blown witch, the frog stuff would
probably come into play, but luckily, no part of matchmaking
ever requires Kermit guts.) I'm not on the valedictorian track
or anything, but I keep my grades high in hopes of snagging
scholarships for culinary school. Plus, getting an A just feels
good, you know?

    You know what doesn't make school exciting, besides being
trapped in a box with people who are technically my peers

but realistically lacking in any sort of redeemable qualities? I'll tell you: group projects. If you are someone who enjoys group projects, then you are probably the reason they are the worst. No matter the subject or combinations of personalities or intelligence levels, there's always one person who completely takes advantage of the others, doing absolutely nothing but still riding the wave to A-town. I am not in the business of maintaining someone else's GPA, but group projects are so evil that they force you to care about other people's incompetence, lest you want to drown by the weight of their laziness. ARGH. And don't try to feed me some garbage about how teamwork will prepare me for the real world: NO. If I encounter bull like this while building my cupcake empire, there will be hell to pay (and trust me, I can get in touch with the right people to make that happen).

But for now, I'm at the mercy of the American school system, sitting in English just waiting to see which batch of Manchester's best I'll be chained to for our next collaborative affair. Ms. Dell announces with annoying glee that we'll be doing group presentations on notable female writers. She assembles the groups herself, ensuring what she believes to be a balance of talents. Amani is in my class, but we never get paired up. No, I'll get whoever is worst suited for me, because Karma is an alcoholic bastard who more often than not is asleep at the wheel.

"Amani," Ms. Dell calls from her clipboard. "You'll be

covering Maya Angelou's works with"—*Amber Sand, Amber Sand, Amber Sand*—"Jeremy and Brian." Damn, foiled again. But she didn't get off too bad: at least Brian works on the school's lit mag.

"Amber"—*oh boy, here we go*—"you'll be covering Sylvia Plath with Brendan and Ivy."

UUUUUUGGGGGGGHHHHHHH.

Ivy shoots me an icy glare from across the room. My skin prickles like it knows something wretched is heading my way.

Ms. Dell finishes the group assignments and instructs us to cluster up and start mapping out our research plans. I wait as long as possible to trudge over to Ivy, whereas Brendan has already pulled his desk up as close to her as possible. He shifts awkwardly in his seat, trying to find the "coolest" way to sit, alternating between a crossed-leg and laid-back slouch. Poor bastard. This must be the happiest day of his life; too bad Ivy hasn't even noticed he's alive, let alone sitting so "casually" next to her.

She's staring right at me, a serpentine smile curling on her glossy lips. I search the room for Amani, who has taken residence in a back corner with her group. She sees me approaching the Ice Queen and hangs herself on an invisible noose, tongue flopping out in imaginary death.

"So, Sylvia Path," I say as I finally take a seat. "Should be uplifting."

Brendan takes no notice of me. If he's not careful, he'll start drooling.

"Well, if anyone knows about eternal suffering, it would be you," Ivy sneers.

"True." I nod. "And luckily, we'll have you as our star expert on human torture!"

Ivy leans forward, French-manicured nails gripping the desk. Her blouse is scarcely buttoned—the bare minimum to keep the girls from escaping—and our male teammate is physically incapable of noticing anything else. "Listen, Amber, you get how this works. No matter what happens, I'm getting an A, I'll see to it. And even though I could, I certainly won't be using my charms to do the same for you."

I cannot stress enough how much of a waste it is to use precious siren magic on something so stupid as a high school English assignment, but hey, the sooner her power's used up, the better for mankind.

"Sure, I get it. I'm a take-action kind of girl anyway; I don't like to rely on the uncertainty of magic," I say.

She scoffs. "Tsk, tsk, Amber. What would your mother say?"

"She'd say the same. Just because you can use magic, doesn't mean you should. That's just a little life tip from me to you."

She lays a limp hand across her heart. "Wow, that means a lot, thanks. Especially when I know you'd do anything to be more like me."

"A siren? Nah. I'd take matchmaking over putting boys like Brendan in a boob coma any day."

She looks at him, as if just noticing he's there. "Oh, that?

The Best Kind of Magic

That has nothing to do with being a siren and everything to do with genetics. An area in which you are clearly lacking."

I'm about to spit fire when Ms. Dell butts her fleshy bottom in. "How's it going, you three?"

"Just wonderful!" Ivy beams, turning up her wattage. "We're all really clicking on a team plan." Her sticky-sweet tone is bringing up my morning waffle.

Ms. Dell just smiles back, brain probably scrambled by Ivy's signals. I have a feeling Ivy could've said, "I'm going to murder these two and feed their livers to my dog," and our teacher's reaction would've been the same. That's some magic trick. With Ivy pulling hypnosis purposely on Ms. Dell and inadvertently on Brendan, it looks like I'll be doing this project all by myself. Perfect.

The bell rings, and I peel myself from my chair. My body feels like dead weight. Being around a siren's energy completely depletes mine. Good Gods, how can it only be the end of second period?

Amani has dashed off; her next class is all the way across campus, so she always has to haul to make it, leaving me to brave the hallways alone. But today when I step outside English, I see Charlie waving at me. About ten girls in the crosshairs nearly faint, thinking his gesture is for them, but they keep themselves off the floor long enough to witness him walking toward me instead.

I've never been so simultaneously loathed and envied.

"Hey," he says. "I'm glad I caught you."

I am too, but mostly because his talking to me is causing other girls crippling pain. "Did you find a picture?"

Charlie grins. "Yeah, but it's not the best shot; her hand is partially blocking her face. Is that okay?"

I shrug. "Maybe. Let's see it."

He swings his bag around and shuffles through. Just as he's about to pull out the picture, Ivy materializes and presses her chest into his.

"Hey, Charlie," she says in a low, bedroom voice. "Looking for that love letter you wrote me?"

He recoils like he just smelled a skunk. "I'm sorry, do I know you?"

She tosses her head back in a fake laugh, golden hair cascading over her shoulders. "You are such a tease!" She tiptoes her fingers up his arm.

"Ivy, I'm flattered, but I'm talking to Amber here," he says, gently removing her tentacles from his suit jacket.

Ivy pops her hip, arms crossed, and makes a disgusted sound. "Why?"

"Because I need her."

The brilliance of his answer floors me and triggers blood lust in Ivy's eyes.

"Gross. I've never figured you to go slumming," she says.

"Only when I'm talking to you," he replies.

My mouth drops in tandem with Ivy's. That was . . .

everything! I've never seen Ivy put in her place before; who knew her siren powers had limits? For a split second, I wonder if Charlie is 1/100th magical in some way and could therefore deflect her advances mystically, but I don't have time to fully process, since Ivy's spazzing and that's much more worthy of my attention. She spins around and disappears into the crowded hallway. Suddenly, I'm having the best day ever.

"As president of the Ivy Chamberlain Is the Worst Club, I'd like to offer you a free lifetime membership," I say, extending my hand to Charlie. He grins, and as we shake, I realize this is the first time I've touched a boy in a non-matchmaking session in a long time. I hope my palms aren't sweaty.

"Is there a membership card?"

"Of course. And buttons."

"Well, sure."

"But before I heat up the lamination machine, please tell me more of your hatred for Ivy," I say, relishing the moment. He laughs, and I notice we're still palm to palm. We release before it gets weird.

"Maybe another time. The bell's gonna ring soon. Can I still show you the picture?" he asks.

"Oh yeah, let me see."

He pulls it out, and it doesn't take long for me to make my assessment. I've known Mr. Blitzman my whole life, and spent plenty of time crystallizing the image of his beloved. And even with only a partial view of this woman Charlie is presenting, I can tell from the curve of her nose to the wave of her hair that things are about to get interesting.

"Charlie," I say, "this is not your future stepmother."

"Really?" he asks excitedly. "Are you sure?"

"Definitely. I've envisioned your dad's match plenty of times, and this is an imposter," I confirm.

"That's great. This is great," he says. I can almost feel his brain bouncing with happiness. It's like when I get an idea for a new recipe and I feel the possibilities opening up to me. I've never seen someone have this reaction to a match negation. I'm glad he's pleased, though I doubt John will be. "So what next?"

"Well, anything moving forward is kind of outside my job description."

"But you've gotten me this far. You can't back out now," he pleads.

"Technically, that's not true—"

He takes a step closer and puts both hands on my shoulders. I'm in such close proximity to his face I notice he missed a tiny spot shaving this morning, and somehow seeing such a minute detail of his jawline makes me squirm for some reason.

"Amber, I don't have anyone else I can go to on this. Regardless of what you just told me, my dad still loves Cass; he's not gonna stop looking for her. If we can find her first, maybe we can convince her—or bribe her—not to come back. And then you can point Dad toward his real match."

"It's just that that's not really how it works, Charlie. Just because I can see who this woman is doesn't mean I have her GPS coordinates in my temporal lobe—"

"Amber, please?" From behind his frames, Charlie's eyes are working overtime, trying to pull off that one-two punch of puppy-dog need and sincere vulnerability. He suckers me in, though I'm not sure if it's due to his devotion to his dad's happiness or my nervousness at standing so close to him. I will say, for someone who's probably used to getting whatever he wants, the boy has serious persuasion skills.

I relent. "All right, geez, I'll help. But I make no guarantees. You probably won't be a satisfied customer."

"I'm already satisfied."

"Great. Then there's nowhere to go but down."

Charlie smiles. Unlike most girls, I haven't dedicated hours of my life to memorizing his physical attributes, though for this feature, I will admit their studies may not have been a complete waste of time. I can't say there's anything truly distinctive about his smile; it's not like he has disproportionately sized lips or dimples that suddenly dot his cheeks. No, it's just . . . I know our interaction is fleeting, and he has surely flashed his pearly whites all over town, but somehow this particular smile seems meant just for me, like I'm the only one he's ever pulled out this expression for. Must be part of that celebrity influence, inspiring me to do his bidding. I better tread lightly here.

The bell rings and everyone starts to scurry, a mad dash

of green plaid. I'll be late for sure; too bad I can't hop on a broomstick (kidding).

"I'll meet you after school, okay?" Charlie asks as he starts walking backward. "We'll come up with a game plan."

"Is that, like, a football reference?"

"Sure." He laughs, before jogging off. "Time to bear down." Maybe I'll have to brush up on my sports terminology if I'm going to be helping one of the game's most famous families.

Nine

AMANI AND I ARE SITTING ON THE QUAD, SHOES OFF, TOES IN the grass. Mom always says it's important to stay connected to the earth: to be aware of the elements around you. That's a very witchy way of suggesting one stop and smell the roses. Chicago has a lot of green spaces tucked within the concrete cityscape, so I do my best to honor the wishes of my Wicca ancestors by occasionally rolling in the grass like a kindergartener. Charlie and I didn't set up a meeting spot, but he's a determined young lad, so I figure he'll find me eventually.

"We had critiques in photography today," Amani says, pulling off her socks.

"For that lighting assignment?" I ask. She nods. "How'd it go?"

She shrugs, picking at a dandelion. "Mr. Espy says I don't have vision."

I laugh. "If only he knew."

The corner of her mouth turns up. "Yeah. Still, I thought I did well."

"I like your photos. What the hell does he know?"

"He's the teacher. I don't know. I just wish I could find what I'm good at. What's the point of being a precog if I can't even figure out my own future?"

"Preach, sister," I say, waving my hands in the air.

"I'm serious, Amber. You already know everything you pull from an oven will taste like heaven; I seem to lack any discernible talent." Her shoulders slump forward. Everyone worries about the future, but Amani's particular situation has made "The Future" a major point of contention for her. She's always worrying, always obsessing about what's to come and getting overly upset when she makes mistakes. It's like she feels she has to master whatever's in front of her; if she doesn't live her life perfectly, her gift will have gone to waste. This is ridiculous because (a) she cannot see her own future, (b) she barely takes the time to see *other* people's futures, and (c) whose life is perfect? I'm convinced this pressure she puts on herself is why she's already planned her wedding, because it's the only thing she knows for sure will happen (because I told her). I wish I could help her chill out and see how awesome she is.

"I think we're having one of those 'grass is greener' moments,"

I say. "Want to do a Freaky Friday so you could find out your career path and I could find out for sure if I end up a spinster?"

Now she's smiling. "Sure. Do you think your mom would notice if her daughter's aura changed?"

"Hmm, probably. I bet she'd whip up a truth serum to be sure."

"Truth *serum*? Ugh. Sounds gooey, like it would stick to the roof of your mouth," she says, making a disgusted face.

"Oh yeah, truth serums are the worst. They taste like tar. It's like you can't help but vomit up the truth," I say.

She's giggling. "And you know from experience?"

"Mom gave me one once, when I was nine. She thought I broke her great-grandma's looking glass. And she was right; I totally did." I stick out my tongue, remembering the thick brown sludge in my mouth. "I haven't lied to her since."

We're both laughing now and don't notice Charlie approach.

"Hope I'm not interrupting," he says with a little wave. His school blazer is slung over the top of his messenger bag, but even in a more relaxed state, he still looks polished.

"No, we were just reminiscing about my time as a criminal youth," I say. "Charlie, you know Amani?"

"Yeah, we're in photography together. I liked your print today," he says to her.

She perks up. "Really? Thanks. Yours was . . ." She trails off, trying to think of something positive to say.

"Not very good," he fills in. "I don't think I'm destined for the arts."

"Me neither," she agrees.

We stand to meet him, brushing stray grass off our skirts. I've been trying to come up with a "game plan" for Charlie all day, but it's been tricky, seeing as how I'm not really built for this kind of work. Being neither a witch nor a teenage private investigator, I'm not sure how to go out into the world and find someone's match. How do people do it? Where do they look? Is this why online dating exists? Still, I promised I would help, and the best I can think of is to find Cass and prove to John that she's not the one.

"So I know my mom tried a locator spell for Cass that went nowhere, which makes me think there's a supernatural element at play," I say.

"Like . . . ?"

"Like, has Cass ever sprouted fangs at the dinner table? Any unexplained scales upon getting wet?"

"You're speaking metaphorically, right?" he asks.

"No. I'm trying to figure out Cass's backstory, and sometimes the supernatural can fend off magical advances."

Charlie's face freezes in confusion as if I removed his batteries mid-thought. I've met so many magical creatures at this point, the thrill behind it is gone, but I guess for someone like Charlie, suggesting his dad's girlfriend could be something from a monster movie is akin to revealing Santa Claus is real. To his credit, he doesn't immediately write me off as others have been known to do, but he's definitely processing at a slower bandwidth.

Finally, he comes back online, saying, "I mean, I've never seen her drinking the blood of the innocent, if that's where you're going with this."

"Doesn't mean it hasn't happened, though," Amani chimes in.

"Right. Let's not rule that out," I say. "What else can you tell me about her?"

Charlie takes a deep breath, trying to keep his feet on the ground. "You guys are joking, right?"

Amani and I share a glance. "I think you'd know if we were telling jokes," I say.

"Yeah, we're really funny people," Amani replies.

Charlie doesn't know what to do with himself. He came to find his dad's missing girlfriend, and now we're talking about vampires and stuff. While he may consider Cassandra a type of monster, I don't think he's ever entertained that as an actual possibility.

"It's okay, Charlie; we're not trying to mess with you. We just need more information about Cass."

He blinks slowly, probably second-guessing every interaction he's ever had with her. "Well, um, she's not very social, mostly likes to stay in with Dad. I don't think she has a job, but somehow she leaves a lot of shopping bags at our place."

"Hmm, not enough. If I had something of hers, something that she touched, maybe that would help," I say.

"Well, I could take you to my place and you could look around," he suggests.

Amani's eyes open wide, her eyebrows up to her hairline. I know what she's thinking: an invitation to Charlie Blitzman's house?! She really wants me to attach myself to a boy—any boy—but if she's still entertaining the idea of me crushing on Charlie, she needs to drop it. Like yesterday. There's no point getting attached to a boy whose future is written with someone else. I subtly sign to her, *Cut it out.*

"Okay, if you want," I say to Charlie. "When's a good time?"

"How about now? You free?"

Today's my one weekday off from Windy City Magic (Mom says I need regular free time to "explore my teenage self," which is slightly unfortunate phrasing). Amani signs to me, *Get it, girl!*

I sign back, *Your subtlety is blinding.*

Charlie notices our silent conversation. "What are you two saying?" he asks.

"Nothing. Uh, Amani just . . . thinks you're hot." Charlie blushes, but not to the extent of Amani's coloration: her face turns so red I'm sure steam will spill from her ears. She is PISSED. "I'm free now."

"All right, my driver is waiting around the corner."

I try not to gag. "Well, we better get going, then. Bye, Amani!" I say sweetly.

"Nice talking to you," Charlie adds as we head off. I look back at my best friend, who is slowly sliding a finger across her neck like she's going to kill me. It's okay. I'll make it up to her with a jalapeño cheesecake.

Charlie opens the door to his waiting black Town Car and lets me in first. He slides in after, setting his bag in his lap and rolling his sleeves up to his elbows, revealing the tail of some sort of reptilian tattoo on his right forearm. Interesting. I'm surprised John let him get such a large tattoo, being underage and all.

"So where are we headed?" I ask.

"The Gold Coast. Where do you live?"

"Wicker Park."

"Cool."

The Gold Coast, as you can imagine, is an affluent neighborhood of Chicago. Lots of old money there. Million-dollar brownstones and elegant high-rises are the name of the game. Picture ladies in heels walking bichon frises and you've got the vibe. My neighborhood, Wicker Park, is more eclectic, bohemian, bordering on hipster. Lots of independent boutiques and funky shops with the occasional Starbucks sprinkled in. I've begged Mom to relocate Windy City Magic there, but she refuses, saying the locals wouldn't support us. I disagree; everyone there is super-committed to being cool, and what's cooler than magic?

"So, tell me more about this supernatural stuff," Charlie says casually.

"I'm surprised you don't already know. You seem like a man of the world," I say.

"I mean, I've traveled with my dad, sure, but he's never taken me to Transylvania or anything."

I choke out a laugh. "Transylvania? That's adorable."

He laughs too. "I don't know! You're implying vampires are real; where are they supposed to come from?"

"Where does anyone come from? We're all just individuals trying to get through our days."

"So, let me see here: witches, vampires . . . Are there any other fictional creatures I should start believing in?"

"Charlie, witches are real, and so are vampires. So are a lot of things."

He's smiling but shaking his head.

I continue. "If you think the things that go bump in the night are only the stuff of fairy tales, then you haven't been observing the weird world we live in."

"Oh, really?"

"Yes, really! Why do you think so many movies and books are littered with monsters?"

"Because those writers are on drugs?"

"No . . . Well, maybe some of them," I concede. "But the truth is, monsters roam among us. To not write about them would be a lie."

He's giving me a pitying look an adult would give a hyper-imaginative child.

"Fine! If you don't believe me, I'll just have to show you!"

"Here in the car?" he asks.

"No, nothing about me would prove the existence of mystical creatures. Being a matchmaker is like being magic-adjacent: close to the cool stuff, yet completely removed."

Charlie considers this. "Okay, then, how do you propose exposing the supposed supernatural underground I've been oblivious to?"

Hmm. Good question. If I were a fairy or mermaid, I could just shake out my wings or tail as proof, but since I don't have any magical appendages, I'll have to take Charlie to someone who does.

"Can your driver take us to the MCA?" I ask.

"Sure, but calling contemporary art 'supernatural' is stretching it."

"Ha-ha," I say with an eye roll.

Charlie asks Dan, his driver, to reroute downtown. Minutes later, we're pulling up to the white flight of stairs that leads to the Museum of Contemporary Art. While this museum is not necessarily my favorite (call me crazy, but piles of discarded printer paper or toilet seats stapled to the wall does not a masterpiece make), one of the curators is a Windy City Magic regular and genuine shape-shifter. My pal Sergio's whole life revolves around art, and who could blame him? When you can transform yourself into any other shape, your body becomes its own canvas.

The MCA's entryway is stark and open: a palate-cleanser for the wackiness ahead. At the front desk, I ask a girl with a shaved head for Sergio, and she informs me he's downstairs in special exhibits. Charlie and I walk down a spiral staircase that circles around an intricate hanging mobile. Thousands of tiny blue squares dangle from almost invisible thread, probably meant to signify the fragility of life or something. Sure enough, when we reach the bottom, I spot Sergio instructing a team about a new installation.

We wait off to the side, next to a sculpture that looks like a piece of chewed gum, until Sergio's team heads down the hall. I give him a wave before he follows, and he greets me with an air kiss.

"Amber, darling! Whatever are you doing here?" His voice echoes through the hall. "Don't tell me Windy City Magic now makes deliveries, because that would just be fabulous." Sergio's dressed in head-to-toe black and wears a winning white smile. He doesn't have to be tattooed and pierced within an inch of his life to prove he's in the art scene; he simply is the scene.

"Nope, sorry, not until the mayor clears the skyline for broomstick travel," I say. Charlie makes an awkward coughing sound. "Speaking of which: Sergio, this is my"—friend? client? boy-shaped person?—"schoolmate Charlie Blitzman."

"Delighted to meet you, Charlie," Sergio says, palm extended. Charlie shakes his hand. "The pleasure's all mine."

"What are you two here to see today?" Sergio asks. "We

have a very exciting new artist who uses black light to draw out emotions and—"

"As tempting as that sounds," I interrupt before he can finish describing what I am sure is a terrifying exhibit, "I actually brought Charlie here for a separate viewing." I take a second to find the right words. The thing about supernaturals—well, everyone really—is that they don't like to be singled out. No one wants to be turned into a freak show. Every creature I know is just trying to go about his or her life, to blend in without protest or persecution. So I don't want to put Sergio on the spot and make him feel like a weirdo. Still, I know he's proud of his shape-shifter heritage and views his talent as a gift worth sharing . . . for a select audience, of course. "He's really gotten into performance art lately, and I told him you're the best of the best." I add a wink for good measure.

Sergio blushes. "You flatter me. Of course, anything for a Sand girl. You know, I have been working on something new and would love a trial audience. I only have a few minutes, though. Here, come this way."

He leads us to an empty, pitch-black auditorium with a small stage. Charlie and I stumble into each other while trying to find seats, while Sergio makes his way to the light room. Finally, he lights a spot and takes his place center stage.

"What is happening?" Charlie whispers.

"Get ready to believe," I say.

Sergio crouches himself into a ball, and for a moment,

nothing happens. Slowly, he starts to stand, but he's no longer a man; he's a bear. A clawing brown bear towering on his hind legs. The transformation was so fluid, so seamless, it's almost unbelievable, except we're seeing it with our own eyes.

"Oh my God!" Charlie gasps, and clutches the armrest between us, incidentally grabbing my hand that was resting there. He squeezes it before realizing he's gripping flesh instead of upholstery.

"Oh, sorry," he says, panicking and letting go. Even in the darkness of the theater, I can see the whites of his eyes.

"It's okay," I whisper. "Keep watching." Sergio has collapsed back down, and this time he elongates into a snapping alligator. The details are really stunning. He's going from fur to scales in a matter of seconds. Must be all those herbs he buys from our shop. For his final transformation, Sergio spreads wings as a bald eagle and flies out over our heads. Even I am shocked by this; I had no idea a shape-shifter could take flight. I clap with much enthusiasm, and Charlie joins in, only with less gusto and more dazed shock.

"Sergio, that was incredible!" I say once my friend has returned to his human form.

"Thank you, Amber. I'm glad you liked it," he says. "I call the piece *Constant Predator*. What did you think, Charlie?"

Charlie looks like his brain has been liquefied, but he manages to respond with "It definitely blew me away."

Sergio is very pleased by this, wrapping us both in a hug.

"I'm so glad you stopped by! It's been a while since I've been able to perform like that. Feels good to keep myself limber."

"I'm sure it does," I say.

"Unfortunately I must get back to an installation. It was nice meeting you, Charlie. Amber, does your mom have those arnica roots back in stock yet?"

"Yeah, they should be in by the end of the week."

"Wonderful! Then I'll be seeing you again soon. Ciao!" He disappears down the hall.

I turn my attention back to Charlie, who still looks like he's seen a ghost. "Am I gonna have to carry you out of here?" I ask him. "Because I'll be honest, I skipped the weight-lifting unit in gym."

He shakes his head, presumably to slosh his brain back in place. "No. I mean . . . whoa. So. That was a . . . ?"

"Shape-shifter. And a damn good one, I might add."

"Wow."

"Want to take a walk? Clear your head before we get back to cracking Cassandra's case?"

He nods.

We leave the MCA and head into the throngs of people outside Water Tower Place. Lots of big-name designers have plonked storefronts in this neck of the woods, so there's always people looking to drop massive cash for meaningless labels. This shopper's paradise is even less my scene than contemporary art, considering I usually get my clothes at the thrift store. But all the flashy merchandise seems to be calming Charlie, who's starting to speak in complete sentences.

"So there's more, right? Like, all around? Supernatural creatures?"

"Pretty much. Chicago is bursting with 'em." I take a quick look to see if I spot any in close proximity. "Ooh, right over there—see the hairy guy with the briefcase? Werewolf, for sure."

Charlie squints, trying to see the signs invisible to him. "How do you know?"

"I just . . . know." I shrug. "It's like a sixth sense."

"And can they detect you too?"

"Oh, sure. But I usually only get approached at the shop. Supernaturals like privacy too. They don't want their love lives discussed on the street."

Charlie raises an eyebrow.

"What? The mystical community isn't so different. Everybody's got their issues; some are just more physically manifested than others."

A smile starts to creep on Charlie's lips. "This is not what I expected when I came to you for help."

"And now you're totally freaking out?"

"Yeah, but in a good way. Who knew the world had so much magic?"

Well, I did, for one thing, but I let him have his moment to revel in this new reality. I guess it's good he's accepting of this, because who knows where this wild-goose chase with Cassandra will take us?

We're walking past the glossy storefronts—Tiffany's, Ralph Lauren, Cartier—when I spot a familiar face bobbing inside a Kiehl's. A face who has no need for expensive eye cream or wrinkle serum because she can easily brew up her own. The sight of her browsing for overpriced cosmetics is so foreign to me, I actually freeze in confusion on the sidewalk.

What is my mom doing in there?

Ten

"CHARLIE, UM, CAN YOU WAIT OUT HERE FOR JUST A SEC?" I ask, eyes trained on the mysterious shopper who shares my mom's face.

"Yeah, sure," he answers dreamily, head still in the supernatural clouds. The way he's looking at all the passing pedestrians, you'd think they were suddenly covered with glitter or flashing arrows pointing to their potential magical mutations. His expression is so pleasantly mystified that I assume I could leave him out here all day and he wouldn't notice I'm gone.

I slip into the Kiehl's and hide out in a corner next to the men's shaving kits to spy on my mom. Could she be doing some comparison shopping, trying to get ideas for new potions? As I look around the store, I realize my mom is not the only familiar shopper. Next to the shampoo shelves are three witches I know I've seen at Windy City; handling the body butter is another Dawning Day coven member. Is this some sort of backward Wicca field trip?

"What about this, Lucille?" says Wendy Pumple, passing over a bottle of facial toner. "It says it contains rosewater."

"Hmm." Mom looks over the label. "Well, rosewater is a known anti-inflammatory. I use it in potions aimed to calm swollen ankles—"

Random laughter interrupts her thought. From behind a mirror emerges a woman I've seen before but not yet met. She's newish to Dawning Day, coming for the last few weeks or so, and she definitely has a much different vibe than the rest of the ladies. Rather than playing into the whole "servant of Mother Earth" look, she's gone the way of a reality-show housewife: hair bleached outside the human limits, skin pulled so tight you can almost see bone. Speaking of tight, there's no way she poured herself into that leopard-print dress without the aid of magic.

"Lucille, darling, rosewater is such an old-world remedy!" the woman remarks in a surprisingly deep voice. She yanks the bottle from Mom's hands. "Of course it *can* work, but its potency is so weak, one might not even bother at all!" She laughs again, as if she's said something truly hilarious. The other witches, though, have turned in her direction, being sure to catch her thought. "On the West Coast, we've tapped into some genetically modified plants that produce amazing results in spellwork."

"Like what?" someone eagerly asks. This stranger has a rapt audience.

From where I'm standing, the fragrance of the foot cream is suddenly overpowering, and I let out a giant sneeze, causing everyone to look my way.

Wendy brightens upon seeing me.

"Amber! Hello, dear!" she sings in her sweet old-lady voice.

"Hello, hello," I say to all the witches who make their way over to greet me. Mom hangs back, pretending to be interested in a display of body scrubs. I keep trying to catch her eye, to signal that I don't have time for a coven meet and greet right now, but she purposely evades me. Finally I'm approached by Ms. Anti-Rosewater, who throws her hands up in musical theater surprise, and fights the Botox to raise her eyebrows in delight.

"So you're Amber! Aren't you the most darling little baby!" She squeezes my cheeks as if I still was one, and I give my best forced-polite smile. For the love of Gods, why isn't my mom coming over to save me? "My name's Victoria," she says, "I've heard so much about you!" She leans in, whispering, "Shame about the whole matchmaker thing, dear. It's so sad when a prominent bloodline is compromised."

If I were a witch, this chick would find herself flame-broiled right about now. But before I can respond, Victoria makes one of those pitying clicks with her tongue and gives my shoulder a condescending pat. She turns and goes back to shopping for lip-plumping products.

I march straight over to Mom, my angry stomping audible over the piped-in classical music. "MOM. WHAT. THE. HELL?"

She grimaces, and pulls out a small rose quartz from her pocket. With the stone in hand, she wraps her arm over my shoulder, and whispers, *"Susurri,"* which puts us in a cone of silence, where no one will be able to hear our exchange. The sounds from the store disappear, and all I hear is our breathing.

"Why is your entire coven shopping at Kiehl's when they should be supporting one of their own?" I yell, to the detection of no one other than Mom.

She sighs. "We're having a coven meeting."

"What? Here?"

"Yes. Victoria thought it would be nice to have a change of venue," she says, clearly annoyed.

"*Victoria* thought? And who the hell is she?"

"She's a recent member, moved here from Los Angeles." I groan. Mom is working overtime to keep her expression neutral, but I can tell there's something else whirring in her head. She continues. "She's had quite an effect on the group since arriving."

"So why don't you just kick her out? I mean, she's clearly not one of you guys," I say just as Victoria passes us by, oblivious to our conversation.

"You know that's not our way." It's true; Dawning Day is certainly one of the more welcoming covens. Some are super-strict, requiring members to give extensive proof of their magical lineage, and even then being put on probation until their mystical worth can be qualified. Dawning Day has always rolled out a metaphorical welcome mat for those looking for magical companionship, a gesture that seems to be biting them in the butt right now.

"Okay, so if you're having a 'meeting,' who is watching the shop?" I ask.

"Bob."

"BOB?! By himself?"

"I'm leaving soon to check on him. The ladies know I have my responsibilities." Mom looks tired, as if simply being at this ridiculous excuse for a coven meeting is draining her patience. She's never been one to cling desperately to tradition, but I know deep down she enjoys the company of fellow witches, and filling up baskets of moisturizers is not her idea of quality time.

"Okay, well . . . see you at home?"

Mom releases my shoulder, and the ambience of the store floods back in. "I'll see you at home," she says with a weak smile.

I don't bother saying good-bye to the other witches; I can't believe that any of them would be down for this scene. Two weeks ago, one of them nagged at me for serving her tea that was bought at a store, not homegrown, so why would they suddenly be stoked for buying commercialized beauty supplies? I'm immediately distrustful of Victoria and make a mental note to get myself a new voodoo doll.

When I get outside, Charlie is calling his driver, who pulls up moments later. I have to say, not having to wait for smelly, overcrowded public transportation is a definite perk of being rich.

I wiggle down into the leather seat, sighing as I push my green-and-blue hair out of my face. For a moment, I'm envious of Charlie, who is still relishing the infinite possibilities of magic and has no idea the annoyances it can bring.

He's looking out the window, a thought churning in his gut. There's a twinkle in his eye illuminated by his lenses. "What about . . . dragons?"

"What about them?" I snap, more sharply than I mean.

"Are they real too?" The genuine curiosity in his question kills me; he's like a little kid wanting to know how airplanes fly or why the sky is blue. I can tell he desperately wants the answer to be yes. I soften a bit.

"I've never seen one, but there's a warlock who comes through our shop; he's one of our suppliers. He says he once saw a dragon in the Himalayas. His product is good and he never tries to cheat us, so I'd like to believe what he says is true."

Charlie leans back, a satisfied smile spreading from cheek to cheek. Apparently, I said the right thing.

"Is that a dragon on your arm?" I point to the tattoo peeking out from his Manchester button-down.

"Oh yeah," he says proudly, rolling his shirtsleeve up even more. "I've always loved them, ever since I saw *Pete's Dragon* as a kid. I mean, how badass would it be to have a pet dragon?" His ink is elaborate, a sleeve starting at his wrist and presumably going up his entire arm. It's a swirl of flames and scales, all bright green and vibrant orange. I had no idea he had his freak flag tattooed on his skin.

"It would be pretty sweet," I answer, "though personally, I'd choose a unicorn."

"I wouldn't turn that down either," he says. I stare at him for longer than I mean to. Since I never really got the chance to get to know him when we were younger, I eventually pegged Charlie Blitzman as a spoiled rich kid, too busy collecting Porsches and swimming in gold coins to even consider conversing with others. Yet here he is, geeking out about dragons and unicorns. It's certainly unexpected.

"Hey, we're here," he says, breaking my spell. Dan stops the car, and we pile out on the street in front of a sparkling highrise. I don't spend a lot of time in this part of the city, so I've lost my bearings.

The doorman nods as we pass by, greeting Charlie as "Mr. Blitzman." Everything here is fancy and perfect, but I guess it should be. It's not like the mayor would be living in a dive. I've just never been serenaded by a grand piano on my way up to *my* apartment.

The Blitzmans live in the penthouse (surprise!), and as soon as we exit the elevator, I go straight toward the window like a moth to the flame. What an amazing view! Sure, I've been to the Hancock Observatory deck, but I love any view of this city. The buildings, Lake Michigan, the hustle of people like ants. So great.

"You want a snack or something?" Charlie offers.

"Sure." He emerges from the kitchen with a bowl of Cheetos and bottled water. Mmm . . . Cheetos.

"I'm just gonna change out of my uniform. I'll be right back," he says.

I wish I had a change of clothes, but I focus on the Cheetos instead. I walk around the living room, artificial cheese dust on my lips, looking at photos. There are lots of pictures of Charlie: baby Charlie, Little League Charlie, stuck-in-a-pile-of-Legos Charlie. Then there's one of John, Charlie, and Charlie's mom; she was in a car accident when he was five. That was so long ago . . . before my matchmaking awakened, before I knew John would one day find love again. I remember John coming to our house sometimes, to talk with Mom, and I'd feel so sad to hear a grown man cry. Seeing this picture makes me want to help him find happiness even more.

Charlie comes back out, dressed in a blue plaid shirt and gray wool tie over dark jeans. He's swapped out his Manchester fox tie clip for another, this one a silver skull. It's the same basic pieces as his uniform, so I don't know why he bothered.

"Okay, so . . . where should we start?" he asks.

"Well, does Cass live with you guys? Does she have a place to store her stuff?"

"She has her own place, but she stays here a lot. I'm sure she has a drawer or something in my dad's room." He leads the way, and we pass by a plethora of blue-and-orange Bears paraphernalia. It's all so shiny, I have to resist the urge to touch everything. Luckily, my orange-stained fingertips keep me in check (damn Cheetos).

I let Charlie take charge of going through the drawers, as the idea of coming across John's boxer briefs horrifies me, until he finds one that's decidedly girly. He pulls out the drawer from the bureau and lays it on the bed, unwilling to touch Cass's unmentionables.

"Can you look through it? I feel weird," he says.

"Yeah, let's find some treasures," I say, wiping my fingers on my skirt. As I dig through a stranger's underwear, I can't help but think what an interesting scenario this is. Here I am, sitting on a bed with Charlie, perusing panties. Ah, if the harpies at school could see me now.

The drawer is mostly filled with undergarments—very soft, silky pieces that probably cost more than my entire wardrobe. But near the back, my hand hits something that clanks against the mahogany frame.

I pull out a locket on a long brass chain. It's tarnished and very gaudy, especially compared to the finery of the underwear. There's an inscription on the top, but it's hard to make out.

"Can you read this?" I ask, passing it to Charlie. He runs his fingers over it, adjusting his glasses.

"It looks like another language."

"I should take it to my mom. She'd know."

"Oh . . . I thought we weren't involving her?" he asks, confused.

"Well, now that we know Cass is not your dad's match, we can. She'll be on our side. She's all about harmony and truthfulness and blah, blah."

"Okay," he says. "I trust you." He places the locket back in my hands, his other hand cupping mine. It's weird; besides Amani, I've never had someone repeatedly put faith in me. My matchmaking services are usually one-time engagements, and no one at school approaches me unless they're forced to. Charlie here is either very trusting or just really hard up for friends. Still, it's nice to be looked at favorably.

"Well then," I say. "I think it's time we have a séance."

Eleven

TONIGHT I TACKLE A BANANA CREAM PIE, SOMETHING I'VE BEEN craving since today's biology discussion on monkeys. I start by popping a deep-dish double-crusted pie shell I stuck in the freezer the other day in the oven. While it warms into flaky, buttery goodness, I get started on the filling. Sugar and whole milk melt in a saucepan as I slice up three ripe bananas. I gently whisk some egg yolks, adding them to my simmering mix, along with flour, salt, and vanilla. Once everything's combined, I remove it from the stove top, letting the ingredients fully blend together. I taste the batter to be sure it's sweet enough just before pulling the browned crust from the oven. The fruit gets scattered at the bottom of the pie, overlapping slightly so not a bite will go without a burst of banana. Then I pour the thick filling on top, spreading it out evenly with a spatula. To finish it off, I whip up a meringue with my extra egg whites, making a nice fluffy cloud to set on my sunshiny dessert. Voilà!

I've been staring at the door for almost ten minutes now, salivating, just waiting for Mom to walk in so I can tear into this treat.

She gets home around 9:45, and I have dinner waiting for her in the oven. I'm not as good a cook as I am a baker, but I hold my own. I always make dinner on the nights I don't work; it's only fair. Having the apartment all to myself also means I can dig my hands into new recipes without interruption. Mom spends a lot of time in the kitchen testing out spells for the shop; living in the city means it's not exactly convenient to fire up a cauldron outside. She usually bogarts the space, but this is also my altar. Baking offers me a release I've never found anywhere else.

When Mom finally gets home, she looks wrecked; I can only imagine what's running through her head after the coven's little beauty shop field trip. As Dawning Day's de facto leader, I know she's troubled about Victoria's "contribution" to the group. Mom's certainly not one to pull rank, but as a legacy member, I'm sure she's feeling torn over the direction of the coven. I decide not to mention it (I've already expressed my frustration), so if she wants to talk about it, she can bring it up.

As she's eating her lasagna and I'm eating pie (baked to perfection, natch), I casually remove Cass's locket from my pocket and place it on the table.

"What's this?" she asks.

"It belongs to Cass. I got it from Charlie." Mom eyes me carefully before I add, "We need your help."

Mom lays down her fork and interlaces her fingers on the table. "Spill."

I tell her the whole thing—no disgusting truth tar necessary!—and when I'm done, she takes several deep breaths, keeping her aura calm.

"And you're sure Cass is not John's match?"

"Completely. One thousand percent."

She takes her time responding. Sometimes I feel like Mom moves at half speed; her gestures and actions are always decelerated, deliberate. I don't consider myself to be hyperactive, but compared to her meaningful movements, I come off like a jackrabbit in heat.

"All right," she says finally. "Then we need to find her and set things right."

"Great!" I say, leaping out of my chair, sugar clearly coursing through my veins. "I'll get the supplies."

"Why don't you call Amani over to join us?" Mom suggests. "I could use the energy of a precog."

"Uh, ooookay. But you know, she isn't exactly practicing these days."

Mom twists her head. "Why is that?"

It's not really my place to share Amani's mystical hang-ups, and besides, jumping into a moral quandary on the pros and cons of magic is not what I'm up for right now. "Not sure. There seem to be some issues there."

"Well, all the more reason to have her join. Do you think she could come now?"

It's getting late, but Amani only lives down the street, a wondrous blessing if there ever was one. "I'm sure it'd be fine."

I call her, while Mom goes in her room to meditate and ready her mind. Amani shows up a few minutes later, dressed in her pink kitty pj's, and doesn't look too happy about being at my apartment instead of her bed.

"I cannot believe you told Charlie I think he's hot," she says as I open the door. "That was the definition of lame."

"I'm sorry. You were making me nervous with all your weird 'ooh, baby' faces."

"Still. Lame."

"I'm sorry, I really am. I will tell him you think he's very unattractive."

"Amber." She crosses her arms.

"I'll . . . give you another clue about your future husband?"

"Better. But also, I don't really want in on this séance."

"I figured you'd say that. Mom wants your chi."

"Why?"

"Because you are an all-powerful precog. She wants you to own it. As do I, by the way," I say.

She groans. "I'm really tired. I don't feel like dealing with the Fates."

"Nobody wants to deal with the Fates, so just sit there like I do and let Mom do all the heavy lifting."

Amani drags herself inside, as if I'm pulling her by an imaginary leash. She's like the walking dead making her way to our office, where we'll perform the séance. The closer she gets, the more stiff her movements become; you'd think we were asking her to mutilate baby kittens or something. All she has to do is sit there and be a magical conduit. I know she's upset with me, but this is a little too melodramatic.

A witch's office, as you might expect, is slightly different from your average work space. Think fewer Post-it notes, more eye of newt. The room is filled from ceiling to floor with the tools of witchcraft; spell books, or grimoires, are stacked and shoved into every inch of shelf space, glass boxes packed with talismans line the floor, and a few culturally significant figurines have been placed wherever they fit. It's more like a very genre-specific library than an office.

Some of the books are crazy old, their leather-bound covers cracked and peeling, while others are pristine, the authors' names clearly inscribed on the bindings. Grimoires are kind of like witch diaries, but instead of filling the pages with personal insecurities and tales of cute boys, witches record spells. Every spell is documented, whether it was successful or not. Keeping track of the failures is just as important as the victories; making a mystical mistake twice is not only embarrassing, but a waste of natural resources. I tried keeping a grimoire in my early match-making days so I could be like the cool kids, but lost interest after a while. Unlike the ever-changing and challenging world of witchcraft, matchmaking is kind of a one-trick pony and not a very compelling read.

The room is overshadowed by a giant oak armoire, where all the good stuff is stored. Hundreds of tiny glass vials filled with everything from dandelion root to bat wings are neatly arranged, with meticulously handwritten labels. Mom keeps this stuff here and not at the shop because it'd take too long to restock in the event of a break-in or disaster at Navy Pier. The armoire is fireproof and waterproof, and can only be unlocked with her command. Bank vaults have nothing on the Sand family armoire.

The room is candlelit when we enter; Mom has outlined a circle of sand on the hardwood floor with three pillows inside for us to sit on. The candles are buttercream-frosting scented, because even though the Fates have been around since the beginning of time and should therefore be above such simple earthly pleasures, they are drawn to sweet smells. The Fates can be total arrogant weirdoes, but we relate on this one point.

"Amani, so nice to see you," Mom says as we enter the room.

"You too, Ms. Sand," she replies sleepily.

"It's getting late, we need to get started." Mom gestures to the pillows.

"Yeah, let's find a hussy!" I cheer. Amani and Mom both give me a "seriously?" look. "Sorry."

Mom huffs in that "I can't believe you're my offspring" kind of way that tells me to take it down a notch. For years and years, I begged her to include me in magical happenings such as séances, so I know my making light of it now is disrespectful in her eyes. She is nothing if not proper.

But here's the thing about séances: they are wildly unpredictable. Every tween sleepover in the history of ever has attempted one, with pajama-clad pals deciding to whip out a Ouija board and contact someone's great-great-great-great-grandmother. Everyone sits around, giggling and chanting, dipping hands into alternate bowls of potato chips and M&Ms, until someone declares she "feels something" and everyone reacts like hyperactive birds. Maybe that girl is full of it, just trying to get a rise out of everybody, but maybe, just maybe, she actually did make contact with the other side ever so briefly. It does happen, even for non-magical folk. Spirits have just as much personality as the living, and some of them are mischievous little suckers who like to stir up trouble. Poking around the subconscious of a willing participant gives them just as big a thrill as it does us, and let's be honest, it must be boring being dead.

If you want to avoid the prankster spirits and really get things going during a séance, you need a bona fide witch in your circle. None of that "light as a feather, stiff as a board" crap. A witch can bypass the hooligans and reach out to the Fates, a much different crop than your regular ol' spirits. The Fates are the ones who set things in motion; they pull all the strings for the big stuff. Fates are real creatures, working with astral-plane levels of sorcery, not just convenient notions that tie up the ends of romantic comedies. As you can imagine, though, Fates are very, very busy and don't like to be bothered unless it's absolutely necessary. They are a cranky bunch, and you don't want to deal with them if you don't have to. Which is why you need a witch.

We each take a seat and join hands. Mom has placed Cass's locket in the center; it will act as a beacon that points us toward her. For Cass's sake, I hope whichever Fate graces us with his/her presence doesn't take a liking to her jewelry, because sometimes they feel they are owed and have a habit of gifting themselves other people's worldly possessions.

Mom takes several deep breaths, in through the nose, out through the mouth. "Tonight we are here to find a missing person. She has evaded advanced locator spells; we are worried she is either in danger or planning mischief toward others. We wish to maintain balance and peace; we come with pure hearts and intentions. Let the energy from this keepsake share its secrets of its owner."

I stare at the heap of brass chain, knowing full well no secrets will be shared with me. My job here is like an anchor, just a blob of flesh keeping all the actual power from getting out of control.

We're quiet, breathing in the scent of birthday cake, looking at a rusty necklace, and I'm sure that any second Mom will call on the Fates for their wisdom or whatever, when suddenly I feel a charge zip through my limbs. It's like a buzz, vibrating my skin and making my arm hair stand up on end. I look over at Mom to see if she's reciting some sort of silent incantation, but no, her lips are still. Our eyes meet—mine alarmed, hers weirdly serene—before we both turn to Amani, whose face is trapped in a voiceless gasp, eyes spinning in their sockets. If we weren't holding her hands, I'm not sure she'd still be sitting upright. There's no doubt about it; she is having a vision.

I squeeze her hand to let her know I'm there, but judging by her suspended expression, there's no way it'll register. She's positively transfixed by the locket, which has taken on a faint glow, tiny tendrils of light peeking through the brass hinge. What the hell? I can almost feel the connection between the necklace and my friend; it's powerful, pulling energy from other elements in the room. The candles are flickering; sand is skittering on the floor. I've seen her have visions before, but this is different. It's like her mind is moving outside herself. I don't like it. I don't know if Mom's magic is somehow intensifying the act, but I feel like my nerves are rubber bands ready to snap. If that's how it is for me, I can't imagine what Amani is feeling. Time for this to stop.

Finally, her eyes roll back in her head, and the buzzing ends. The locket stops glowing, the flames extinguish: Amani releases our hands and starts to tip backward. Mom quickly levitates another pillow and places it under Amani's head just before she hits the hardwood. She lies like a corpse, very still and pale. I crawl to her side.

"Amani! Oh my Gods! Are you okay?"

No response.

Twelve

"MOM! WHAT THE HELL JUST HAPPENED?" I YELL.

"Amber, calm down," Mom says in that infuriatingly monotone voice she uses during emergencies. Just because you speak in a serene manner doesn't mean your vocal cords will actually soothe the drama before you. "She will be fine."

"Fine? Fine? She sure as hell doesn't look fine!" I try shaking Amani's shoulder, which feels cold and heavy. I've never seen her go catatonic after a vision; something is wrong with my best friend, and I won't be able to live with myself if she doesn't wake up.

"Stop saying hell."

"Mom!" Good Gods! This is no time for an etiquette lesson!

"Amber, trust me. Clearly it's been a while since Amani has

had a vision; she must have overloaded. But she's built for this; she'll recover. I'll go make her some tea."

Tea? Seriously? I'm about ready to stab Amani's heart with pure adrenaline to wake her up, but sure, I bet water and leaves will do just the trick.

Mom sees the skepticism in my face. "I'll add a drop of rejuvenation potion to it," she offers.

"Thanks." I sit with Amani while Mom disappears to the kitchen. I push a few strands of damp brunette hair from her forehead; her skin is so clammy. No wonder she's been repressing her talent; it doesn't just momentarily flood her system like mine does. It completely overrides her.

Mom comes back with the tea, but Amani is still out. She begins clearing the sand and candles from the floor, yet she's very blasé about the unconscious girl in the middle of the room, and honestly, it's pissing me off.

"Why didn't you call on the Fates?" I ask as Mom picks up the locket.

She runs her fingers over the necklace, examining the details. "Such a strange inscription; I believe it's Latin," she says, completely ignoring my question. "*Felicitas ubi lux tangit.* Hmm."

"Mom?"

She sighs. "I was about to, but then Amani took over."

I find this hard to believe. "Really. She just happened to jump in and do the one thing she actively tries to avoid on a daily basis?"

Mom stands up straight, towering over me in my seated position. "What are you implying?"

I'm swimming in dangerous waters here, so I steer clear of the deep end. "It's just that I think it's weird my friend is suddenly unconscious."

"I'm concerned about her reaction as well," Mom says. "Suppressing her talent is not doing her any favors; if she worked on regularly channeling her energy, she wouldn't have these kinds of extreme side effects." She stops cleaning and takes a long look at my friend. "Think of your younger self, Amber, when your talent took over your ability to function. Your matchmaking was at the forefront; you couldn't stop it even if you wanted to. It took years, but you learned to channel your gift so it could be present but not all-consuming. Amani needs to do the same, or else one day, her talent could devour her."

I'm beyond annoyed at her right now. She's acting like she did Amani a favor by inviting her to this séance and knocking her out. Maybe in the long run, she did; I don't disagree that Amani needs to get a better grip on her visions. But . . . Mom always thinks like a witch first and a mother second, and a lot of the time, I wish it was the other way around. I mean, magic is important, but not more than someone's well-being. My mom seems to nurture everything except the human heart.

I could never tell her that, though. Instead, I just say, "That's really ominous, Mom."

"It's the truth." Amani's head slowly rolls to the side. "Look, she's coming to."

Her brown eyes flutter open. She groans, trying to pull herself to a seated position, rubbing her forehead like she's been hit by a brick. "My Gods, what happened?" she asks groggily.

"You had a vision that knocked you out. Are you okay?" I ask.

"I feel like I got stuck in a trash compactor."

"Here, drink this," I say, handing her the teacup. "Mom spiked it with rejuvenating potion."

"Thanks," she says quietly, taking a small sip. She winces at the bitter taste.

"Can you remember what you saw?" Mom asks after a minute.

Amani swallows hard, color returning to her face. The potion is probably waking up her cells one by one. "Um, kind of. It was a place I'd never been, with lots of creatures and randoms hanging around. A bar, maybe? Or a restaurant? Cass was there, meeting with some guy. . . . At least, I think it was a guy. His face was covered in shadows. He gave her something: a little slip of paper. That was it."

"This place . . . any distinguishing characteristics you can describe?"

Amani runs her finger along the teacup rim, pinching her face in thought. "It was dark—no windows—but there was a certain shimmer to the place, like gold and stuff."

Mom tips her head back knowingly. "Like . . . golden table-tops?"

She closes her eyes, trying to envision it. "Um . . . yes. Yes, I think so. And there was a long chandelier made out of—"

"Champagne flutes?" Mom offers.

"Yes. Wait, how did you know that? Did we all have the vision?" Amani asks, confused.

"No." Mom shakes her head. "I happen to know the establishment."

"Well, that's a major stroke of luck," I say.

"It's not luck. Luck is a social construct designed by humans to amplify pleasant happenstances. No, I know this place Amani describes because it's a hot spot for Chicago's underworld of paranormal activity."

"Reeeeeally," I start, "and you just happen to know where all the city's creepy-crawlies hang out?"

"Of course I know. It's my responsibility."

"Responsibility . . . to party?"

"Amber, please. You know full well about the paranormal population. Don't you think they'd create a social space for their own?" Mom asks.

"I guess. I never thought about it before."

"So Cass went there, or is going to go there, because she's supernatural?" Amani asks, trying to get us back on task.

"Perhaps," Mom says, "but it's also a place people go when they need magical assistance."

"Isn't that what Windy City Magic is for?" my friend asks.

If I had asked, Mom would've given me the "don't be so naïve" look, but because it's Amani, who Mom is trying to bring back into the magical fold, she answers with patience.

"To a degree. I am willing to help clients who come to me with pure intentions. But the dealings at the Black Phoenix are of a more sinister nature. Any witch who's worth her salt would not surround herself with such negative energy. Witchcraft is about balance, not cheating the system."

"Okay, well, where is this place? If Cass is stopping by in the very near future, we need to be there," I say.

"No, Amber, no," Mom states. "I will not have you girls getting mixed up with this unsavory element."

"Mom, don't be so speciesist. Just because someone has scales does not mean he's unsavory."

Mom picks up the locket and stands to leave. She's had enough; I've pushed her too far. "That is not what I mean and you know it. The individuals who populate that restaurant are dangerous, and you do not have the ability to protect yourself. Amani, thank you for your assistance, but I will take it from here. End of discussion." She storms out, leaving a tangible trail of frustration for us to take in.

"Well, I guess that's that," Amani says.

"Yup. Put together your most vamptastic outfit, my friend; we're going to the Black Phoenix."

Thirteen

FINDING THE ADDRESS FOR THE BLACK PHOENIX WAS laughably easy. While a Google search brought up nothing (the best secrets evade search engines), I only had to call Willie, a fourth-generation Chicago minotaur who I set up with his wife over a year ago. She is a florist who specializes in bizarre botany and supplies Windy City with rare cuttings; Willie is one of those recovering man-beasts who definitely spent time pillaging and plundering before settling down for a life of book clubs and herb gardens. After interacting with both of them separately and seeing the other in each other's eyes, I arranged for them to meet, and now he is forever in my debt (his words, not mine). I figured of all the creatures I've counseled over the years, Willie would be most likely to be in touch with the criminal element.

In true telling of his cohabitation rehabilitation, he did warn me to be careful and take backup. I love it when monsters show their sensitive sides.

It's Saturday night, and I'm waiting on the sidewalk outside Charlie's high-rise. Amani has punked out, citing a mystical migraine, but I did stop by her place on the way to drop off some cinnamon-chili brownies. Maybe there's no scientific evidence of desserts curing what ails you, but if you ask me, the jury's still out on science anyway. Even though she was laid up on the couch, she still tried to accessorize my outfit as I walked out the door; you'd think *she* was the matchmaker. But it's not like tonight is a date or anything. Willie did tell me to bring backup, and since I can count my number of friends on one finger, it's not like I am exploding with options.

"Hey," Charlie calls as he walks through the revolving door. "Am I dressed appropriately for a monster eatery?" He spins on his heel to give me a 360-degree view. I will give it to him; the boy can dress. In a crisp white button-down with black tie, embellished suspenders, and black jeans, only his grommet earrings and tattoo keep him on the modern side of a barbershop quartet. Which is not a bad thing; I actually like his skateboarder-meets-speakeasy look. I myself don't spend a lot of time thinking about clothes since I'm usually wearing one of two uniforms. Tonight I tried to pull together a black tank top and skirt that didn't scream "I don't belong here!" but clearly when I'm with Charlie, I'll have to step up my game.

"You look positively biteable," I say.

The color from his face drains. "What?"

"That's demon speak for 'you look good.'"

"Should I be taking out an extra life insurance policy or . . . ?"

"Nah, most monsters I know like to keep a low profile," I say, trying to assuage his fears. "They wouldn't have the balls to munch on a local celebrity."

"This probably isn't the manliest thing to admit," Charlie says, "but I'm kind of nervous. I've never knowingly met vampires and whatnot."

So precious. "First of all, don't refer to them as 'whatnot.' That's a good way to get your head bashed into a wall," I instruct.

"Right. Good point."

"Second, just relax. We've got trolls and other baddies at school, so just think of this as Manchester Prep with less homework and more potential for bloodshed." I reach forward and straighten his tie, before realizing it's not exactly my place to do so. He doesn't flinch, though; in fact, his cheeks are starting to regain their human coloring.

Looking up at him, I'm treated to yet another glimpse of his future love. The more I hang out with him, the more I get to know not just him but his girl-to-be. She really is quite cute; I watch a scene of the two of them getting dressed for a black-tie event. She's in a gown covered in sparkles, he's in a formal tux with tails, and she's giggling as she fixes his white bow tie. Seeing this jolts me back to the present, and I quickly glue my hands back to my sides. Clearly, this is a sign for me to back away; it is another girl's business to be adjusting his appearance.

"Wait, who at school is a troll?" he asks.

"Michael Barrister. Total troll," I reveal. Charlie considers this.

"Oh. I just thought he had a really bad complexion." He laughs to himself. "Okay. Forget what I said. I'm totally psyched to throw myself to the wolves."

"That's the spirit!"

We start walking east. Of course the Black Phoenix is in the Gold Coast; who would suspect violent supernatural crimes happening with Gucci being sold down the street? We pass several brownstones, an art gallery, and a fur coat shop. I've never understood the appeal of fur nor how it became such a status symbol. "Look at me and my financial ability to wear an animal carcass on my back! Huzzah!" Gross. Since Charlie is rich, I'm about to ask him to crack the code, when we come across a familiar-looking sign. It's tucked away, basement level, painted on a blackened-out window: a charcoal bird's wing with an even darker shadow. If you weren't looking for it, you'd never notice, and even though I can guarantee I've never in my life set foot on this block, I know for sure I've seen this before.

"Whoa, I know this place," I say, stopping Charlie in his tracks.

"I thought you said you'd never been," he says.

"I haven't, but . . ." Where have I seen this? For some reason, Amani's face keeps popping up as I scroll through my mental hard drive and then—oh my Gods! Amani! Suddenly, everything snaps into focus; why I know I've seen this place before—I see it every time I hang with my best friend. "This is the place! The restaurant! With the vampire!" I exclaim, doing a weird dance on the sidewalk.

"Uh, I feel like I'm getting the CliffsNotes version here," Charlie says, confused.

"This restaurant—Black Phoenix—is owned by a vamp named Vincent, who is Amani's future husband. I've been seeing his face and this place for years, but I never knew what it was called or where it was!"

"Amani is going to marry a vampire?"

"I told her she should've come tonight, but nooooo, she just had to play the 'I'm too maxed out from my psychedelic trip to the future' card."

"I play that card all the time," he says, smirking.

I do a sort of half laugh, half snort. Charlie's a good sport. He's been thrown into this whole paranormal world he didn't realize was around him all along, and he's handling it well.

"So, are you going to tell her?" he asks. "That he's here?"

My mouth moves to say yes, but my voice catches in my throat. As a matchmaker, it's my job to bring soul mates together. It would be unethical of me to keep love from happening. But as a friend, I've promised not to interfere with how the future unfolds. We made a pact to let each other's lives happen naturally, wherever the Fates may lead us. But this has to be part of the plan, right? Me coming here is not an accident. If I don't say something, will Amani and Vincent ever meet? I can't keep a secret like this!

"You'd want to know, right? If there was a guaranteed path to your true love?" I ask Charlie.

"Sure, who wouldn't?" He shrugs. And yet, he's never asked me. He knows I'm a matchmaker, yet the subject of his love life has never come up. Everyone asks me; strangers on the street ask me. But not Charlie. "I'd like to think, though, that if there was a girl for me, I'd be able to spot her on my own."

Well, that is certainly admirable.

"Let's just focus on finding Cass tonight," I suggest.

We walk into the Black Phoenix without hassle or question. I expected there to be a bouncer at the door, like a giant or some other super strong brute, but I guess if you're resourceful enough to find this place, they figure you can handle yourself. From the outside, it was an indistinguishable hole in the wall, but inside, it's like Jay Gatsby's daydream. Gold tabletops and the champagne chandelier are here as Amani described, and the rest of the décor only adds to the glitz and glamour. Upon first glance, you'd be hard-pressed to find any supernatural tells; everyone is dressed like it's New Year's Eve, keeping any tails or wings under sparkly dresses and well-tailored suits. If I felt underdressed next to Charlie before, now I'm really wanting a wardrobe upgrade. (I should've let Amani accessorize me after all. Dammit.) I shake my hands through my hair, letting the blue, green, and black strands fall haphazardly in a messy, "I mean trouble" kind of way. No one here looks up for a fight—the crowd's too busy eating and laughing—but I need to be ready for the unexpected.

"Do you see her? Cass?" I ask, having to raise my voice over the crowd.

His dark green eyes are wide behind his glasses, undoubtedly trying to discern what kind of creatures are among us. "No," he shouts back. "What about Amani's guy, Vincent? Do you see him? Maybe he could help."

"Good idea." I scan the room and quickly spot Vincent in the open kitchen in back, chatting with his staff. It's surreal, finally seeing him in the flesh. Of all the matches I've made, my perception of him has been most clear, thanks to my constant companionship with Amani. I never doubted he'd eventually materialize, but it's always satisfying to see how accurate my gift is.

"He's over there." I point. Just then, the server, a gorgeous part-sphinx in a golden dress matched to her wings, approaches us.

"Table for two?" she asks with the purr of a lion.

Being the professional I am, I try to keep a neutral face, but I have to say it's been quite some time since I've seen a sphinx. With Vincent only a few feet away, I'm starting to get overwhelmed with this whole scene, but then remember that I am Charlie's guide and cannot fail him.

I clear my throat. "Yes," I say awkwardly. "Two, please."

"Right this way." She leads us through the crowded room, Charlie tracking her tail as we follow. I know Mom expressed the inherent danger of this place, but from what I can tell, the only real threats are on people's plates. I have never seen such exotic entrée offerings. Heavily salted eyeball soufflés; a green bowl of mush that looks (and smells) like sewage. Fried lizard skewers; candied cow tongues: I know supernaturals have demanding taste buds, but this is pretty crazy.

Charlie and I take a seat and I run my finger over the golden tabletop. It's so shiny I can see my reflection staring back at me.

"Should we order something?" I ask Charlie. I take a quick look at the menu and don't see anything close to edible.

"I guess that's how it usually goes. Do you . . . want a drink or something?"

"Not really. I'd rather save my calories for cupcakes. You?"

"Same, actually." He smiles.

"C'mon," I say, nudging his shoulder. "Don't you want to live up to your given stereotype? Rich kid with a substance-abuse problem?"

"Nah, I'm saving that for my mid-thirties. Besides, I really do like cupcakes."

Before I can stop myself, I say, "Have you ever been to MarshmElla's in Wicker Park?" I can't believe I shared that so easily. Not that Ella and her desserts don't deserve to be promoted, but MarshmElla's is my place, my sacred little haven, my private escape. Where I can just sit back, stuff my face, and never be judged or ridiculed. It's not that I don't want Charlie to know about it, I just never tell anyone. Ever.

He's shaking his head no, so I add, "Well . . . then you're missing out."

"Maybe you could take me there sometime."

The question hangs in the air like a speech bubble from a graphic novel. I have trouble processing the words, as if the way they're strung together is in another language. What is going on here? Did Charlie just ask me . . . ?

"We need to get Vincent over here," I say, changing the subject.

"Excuse me." Charlie flags down a server. "Can we speak with the owner, please?"

"What should we say when he comes over?" I ask.

"I thought you knew this guy?"

"Just his face. We've never actually met."

"Okay then . . . I'll start, I guess. People usually want to talk to me," Charlie admits.

I cross my arms, giving him an "oh really?" face.

"Trust me," he says without humor, "it has nothing to do with me."

Before I can reply, Vincent is sauntering up to us, and he definitely looks the part of a paranormal restaurant owner. Dark, slicked-back hair, a custom-cut three-piece suit with black diamond cuff links: he could be the James Bond of the vampire scene. He greets us with a wide toothy smile, fangs retracted.

He's very handsome; Amani is going to lose it when she meets him. Despite being Gods know how old, he only looks a few years older than us. Eternal youth: gotta love it.

I'm suddenly overtaken by a bout of nerves. I'm about to meet the guy who will eventually steal my best friend's heart and will therefore be a constant presence in my life. I know it shouldn't matter, but what if I can't stand him? What if Vincent's personality is completely endearing to Amani but super annoying to me? The most important thing is that he makes her happy, but if he makes *me* crazy, will I have to hide my contempt for the rest of time?

"Can I help you two with something? I don't believe we've had the pleasure of meeting," Vincent says in a smooth baritone voice.

Charlie extends his hand. "Charlie Blitzman," he says in a more businesslike tone than I'm used to hearing from him. Suddenly, Vincent, who was already being very hospitable to begin with, stands even taller, shaking Charlie's hand with extra vigor. It's like somebody blew a celebrity version of a dog whistle, alerting all interested parties to take extra care.

"Well, well! The young Mr. Blitzman! Welcome! It's an honor to have such a special guest at the Black Phoenix! I'm Vincent, and this is my place, so anything you need, anything at all, please don't hesitate to ask," he says with a little bow.

Charlie gives a gracious yet tight-lipped smile. Everything about his body language has changed, as if just saying the

Blitzman name has sprouted steel rods through his bones. I guess it is weird being regarded as special after only having revealed something as insignificant as your name.

"And this is my friend Amber Sand," Charlie says, gesturing my way.

"Hi there," I blurt out more forcefully than I mean. I'm just so revved up to tell Amani about this, I'm mentally skipping past the first impression to their nuptials. A quick look into his ageless eyes, and there's my best friend, looking back at me.

Vincent doesn't seem to notice my weirdness. "Sand, huh? Any relation to Lucille?" he asks.

"Yeah, she's my mom. You know her?"

"Oh, she's infamous in these circles," he says, motioning to the room. "I sense the apple didn't fall too far from the tree. You're a . . . ?" He looks me up and down, not in a bloodthirsty way, but trying to sniff out my supernatural scent.

"Matchmaker," I say, saving him the trouble. "So I'm a bit down the valley from the tree."

"Really?" he says, delighted. "That's fascinating. Do you do readings?"

"Of course." Duh.

"You know, my jazz quartet canceled last minute, leaving me without entertainment for the evening. I don't suppose you'd like to offer the crowd your talents?"

Oh boy. I don't know if that's a good idea. I scan the room; everyone seems chill, but in a place like this, talons and teeth could be bared at any moment. This would strictly violate my "no matchmaking in the wild" policy, and yet, I don't want to disappoint Amani's future beau on our first meeting.

Charlie jumps in. "I'm sure Amber would love to, but we're actually in need of some help ourselves. Maybe we could do a trade of services."

"Careful Blitzman, your inner politician is showing," I tease.

Vincent smiles with amusement. "I'm listening."

"We're looking for someone. Have you ever seen this woman in here before?" Charlie pulls the picture of Cass from his back pocket.

Vincent considers the photo. "You're in luck, my young friends. She was here earlier, conducting business with Mr. Hollister over there." He points to a tiny man with a long, pointy nose, his ears conspicuously tucked into a black bowler hat. More limbs than torso, he has spindly fingers wrapped around the bone of whatever animal he just polished off.

"Elf?" I ask. The ears are always a giveaway.

"Goblin, actually. Not a very pleasant fellow. Comes in once a week to drink dirty martinis and meet with dirty folk."

"What do they talk about?" Charlie asks.

Vincent throws his hands up. "Not my business. You can try asking him but I doubt you'll get very far. When you're done, come back over and tell me some love stories."

I decide to let Charlie take lead on this one too—it's his quest, after all—and I don't doubt Vincent's assessment that

Mr. Hollister will prove fruitless. I've only come across a few goblins in my day, but they could all be described as cantankerous. There is serious misanthropy coursing through that bloodline.

"Excuse me, Mr. Hollister?" Charlie says, bending considerably to meet the goblin's eye line. Mr. Hollister stays still except for his eyes, which track like menacing storm clouds.

"Uh . . . sorry to bother you, sir, but I'm looking for a family member. She's been missing for a week. Have you seen her?" He presents the photo.

The goblin looks at it with disinterest before saying, "My plate is empty."

Charlie and I share a glance. Was that a hint? "Oh, uh, let me get you another," Charlie offers.

"No, let me," I say, walking away before Charlie can object. This creep is giving me the creeps.

"Another helping of . . . whatever this was, for Mr. Sunshine," I say to Vincent once I reach the kitchen.

"I probably should have sent you over with an offering to start with," he admits.

"Yeah, thanks for that," I joke. I like this guy. What a relief.

"So," he says as he passes the plate back to a chef, "you can really find people's soul mates?"

"Yup. I'm a vending machine of happy endings."

"I've never been very lucky in that department."

"That makes two of us."

He frowns as he watches a plated ox brain pass by. "Too bad you don't get to use your talent on yourself."

"It's a cruel world."

Vincent shakes his head. "Those Fates. Tricky fellows."

"You've met them?"

"Not personally. But when you've been around as long as I have, you hear things." A cook returns with a heaping serving of unidentified fried animal parts. He slides the plate across the golden tabletop to me. "You better go rescue your boy."

"Oh, he's not . . . I mean, he's not mine or anything," I stammer. Vincent just smiles. "Thanks."

Charlie has not made any progress with Mr. Hollister by the time I return. The goblin sits, practically a statue, bony fingers awaiting his order. Once I give him his food, he slowly lifts a bite to his cracked lips, making such an elaborate showing of his ability to consume solids, I actually feel the passage of time. My life is wasting away while this cranky curmudgeon gets his chow on.

Finally, he turns his stone head toward us and asks, "Was there something else?"

I'm fuming, but Charlie stays cool like a PR rep during a scandal. "Yes, actually. We're looking for Cassandra Callaghan." He shows the photo again.

"How unfortunate for you," Mr. Hollister sneers.

"We know you saw her tonight!" I burst. "What did she want? Where did she go?"

"I believe this young man already knows what she wants," he grumbles, looking at Charlie. "It's the very reason he doesn't want her around. As for where she went, I would follow the gold."

"What? Is that some kind of goblin riddle?" I ask. He takes a sip off his drink and offers nothing more. I want to shake his freakishly small shoulders, but Charlie guides me away, admitting defeat. "That was so pointless!" I yell.

"Well, not entirely. He did confirm that Cass only wants my dad's money."

Before I can respond, a woman in a red satin dress pops up in front of me, with one of those smiles that have been curved by too many cocktails. "Heeeeeeey," she says, like we're sorority sisters. "I heard you can find me a boyfriend."

Now there's a tall order. "Sure thing. Let's see who's waiting round the bend."

And so begins my repayment by doing readings for everyone in the restaurant. It starts slowly, one or two at a time, but eventually there's a line wrapping around the room. All the paranormal guys and gals anxiously wait to take my hands and hear about their true loves. I don't know if it's because they've been drinking or if they're all just genuinely overjoyed to learn about their romantic futures, but each patron is more excited than the last, letting out shrieks and roars of delight. If I was at the shop, I'd have made a pretty penny, but the Black Phoenix's regulars are having such fun, I don't think about my fee.

Charlie sits beside me the whole time, never interrupting

my process, just silently observing. I look his way every now and then—matchmaking is not usually a spectator sport—but as far as I can tell, he's enjoying himself. When my matches elicit happy reactions, Charlie laughs or applauds right along with them, sharing in the celebrations. I feel giddy from all the joy in the room, like there's been a nitrous oxide leak. I've never done a mass matchmaking before, and my talents are getting rave reviews. Patrons are clinking champagne glasses and making out in dark corners; I'm getting slaps on the back and kisses on the cheek, some of which are more slobbery than others, but that's okay. Tonight I'm a hero, and the feeling's intoxicating. And maybe I'm just imagining it, but as the line dwindles down, Charlie's chair seems to be scooting closer to mine.

With only a few more hopefuls to go, Charlie leans in, whispering in my ear, "Can you do me next?"

"Excuse me, what?" I shout back in surprise.

"A *reading*," he emphasizes with a laugh. "I don't want to be left out."

My heart goes into an unexpected tailspin. It shouldn't make a difference, me doing a reading for Charlie; he'd be just another patron in line. And I already have a clear vision of his beloved; I can picture her without even looking in his eyes. But for some reason, I don't want to share any details, not yet, which is weird, because why should it matter? Charlie deserves love just as much as these bloodsuckers, so why would I withhold that from him? It goes against my personal code to keep lovers apart.

"Charlie, I . . ." But I don't get to finish because an unhappy customer from my past has cut to the front of the line.

I recognize him instantly. Even though our meeting was brief, it's an encounter even hypnosis could not erase. It's him: the vamp who cornered me years ago after I confirmed he killed his true love. What are the odds he'd be here tonight? His giant frame lurches forward, murder in his eyes, and I spring up to try to back away. He's much faster than me, though, throwing tables and chairs to get to me. Every morsel of happiness I was just feeling has been replaced with paralyzing fear.

"You!" he bellows, fangs bared. Vincent tries to charge him, but the larger vamp pushes the restaurateur away with ease. He's like a pro wrestler hopped up on too many rounds of steroids. I'm backed against the wall with nowhere to go, trying to stay calm, but my lungs feel like cinder blocks beating on my insides. "I always knew I'd see you again. You just spread love wherever you go, huh? For everyone but me, right?" His face is inches from mine; I can smell blood on his breath. "Well, if I can't have a happy ending, neither will you."

His mouth opens wide like a jungle primate, and I squeeze my eyes shut, knowing my pepper spray is in my purse and out of my reach. But I don't feel a bite; instead, I'm pulled downward, knees hitting the ground as the vamp's head hits the wall. Charlie, on his hands and knees, has crawled over to me and pulled me down toward him. As the vamp yells out in frustration, Charlie wraps himself around me like a human shield, giving the crowd just enough time to rally and overpower my attacker.

Three burly brutes drag the vamp toward the door; he tries to fight back, yelling about how I'm a destroyer of dreams and so on, but he's outnumbered now, and as soon as he's pushed outside, a witch says a sealing incantation, forever barring him from the Black Phoenix. He tries to barge back in, but the invisible screen holds tight, bouncing him backward. After a few attempts, he gives up and disappears into the night.

"Are you okay?" Charlie asks, still hovering above me. He's propped up on his forearms; I can feel his panicked breath on my neck. Our legs are tangled together, and if I moved my head to the side, my cheek would be resting on his hand. His glasses are dangling on the tip of his nose, and all I can think is, *I can't believe he saved me.*

"I . . . I'm fine," I manage to say. I sit up slowly, head throbbing from the fall. Charlie sits back on his heels and pulls out his phone.

"I'm calling for my driver," he says.

"We're only a few blocks from your place," I croak out.

"Yeah, well, after a night of mortal danger, I think I'd rather have the car service."

Vincent fusses over me. The vamp's attack happened so quickly, it seemed like everyone (except, somehow, Charlie) was frozen in time, unable to help. But now the crowd is reanimated, picking up chairs and making hushed conversation.

"I'm so sorry this happened. Is there anything I can do? Can I offer you a drink?" Typical vampire, always thinking about drinking. But call me crazy; after nearly having my throat ripped out, the last thing I want to do is hang.

"I'll be fine," I reassure him, trying to shoo him away.

"The car will be here in a minute," Charlie says, standing over me. "Here." He offers me his hand and pulls me up; again, we're merely inches apart. Multitudes of thanks are piling on my tongue—*I owe you my life, I'm forever grateful, how can I ever repay you?*—but I stay silent, unable to choose the right string of words to convey my swirl of surprise and gratitude.

I'm approached over and over again by the concerned patrons. Werewolves and shape-shifters run their paws over me, looking for injuries. I keep reassuring everyone I'm fine; I feel a lump forming on the back of my head, but it's what's going on in my mind that really concerns me.

I've never been a damsel in distress before, and I feel uncomfortable with the role. Like my mom, I don't like having to ask for help; I'd rather flail on my own than be in someone's debt. But without Charlie's bravery back there, I'd have been nothing but a blood bag. So what do I do now? How does one give thanks to a knight in shining armor? Because that's the part Charlie's played here. What's the standard token of appreciation? A dowry? A flock of sheep? My firstborn child? My head is spinning to ridiculous places.

After giving Charlie's driver my address, I realize how close we came to a bloody end. I shouldn't have brought him here, not Charlie Blitzman, son of our mayor. Can you imagine the headlines had Charlie been hurt? In the movies, they always blame vampire attacks on wild animals, but in downtown Chicago, the only animals that would be roaming the streets would be escapees from Lincoln Park Zoo. I doubt anyone would believe a lion busted from its cage and happened to find the most famous teenage victim possible. Bringing him here was wrong; I got lulled into a false sense of security during the feel-good matchmaking marathon, but like Mom warned, I had no way to protect us. I have no magic shield.

We sit in the Town Car in silence, as the high-rises give way to three-floor walk-ups. I know I should say something, but what? New questions pop up with every passing streetlamp. Why did he save me? What does that mean? Does it have to mean anything? Should I say "thank you" or "I'm sorry" first?

Charlie says nothing either. He glances my way from time to time, but I'm too consumed with guilt and frustration to meet his gaze. Eventually he gives up, and stares out his window. He's probably pissed off that he put his life on the line for some ungrateful mute wench. The only word that's spoken is "good night" as I exit the car. I watch him drive away, my stomach dropping at the thought of my selfish, childish behavior.

Ugh. And things were going so well.

Fourteen

I AM IN EMOTIONAL TURMOIL. IT'S EARLY SUNDAY MORNING, which means I'm restocking the shelves at Windy City Magic. The weekends are our busiest time, with tourists piling in their SUVs and heading toward the big city, and we have to make sure we have enough supply for demand. Not that honey-coated night-vision drops are necessarily flying off our displays, but it's better to be safe than sorry. Especially because this weekend Navy Pier is hosting a weekend-long "Rock Around the Clock" 1950s sock hop. (The things they come up with, seriously.)

I'm in the back room, which I'm not particularly fond of anyway due to its permanent pickle smell, but today it's worse because the cramped space is making my crowded brain seem even more claustrophobic. What the hell was wrong with me last night? Why did I turn silent after Charlie saved me? Have I become so jaded that having someone actually do something nice for me rendered me speechless? Was it the adrenaline, my survival instinct? I mean, WHAT? No matter the reason for my short circuit, my behavior was garbage and I'm really frustrated with myself.

Worst of all, since I'll be stuck here all day, there's nothing I can do but spin my wheels. I can't sneak off and call Amani (this issue exceeds the limits of texting), and I definitely cannot talk to Mom because she would LOSE IT if she found out I went to the Black Phoenix against her direct orders (keeping this from her, by the way, will not technically be a lie but rather an omission of facts).

Clearly, this insanity is my punishment for my awful behavior, and I'll just have to suck it up and deal.

Hours later, things are finally starting to die down. Thanks to this sock hop thing, our shop was extra busy; I did over a dozen readings, and Mom sold a bunch of her mind-concentration elixirs, a spell she recently mastered for the means of mass consumption. Due to the '50s theme of the weekend, more than one poodle skirt twirled through the shop, and during the lunch hour, a kiosk a few doors down was passing out free hand-scooped milk shakes (of which I forced Bob to get me one . . . okay, two . . . OKAY, five). Since the sun is starting to set and suburbanites are terrified of Chicago traffic, the pier is slowly clearing out, though there are still a few greasers cruising around outside.

"Nice job today, Amber," Mom says as she sweeps fallen milk shake straws from the floor. "You really handled all those matchmaking requests with ease. I don't think I've ever seen you perform so many at a time."

No, you definitely haven't, I think. Still, motherly compliments are few and far between, so I make sure not to repeat last night's offense and say, "Thank you."

Bob trudges over from Windexing the crystal balls. His massive feet just barely miss knocking over a basin of candles. "So next weekend is the autumnal equinox," he starts. "I was thinking we could set up a display or something."

This gives me pause. Usually, Dawning Day would have already set something up, using a meeting to decorate the shop with an altar in the colors of the season. The fact that this hasn't already happened is not good.

Mom shakes her head gently. "I appreciate your initiative, Bob. But no, we won't be recognizing the Mabon at this time."

No equinox celebration? We've never been the best at sticking to Wiccan traditions, but I can't believe something like this is falling by the wayside. What's next? No more cauldrons? No more magic? I try to catch Mom's eye to say this very thing,

139

but she's already left the conversation. Bob shrugs his giant shoulders, and I go back to tidying up the shop, untangling the "bewitching" necklace display, and straightening the awful knickknack area. From the main pavilion, I hear the live band play some bouncy rock 'n' roll, but it's not so loud that I can't hear Mom talking with a customer at the front of the store.

"Charlie," she says, causing me to whip around so fast I almost knock over a porcelain gnome. "What an unexpected surprise!"

"Hello, Ms. Sand, it's nice to see you," Charlie says warmly. He gives me a quick look before refocusing on Mom.

"You've gotten so tall since the last time we met," Mom says. That is such a parental thing to say. "I spoke with your father last night; I'm doing everything I can to bring Cass home."

"Thank you. I appreciate that."

"So to what do we owe your visit here today?"

"I'm actually here to see Amber, if that's all right. Does she have a break coming up?" he asks.

"I think that can be arranged," she says. She turns around and calls, "Amber, you have a visitor." As if every cell in my body wasn't already vibrating.

Amber, for the love of Gods, calm down, I tell myself as I walk over. *Just tell him you're sorry and thankful for what he did; then things will go back to normal.*

"Heytherehow'sitgoingfriend," I spit out like a verbal machine gun. Sheesh. Mental face palm.

"Walk with me?" he asks, gesturing outside.

Navy Pier may be the ultimate collection of the tacky and overpriced, but even I can't deny how nice it is to walk along Lake Michigan at sunset. The Chicago skyline changes from steel to sparkle, and with the shade of darkness coming down, the pier's cheesy carnival rides start to take on a more enchanting glow. Everything looks better under twinkle lights.

Staring out onto the string of tour boats bobbing in the water, I decide I better speak first or I'll explode from guilt.

"Charlie, I'm so sorry about last night. I shouldn't have taken you there in the first place without protection, and I definitely shouldn't have forgotten to thank you for helping me. I don't know what came over me."

He shrugs. "You were scared. A vampire tried to make you his dinner. It was terrifying."

"Yeah, but you were all brave while I had a mental break-down. It should have been the other way around; I mean, I at least know more about that whole world."

"Well, I had naïve stupidity working for me," he says.

"I wouldn't call it stupid—" He puts his hand over my mouth to shut me up.

"Amber, I'm not upset with you." He lowers his hand.

I'm confused. "Why not? *I'm* upset with me."

"It's not like you lured me into some trap. You took me there because I asked you to help me, and that was the next breadcrumb on the trail. Up until the undead came in and killed the vibe, I was actually having a good time."

"Really?"

"Yeah. Nobody was pressuring me about my future, or asking me about my dad's chances for reelection. In fact, nobody cared if I was there at all."

I open my mouth, but he covers it again before I can speak.

"What I'm saying is, a lot of the time, I'm seen more as a platform than a person. And I get it, I do. But it's kinda empty. And last night, it wasn't like that. So we almost got eaten alive, so what? Somehow being around a bunch of monsters made me feel like more of a person."

Well, that went differently than I imagined. I spent the past ten hours daydreaming many possible scenarios: some of them involving faceless prison guards taking me away for endangering the life of Chicago's first son, others having our shop close due to sudden permit problems relating to mystical misconduct, resulting in losing our business license and becoming homeless. But none of them involved Charlie thanking me for almost killing him and checking on my well-being. A precog I am not.

We're leaning against the guardrail, the smell of popcorn and cotton candy wafting through the air. Now that I know Charlie doesn't hate me, I can breathe easier.

"Well, I'm glad we're both not dead and also not angry. But this is exactly why you don't put a matchmaker on a missing persons case," I say.

Charlie shakes his head. "You keep selling yourself short, but you were killing it last night. Did you see how happy you were making everyone?"

I think of all the joyful faces and can't help but smile. "Yeah, that was pretty awesome. But that's my thing: I could match people in my sleep."

"I don't know how it all works, and maybe it seems like nothing to you, but watching you do it"—the corners of his mouth tug upward at the memory—"you were basically taking away those creatures' fears of being alone by giving them the promise of love. Do you have any idea how incredible that is?"

Huh. I can honestly say I've never looked at it that way: that by giving someone their match, I'm also taking away isolation. I guess I take it for granted that love is a concrete reality, and others might not have that innate understanding.

"Wow, Charlie, you really know how to deliver a compliment," I say, feeling my face betray me. *Damn you, cheeks—don't blush!* But it's too late; I'm all flushed. He just smiles. "Thank you," I add.

"How'd you get into this anyway? The whole Cupid scene?" he asks.

"Are you asking for my origin story?" I joke.

He rests his cheek on his propped up palm. "Yes, please."

I snicker, looking up at the stars, trying to think on where to begin.

"Well, I guess it all started at my uncle Seymour's wedding,"
I start. "I was five, and I'd been picked to be the flower girl,
which was semi-ridiculous because I barely knew anyone on
my father's side of the family." I pause, trying to dampen the
inevitable feelings of frustration when I think about my dad.
"They were never super-down with my mother's magical ways."

"How very Salem of them," Charlie remarks.

"I know, right? But anyway, I guess I was the only blood
relation under four feet tall who could take on the arduous task
of sprinkling pink petals before dainty bridal toes. The whole
clan lived in Milwaukee, so leading up to the main event, I never
got a chance to actually meet Seymour's wife-to-be. Somehow,
though, I started picturing what she was like." I remember it
to this day: visions I couldn't explain flooding my head. I saw
her: long black hair, soft brown eyes, fingernails filed in even
little ovals. A stranger I could size up, clear as day. "Then, to
my surprise, a completely different woman came beaming down
the aisle.

"I was crazy confused, but then"—I raise a finger and eyebrow to heighten the drama—"an opportunity. The minister
asked for objections and—"

Charlie covers his mouth, knowing where this is going. "Oh
no, you didn't!"

"Of course I did! My uncle was about to marry the wrong
woman! I couldn't just let that happen! Picture a sweet little
flower girl, hair in ringlets, ribbons around her waist, screaming

at the top of her lungs that she protests the marriage. At first, there was laughter—nervous giggles from a crowd unsure of how to process such an unprecedented scene—but when I wouldn't stop, the chuckles turned into angry yells, demanding I be removed from the church. My father had to throw me over his shoulder and carry me out, kicking and screaming the entire way. Total nightmare."

It was . . . not the best, and certainly another check in the "magic is horrible" column for my dad. My mom has never said it (and never would), but I feel certain that wedding was the beginning of the end of my parents' relationship.

Charlie's laughing, doubled over with his forehead planted on crossed arms. "You were the only one with the guts to speak up!"

"Yes! Thank you! I was doing them a service."

"And I guess the rest is history," he says, wiping away a few stray tears.

"Yeah, well, it wasn't exactly smooth sailing. In the supernatural community, once a gift is unearthed, it's next to impossible to bury it back down. I've definitely put my foot in my mouth an inconceivable amount of times. But I've cooled it to the point where I no longer offer my opinion unless asked. Or paid."

I can't tell if it's because I just shared a pretty personal story, or because a chill is setting in, but Charlie has definitely leaned in closer. The twinkle lights have given his eyes extra sparkle, and I detect a hint of cologne. Suddenly, my arms are covered in goose bumps.

"I should head back in," I suggest, and we push away from the guardrail. On our way back to the store, we're bombarded by the sounds of rockabilly guitars and drums.

"What's with the music?" Charlie asks.

"Oh, it's a Navy Pier theme night. Doo-wop, or something."

"Sounds fun."

"I promise it's not."

"Let's go look."

We enter the main pavilion, and even without the echoing melodies of the live band, the space is a cyclone of sensory overload. Every square inch is screaming and fighting to grab attention and dollars; an IMAX theater, several chain restaurants, a children's museum, and staggered kiosks are jammed together in one neon-lit cluster of crazy. I pass by here daily and still can barely make sense of it. I'm so glad our shop is farther down the pier and not in the belly of the beast; I'd have to achieve a major level of Zen to deal with this every day.

We're standing on the top level, looking down at the madness. There's a decent-sized crowd clustered around the band, doing their best to imitate moves their grandparents did when they were young.

"Okay," I say, my tolerance for public gatherings waning, "we checked it out. Now let's—"

"Dance," Charlie chimes in.

I stare at him blankly. "I'm sorry, the music's really loud. Did you just say we should dance?"

He nods, grinning from ear to ear.

"You're insane if you think I'm going down there." I cross my arms to emphasize my stance.

"Well, when the nice men come to fit me for my strait-jacket, you know where I'll be." He gives me a little bow before heading for the escalator. He waves as the stairway carries him down.

Is this really happening? Is he for real? I watch as he willingly enters the mass of bobby socks and saddle shoes. He looks up at me expectantly as he starts to twist and shout, motioning for me to join him. I can't just leave him there dancing like a dork by himself, can I?

Man, you know the past twenty-four hours have been severely messed up if somehow being nearly eaten by a vampire has dropped to only the second-weirdest weekend occurrence, because here I go, marching into the crowd after him.

Charlie's worked his way to the middle of the dance floor, so I have to squeeze past hordes of letterman jackets and pedal pushers to find him. When I finally do, he spins toward me and beams.

The song comes to an end and everyone applauds. The Buddy Holly wannabe singer says a few thanks while the band cues up their next number.

"May I have the next dance?" Charlie asks.

"Sure thing, daddy-o. But only one." No way I would be here if I didn't owe him my life.

The band starts up again, another swinging upbeat rhythm. Charlie pulls an imaginary comb from his back pocket and pretends to slick back his hair like Danny Zuko. Not to be outdone, I pull my hair out of its ponytail, shaking out the strands to the beat of the drums. Charlie purses his lips to make an "ooh" face, and takes my hand to spin me around.

I can't believe I'm doing this. We jive, we jitterbug, we laugh and flail about. At first I feel silly—I've never danced in public before—but Charlie has his full attention on me, so I reciprocate, and the other lindy hoppers fade away. I have to say . . . Charlie is pretty good company. He's certainly not the sullen boy who lurks around Manchester Prep, waving off advances from starstruck schoolgirls. I would've never expected this from him, nor would I have guessed I'd find myself in this situation. But no one else has ever asked me to dance, so why not? I'm not hurting anyone.

But then . . . Buddy breaks from the chorus and instructs all the guys to grab their gals, and Charlie does; he puts his hands on my hips and pulls me into him, our torsos touching. Suddenly, we're not just two people dancing around the same space; we *are* the same space, moving as one. I don't know what else to do except hold on, wrapping my arms around his shoulders. I feel tiny beads of sweat on his neck, his fingers clutching my lower back. My heart is pounding so ferociously I no longer hear music, just the white noise of all my senses exploding.

Charlie, perhaps sensing my inward implosion, says into my ear, "Is this okay?"

Is it? I can't say for sure. Minutes ago, I was up on the balcony, refusing to be part of such a ridiculous scene, and now I'm here, dancing in the arms of a boy who not only saved my life, but also does not seem turned off by my supernatural freak flag. I can't deny it feels good; it's been ages since I let myself get so physically close to a boy. And I'd be lying if I said this particular boy wasn't appealing.

Just before the song ends, Charlie leans in so we're eye to eye. His face is glowing from all the dancing, and I become acutely aware of how warm I am. But our locked eyes also remind me of something else: Charlie's future wife. With his fingers still clinging to my body, my brain is flooded with this girl: the way she lights up when Charlie enters a room, the way she complements him in every way. And it hits me hard—this *isn't* okay. Charlie is not my guy; he belongs to someone else. Whether he meets her tomorrow or ten years from now, the outcome will still be the same. He'll skip off into the moonlight with a beautiful lady at his side, and I'll be left alone. There's no messing with the Fates.

I have to stop this. Immediately. Before it's too late. I try to subtly shimmy away, but then he smiles, that magical "I'm only this wholeheartedly happy when I'm looking at you" smile, and I actually feel myself go weak in the knees. Is that a real thing?

I thought it was just a cliché expression used by lazy lyricists, but no, my legs are legitimately shaky, and if his arms weren't wrapped around me, I'm not confident I could stand on my own.

Good Gods, what sorcery is this?

Fifteen

SOMEHOW I MANAGE TO HELP MOM CLOSE UP FOR THE NIGHT,
even though my feet are barely touching the floor. (Not literally, of course. I didn't randomly develop levitation powers
nor sprout a pair of pixie-dusted wings. But figuratively, I do
seem to be walking on air.) I don't even mind wiping down
the Brew Your Own Potion station, a chore I usually despise
because getting even a drop of those liquids on any square inch
of skin means living out the side effects for hours afterward. But
tonight I push on, since every part of me is already tingling.

It's weird, honestly, that engaging in a Navy Pier–sponsored
event could have this kind of effect. I usually avoid their functions like the plague, and now here I am, relishing the after-
glow. Is this why people participate in things like this? Are

all outwardly obnoxious gatherings secretly entertaining and uplifting? Do all people know this? Did Charlie? Charlie . . . A smile sneaks on my face without permission. *No! Stop it! You're being stupid!* I need to figure out how to nip this in the bud, and clearly I am not to be trusted. I need additional assistance.

I head straight to Amani's house after work. A lot of households might have picturesque family dinners on Sunday nights, but not mine; the weekends are so busy at Windy City Magic that Mom usually only has enough energy to flop into bed. The shop is closed on Mondays (unless it's a holiday), so those nights tend to be more successful for a sit-down meal. More often than not, I dine with the Sharma family on Sundays, because even if there's nothing cooking, there's always a lot of food in the house.

There has to be. Amani is one of six kids; her parents tried for years to have "just one more" after her, then wound up getting pregnant with triplets. Then two years later they had a bit of a whoops and ended up with twins. All boys, of course, leaving Amani as the reigning female sibling. Walking into the Sharma house is like entering the thunder dome: always loud, always chaotic, always the sound of something breaking in the background.

My head is swirling with thoughts of supernatural rescues and sock hops, but all that fades away when my best friend opens the door, looking like she just escaped the nine circles of hell.

"Please, wake me up from this nightmare," Amani says,

leaning on the doorframe. From her clothes alone, I can tell things are not good. Instead of one of her usual flouncy dresses, her jeans and hoodie are stained with multiple unidentified substances, and her hair is barely hanging into a lopsided bun. She looks haggard, like she pulled herself out of a war-zone trench.

"Sorry, I ain't the sandman and you ain't asleep. What's going on?" I ask.

"My parents had an emergency session and left me to watch the pack," she says, growling coming from the other room. "They've been gone for hours."

"What can I do to help? Want me to call Bob and have him sit on them?" I offer.

"Actually, can you order a pizza? I've lost all will to communicate with the outside world."

"Ooookaaaay. Lou Malnati's? Half sausage, half cheese?"

"Yes. Extra cheese. All the cheese. I need it." She flops onto her couch and buries her face, one arm hanging lifelessly off the side. I hear what sounds like snoring, but no, she couldn't have fallen asleep that fast, could she? I nudge her hand with my foot to no response. Wow, that has to be some sort of record. I leave her to rest while I pull up the number for Chicago's most delicious pizzeria (saved in my phone, because duh).

There's a symphony of stomping and screaming coming from upstairs, so I head up after placing our order. One hour until delivery means I'll need to keep these rascals under control for sixty minutes so my friend can have a break.

The five boys have managed to round up every mattress in the house and lean them up against one another like a giant, memory-foamed teepee. I'm not sure how they dragged a king-size mattress all the way from their parents' room; it's kind of amazing.

"All right, you hooligans, I've found your secret war base," I call out, prompting five tiny heads to poke out from the teepee. I stick up two finger guns. "This means war!"

"Amber!" they shriek, clamoring toward me. Suddenly, I'm covered in tiny fingers and toes, each determined to find all the ticklish parts of my body. Palak, the little guy with the hearing troubles, signs to me, *Gotcha!* so I tackle him down until he's laughing uncontrollably.

We play while we wait for the cheesy deliciousness to arrive, and even though I'm tired and their childish energy knows no bounds, I enjoy their silly roughhousing. The good thing about hanging out with kids is that their romantic destinies are still baking, meaning I'm free from witnessing the final products (for now). Sometimes it's nice to just be, without my matchmaker switch active.

Eventually the doorbell rings, and the six of us run to claim our deep-dish prize. The sound of twelve feet pounding down the wooden stairs rouses Amani, whose panicked face resembles someone afraid she left the oven on.

"Did I fall asleep?" she asks, wiping drool from her cheek.

"Yeah, in like five seconds. It was impressive."

"And everyone's still alive?"

"No human casualties to report."

She sits up, her body heavy against the couch cushions. The boys carry the pizza into the kitchen, where the sounds of open-mouthed chewing echo. I imagine them all huddled around the pie, digging into it with their bare hands, like vultures cleaning a carcass. Good thing I ordered a separate, smaller pizza for Amani and me to share.

"Did you ever know you're my hero?" she says as I pass her a plate piled with melted mozzarella, along with a bottle of Tabasco.

"No, but I accept the title with honor." I do a little bow before my next bite.

The nap and the pizza have helped to revive her, but still she says, "I'm never having kids."

It's an offhand comment, one she's made several times before (usually after a babysitting apocalypse), but having just come face-to-face with her future undead husband, it hits me: no, she really won't ever have kids. Falling in love with a vampire means gaining an eternal love, but losing the ability to procreate. I know her little brothers are a lot to handle, but I hope her desire to forgo childbearing lasts her the rest of her life.

"Um, about that . . ." I start, setting down my plate. I have to tell her about Vincent. At the very least, I have to give her the choice about knowing; I can't keep this from her. "I have some information, should you choose to accept it. It's in direct violation of our pact, but you should be aware that new evidence has been brought to my attention."

"You're being very cryptic all of a sudden," Amani says, one eyebrow raised. "Do I *want* this information?"

"I don't know, that's why I'm asking."

"Well, you know me best. Do you think I'd want to know?"

I don't even hesitate. "Yes you would. But it will change everything. Forever." I refrain from adding a *"dun, dun, DUN!"* but it would totally apply.

Amani sits up straight, legs crossed, hands on her knees. It always amazes me how even at her shlubbiest state, she still looks like a graceful yoga instructor: long and lean and ready to effortlessly slide into downward-facing dog. She closes her eyes and takes one long deep breath. On the exhale, she says, "Tell me."

I hope this is the right thing, telling her like this. There's no matchmaker guidebook that lays out the proper ways to bring people together. Do I facilitate the blossoming of love, or step back and leave it to chance? If I intervene, there's no meet-cute story to tell at their wedding, like bumping into each other at the pharmacy check out, or accidentally climbing into the same taxicab during a snowstorm. But does that matter? All I can do is go with my gut, and my inner five-year-old still wants love to happen so badly that the circumstances aren't important. Love is love, regardless of how it comes out the gate.

"I met your husband."

Amani doesn't move, except for her mouth falling open.

When no words come out, I continue on. "Charlie and I, we met him last night. At that restaurant you envisioned. He was there. I recognized him right away." Still she says nothing, blinking slowly. This is not the reaction I expected. "Um, please tell me you're not having a stroke."

She snaps back to life, out of her trance. "You . . . you met him? And you talked?"

"Yeah, he's great. He gets my stamp of approval."

The initial shock is melting into excitement. A smile creeps across her face, and she looks up at the ceiling with relief. I can tell what she's thinking: *Yes, it's happening. Things are finally setting into motion.* This is what she's always wanted. Her love story is beginning. I'm beyond happy for her.

"Wow," she says, glassy eyes staring off into the future. "I can't believe it."

"I know. It's crazy."

"When do I get to meet him?"

"Well, I'm not the one with the window to the future, but now that we know where he is, it shouldn't be long," I say.

Amani springs from her side of the couch onto mine, knocking me over with an aggressive hug. I can actually feel her happiness; she should be crushing me, but her euphoria is making her weightless. I think about what Charlie said, about my matchmaking taking away loneliness. Amani already knew she was destined for someone, but somehow my meeting him clinches it. She's giggling uncontrollably, pulling me up to stand.

We simultaneously break into a ridiculous happy dance, whipping our hair all around and flailing our limbs just as crazily. The boys come in and join us, jumping up and down, throwing pillows in the air, all of us moving to a nonexistent soundtrack. It's one of those moments you know you'll look back on in slow motion, as part of a warmly lit, perfectly orchestrated montage of happy memories.

Needless to say, this dance is much different than the one I shared earlier, but I decide not to tell Amani about that right now. This is her moment, and she deserves to fully live it.

Sixteen

ISN'T IT WEIRD HOW YOU CAN HAVE AN AMAZING WEEKEND AND still find yourself surrounded by the same wooden desks and wooden people come Monday morning? The future is awakening all around me, yet I'm very much stuck in the present, balancing quadratic equations and picking at polyester plaid fabric. Not that school has ever been exciting, but after almost being decapitated by the undead, it's considerably less so.

Amani, for her part, is doing her best to keep our minds outside the walls of Manchester Prep. Our forty-five-minute gym class has been like an intense job interview, only with every question pertaining to a particular vampire. Today we're doing a yoga unit, which is easy enough to fake. We've assumed our usual post of sitting aside from the action, pulling our mats to the back so we can stay in *shavasana* the whole time. Our teacher is dressed in questionable spandex and has drenched the gym in soothing music and dimmed light to set the mood.

Apparently, my visual confirmation of Vincent's existence has made Amani's and my pact null and void, at least as far as my abilities are concerned. Their meeting is imminent, so might as well build the anticipation to an earth-shattering level. At one point, Amani squeals so loud, the entire class stops and stares from their downward dogs. The girl is excited, and who could blame her? Not me, which is why I keep egging her on.

"Not only does he look like a retired male model, but he was ready and willing to throw down during the attack," I whisper as we sit on the gym floor, "stretching."

Amani looks up from what could maybe pass as a lotus pose. "Wait, what attack?"

Oh, right, I still haven't given her the details of that night. Well, I guess since we're in full-blown sharing mode, and not even pretending to be meditating, this is as good a time as any.

"Remember a while back when that vamp with the drinking problem tried to blame me for his murder spree?" She nods. "He was there Saturday night, just as unhinged as before, and he tried to take my head off. Like actually."

"Holy crap, Amber! That's terrifying! Why didn't you tell me?"

"I don't know, I didn't want to ruin your excitement about Vincent."

She rolls her eyes. "Don't be stupid. Talking about a boy is not as important as your life."

"You're right. I just liked seeing you all twinkly."

"So what happened?"

"Vincent tried to stop him, but actually, it was Charlie who got me out of the way."

She blinks a few times. "Hold on. Charlie . . . saved you?"

Oh boy, here it comes. "Yes."

"Charlie Blitzman took on a rabid, lunatic bloodsucker to ensure your safety?" Her eye is twitching.

"Well, he didn't whip out a crossbow or anything, but basically, yes," I say.

"Do you know what this means?" She's practically salivating.

"I'm lucky to be alive?"

She shakes my shoulders. "He likes you!"

I look down at the shiny wood floor to avoid her eyes, which are moments away from having tiny pink hearts fly out of them. "There's more," I say.

"THERE'S MORE?!" I tell her about our dance at Navy Pier, making sure to detail exact hand placements and levels of sweatiness. Somehow, I think this is making her even happier than the Vincent details. She gets up and kicks her leg in the air; I'm not sure if she's aiming for a particular pose or is just excited, but I think it's the only time I've ever seen her do anything athletic in gym class. Amani has been waiting years for this; she loves talking about this stuff, and I have a hard time giving it up for her. Sure, I talk about love all the time, but never with myself in a starring role.

Yet the conversation comes to a screeching halt, thanks to Ivy moving into our bubble.

"Excuse me, this is a Zen space. No negative chi allowed," I stress as she sits down.

"Did I just hear you two losers talking about dating Charlie Blitzman?" Ivy says incredulously. "I mean, you both aren't that naïve, are you?"

Amani starts to pounce, but I hold her back. "Honestly, Ivy, I know you're used to everyone submitting to your every whim, but this is none of your freaking business."

"Oh, I'm pretty sure it is," she says, a nasty smile spreading on her face. "I think you're meddling in the wrong scene."

"Oh my Gods, Ivy—back off!" Amani yells, her outburst breaking the serenity of the piped-in pan flute. Our teacher looks over from his warrior pose and asks Amani to approach. Her punishment is to finish the class in front, demonstrating the final progressions. That girl's a martyr, I tell you.

"Seriously, Amber, do you really think that would work out?" Ivy continues. "You're a matchmaker—you'd have to know you two would be doomed to fail. A guy like Charlie can't be satisfied by one girl, especially a girl like you."

"And what kind of guy is a guy like Charlie?" I ask.

"You know, a guy who's close to power, to the finer things in life. From one girl to another: you're just not in his league."

"Well, thanks for the advice, friend. Now, please go back to the sea urchin you crawled out from."

Ivy just smiles, then bends backward into a camel pose, her breasts pointing perkily to the sky, while her shirt rides up and reveals her midriff. One guy actually falls out of his plank at the sight of her, and there's a collective sigh of admiration across genders as everyone takes in her perfect body. Feeling ill, I roll up my mat and go to the locker room, where I sit and wait for class to end.

Alone with the smell of bleach tile cleanser, I think about what it'd be like to truly let myself enter a relationship without all my mystical baggage. It's not like I haven't dated. There have been sporadic romantic encounters over the years; I've kissed a few toads (not actual toads, mind you). But it's never really meant anything to me, and judging by the other girls dancing in those boys' heads, it didn't mean much to them either. Do you know how hard it is to make out with someone when all you can picture is his wedding to someone else? I'd have to be blackout drunk to keep those visions from coming, and what would be the point of that? No thanks.

I've gotten pretty good at shutting down my heart before it grows attached to others; it's too exhausting, too pointless. And I know that sounds extremely discouraging coming from a "love professional," but I'm not questioning the existence of love. The certainty of other people's love stories is completely thrilling. It's just that my story's a blank: no beginning, middle, or end.

I'm so used to extinguishing my feelings before they build into a flame, I wouldn't even know how to stoke the fire without letting it burn out.

Because . . . for all her horrible intentions, Ivy does have a point. I can't date Charlie, and it has nothing to do with class status. Wouldn't knowingly starting up a relationship with someone who is not your forever and ever be wrong somehow? Like, pre-cheating? I know most single people don't start dating with the preloaded awareness of who their beloved is, so they try on suitors until they find a match, but I am not most people. I have a responsibility to use my talent for the betterment of mankind, and this—my possible interference—feels dirty. Not in a hot way, but in a "you're going to get burned at the stake" way.

Still, I can't deny that Charlie is good company. We get along well, and he's surprised me again and again; when I'm with him, I even surprise myself. I mean, willingly participating in a Navy Pier–organized function and enjoying it? Are you kidding me? Before that happened, I would have sooner believed I was growing a tail. While we were dancing, there was a brief moment where I was totally present with him. Not staring off into his future or visualizing his nuptials, just being with him: feeling his arms, hearing his laugh. It was . . . Well, it doesn't matter what it was. Because I can't. Right?

My moral dilemma is causing me so much torment, I consider presenting my case at the coven meeting that night. Normally the shop is closed on Mondays, but this week's meeting had to be moved up a day since tomorrow night we're expecting a shipment of stink root, which, if not handled with care, can make the whole place smell like a skunk butt. The witches often go around and list the pros and cons of various magical gray areas; you'd be surprised at how often it is unclear whether or not magic should leak into everyday life. But standing in front of the group and confessing my sins would be admitting to feelings I'm not even supposed to have—in front of my mother, no less—so I just keep silently spazzing in the background while my brain continues to spin.

The pillows are set, the candles are lit: she didn't say it, but I think Mom is relieved to be having a "normal" night with her people. As the ladies filter in, I excuse myself to the back room to assemble a little dessert tray I put together last night. I couldn't sleep, so instead I experimented with some flavored mousses; Dawning Day has long been a receptive audience for my exploratory recipes.

I'm bringing out the cups of whipped cream from our mini fridge just as the magical round table is coming to a close. One of the younger witches, Julie, is finishing up a story to a rapt audience.

". . . and I know this doesn't particularly pertain to magic, but the thing is, I love him," Julie says, to the background of approving sighs. "And I don't want my being a witch to get in the way of that. He says he loves my abilities, even if he can't completely understand them. And, I guess, I'm just curious if any of you have gone down this path." The circle is buzzing with opinions.

"I've never dated someone who wasn't supernatural, but I don't see why it'd matter," says one. "As long as you're open about it."

"I don't know," pipes in another. "My first serious boyfriend said my being a witch was a turn-on, but it turned out he was more interested in my magic than me." The crowd groans. "People just don't understand what being a witch means."

I'm on the outskirts, silently passing out my raspberry-and-mango mousse, when I notice Victoria has curiously taken her seat at the head of the circle. While this coven is decidedly "leader-free" and anyone can sit wherever they choose, it's been an unspoken understanding that my mom—owner of the shop and legacy member—sits at the head. Yet currently, she's tucked away in the middle, almost unnoticeable. I had to scan all the faces just to find her. This isn't right.

The seat-stealer decides to throw her theory into the ring. "I'm glad you brought this to our circle, Julie, because your dilemma is not uncommon. In fact, you remind me of a young witch I used to know." She crosses one fishnet-stocking-covered leg over the other, casually shooting a smug smirk in Mom's direction. Mom doesn't flinch. "It was a tragic story, really. A powerful witch in her prime, who turned her back on her calling, all in the name of love."

Julie shakes her head. "Oh, I wasn't saying I would give up my practice for him, I just—"

"Of course it never starts that way," Victoria continues. "Who in her right mind would neglect the deep well of power established by the goddesses before us, especially for something as trivial and fleeting as love?" She makes a gargled sound that I think is supposed to be a laugh but registers more like "tortured walrus." "But love, no matter how ridiculous, has its own power. It can change you, make you do things you never even considered, making your choices and personality completely unrecognizable, even to yourself." She's speaking to Julie but still looking at Mom, with one eyebrow perilously perched. I can't believe she can even make facial expressions, what with all the chemical fillers that must be coursing beneath her skin. Mom is locked into her poker face, but I can tell this soapbox moment is ruffling her feathers. "It's a dark art so ancient, no one can stop its magnetic hold once it has begun. In my opinion—"

"And who made you the expert?" I blurt out, instantly regretting it. Because while most of the eyes that turn my way are in desperate need of positivity, two pairs—Victoria's and Mom's—only show frustration. But I already opened my big mouth, so there's no turning back now. "I just mean, you're painting a very one-sided picture here."

Victoria sizes me up. "Oh, am I, matchmaker?" She says "matchmaker" like it's equal to "puppy killer."

"Yeah. You're making love sound like some kind of living nightmare, and it doesn't have to be that way. If Julie wants to know if this guy is worth pursuing, I can tell her right now."

"Oh, Amber, that would be wonderful!" Julie exclaims, while some of the witches nod in agreement.

"That's what you're going to hinge your entire future on? Some inane reading?" Victoria asks, incredulous. "She has less magic in her entire body than I do in my pinkie finger."

"Leave Amber out of this." Mom finally enters the conversation.

"I'm sorry, Lucille, of course it's not my place," Victoria concedes, yet her face is still twisted in a wicked expression. "And yet, this really isn't Amber's place either." She turns to me, lips pursed in fake sympathy. "This is a coven meeting, sweetheart, and if you aren't a witch, you shouldn't attend."

"This is our shop! You are our guest! Who even are you, barging in here and messing up the vibe with your over-perfumed aura?" I yell.

"Amber," Mom starts.

"No! This is bull! Maybe I'm not an official member of Dawning Day, but I belong here more than her!"

Victoria makes another unpleasant laughing sound. "You can't really believe that. Just because you provide the 'refreshments'"—she actually uses air quotes, as if she didn't just scarf down my mousse seconds ago—"doesn't mean you're really involved."

At this, I drop my tray, breaking the remaining dessert flutes. Some of the witches gasp, but I don't care that I'm making a scene. I'd rather listen to shattering glass than this wench's voice for one more second.

"You are ridiculous! Literally no one in this room feels the way you do!"

"Amber," Mom repeats, with more force.

"No! And there's nothing wrong with being a matchmaker. I *like* what I do. At least I help people, which is better than spending precious cauldron time trying to gain back the youth that obviously disappeared years ago," I snap with sass.

"AMBER!" Mom yells, standing now. Most have diverted their eyes, yet I know I'm still the center of attention. "That's enough."

"Mom, she—" Before I can get out another word, Mom spins around and silences me with a flick of her wrist. I try to spit out a stream of obscenities, but I've been muted, my voice temporarily stolen. This enrages me even more; for Gods' sake, I'm trying to stand up for myself! For the coven! She doesn't say a word, standing firm in her decision to keep me quiet. There isn't even an apology in her eyes, nothing to indicate any remorse.

"She's right. You are out of line. You need to leave," Mom instructs me. I've been thrashing about in my own little bubble of silence, but this freezes my fight. Victoria is brainwashing the group to think that love is a curse and I'M the one who needs to leave? Well, you know what? FORGET IT. If I'm not magical enough to have a say, then I want no part in whatever's to come. I charge through the group, making sure to glare at Mom as I pass; Victoria may be the clear villain here, but I absolutely cannot deal with Mom's dismissal. She tries to stop me as I pass, her steely demeanor cracking slightly, but I shake free of her grasp and tune out whatever stupid consolation line she tries to feed me. I don't want to hear her reasoning; there's nothing she can say to erase this sting.

Just before I leave the shop, I hear the group resuming their conversation as if I didn't even speak up at all.

I text Amani to meet me at MarshmElla's for emergency salted caramel cupcakes, and when I arrive, she's there with two plates ready. My voice doesn't come back for a full thirty minutes, so we sit and sign instead.

Why does she always do this to me? I ask with my hands. *She keeps me at arm's reach from anything important, like I'm a kid you can't trust around a stove.*

Maybe she's trying to protect you? Amani signs back, but even without vocal inflection, I can tell she doesn't believe that.

No. I'm not a witch, so . . . I'm not enough, I sign with a shrug. It's not really a shrug-worthy subject, but I'm so tired of feeling this way. It's not my fault I was born without full Sand magic; I didn't ask to be a matchmaker. But considering the circumstances, I think I've done okay. I've honed my skill the best I can; I've made the most of it. I can deal with kids at school hating me or customers being dissatisfied with my readings, but having my own mom look at me as less than? There's only so much a girl can take.

Amani leans her head against my shoulder, and I lay my head on top. "You're enough for me," she says quietly, and I pinch back the urge to cry.

Seventeen

I SPEND THE NIGHT AT AMANI'S AND DON'T BOTHER CALLING MOM
to let her know where I am. Let her worry . . . if she even cares.

To lighten the mood, Amani changes the subject to her
topic of choice: boys. I should have known that as soon as I
told her about Vincent, she wouldn't stop bouncing like a rabbit until we met him, so we spend the evening planning an
outing to the Black Phoenix. She agonizes over what to wear
and what to say, and I can't even tease her about it, because
really, if you knew for a fact you were about to meet someone who would change your life forever, wouldn't you want to
make the best possible entrance? I suggest visiting next weekend,
but that's apparently too long a wait, so we settle for tonight.
Even though the beginning of the week might make for a

night when the restaurant would be completely dead (no pun intended), she insists she doesn't care, saying there's only one person she wants to see anyway, so what does it matter how crowded it is? You can't compete with logic like that.

And now we're here, standing on the sidewalk outside, me dressed in Amani's girly wear, and her decked out from head to toe. "How do I look?" she asks before we walk in. She spent hours trying to find that unattainable blend of meticulously thought out yet effortlessly casual. She looks adorable: her dark brown hair left wavy, her long legs emphasized by a short black skirt and ankle booties. Her young-looking features can't hold a lot of makeup, so she's added just a touch of pink lip gloss.

"You look ready to make a lasting impression," I assure her, giving her a big hug. She squeezes me back even tighter. Although I am always her best friend, tonight I am playing my official role as matchmaker, bringing together yet another couple, as I am destined to do. She's asked me to stay for moral support, but experience has taught me that once these two lock eyes, I'll become an afterthought, another blob in their hazy amber glow. It's fine; I've tucked a Sylvia Plath book in my bag, because if you're going to sit alone at a restaurant, you might as well do it up right.

The place is far less occupied than last Saturday night, but there's still a small crowd lingering about. It's definitely a different vibe, though, and I kind of wish Amani could have seen it over the weekend instead; whereas Saturday was all glitz and

glamour, tonight is way more laid-back: beers instead of cocktails, jeans instead of ball gowns. Even Mr. Restaurateur himself
is more subdued, having traded in his tux for a more relaxed
button-down.

Look at him, wiping down the golden tabletops like it's
just another night and not the first encounter with the love of
his life. I have to admit, I love this part. I don't always get to
actually witness a matched couple's first meeting, but when I
do, there's a certain magic in the air that not even the most
powerful Wicca could replicate. The merging of two lives, the
threshold of possibility: it's an energy unlike anything else. I'm
so happy I get to do this for my best friend.

Vincent spots me and gives a little wave, but his eyes quickly
move to Amani. She sees him, and I know that she knows;
every part of her is suddenly pulled upward, her smile and heart
both lifting to the sky. You can almost hear an orchestral swell
narrating the moment, pulling these two souls together. I have
to grab her hand so she doesn't float away from excitement.

"Amber, hello," Vincent says to me, but clearly enchanted
with the creature beside me. "I'm glad to see you're doing all
right."

"Oh yeah, I'm super. Vincent, I wanted to introduce you to
my best friend, Amani Sharma."

Like a princess, she offers her hand, which he kisses lightly.
"It's nice to meet you," she says.

"Believe me, the pleasure is all mine," he answers, clearly

bewitched. They stare at each other breathlessly, undoubtedly blinded by fireworks, and I excuse myself to a solo booth. They don't notice my exit, nor would I want them to. My job here is done; the rest is up to them.

I'm not a big drinker, and who even knows if my stomach could handle any of the offerings here, so when a waiter comes by my table I order a cup filled with maraschino cherries instead. Hey, if I'm going to sit alone, I might as well satisfy my sweet tooth. As I munch on my syrup-soaked fruit, I watch Amani and Vincent chat. I can't hear what they're saying, but it looks like it's going pleasantly enough. Like me, Amani has had a few flings but nothing serious. She's been more open to dating than me, however, since she doesn't have the same disadvantage to deal with. She likes to talk and joke about guys, but she still keeps them at a distance, knowing they aren't truly worth her full emotional investment. I can't wait to hear what she thinks about her future husband.

I should be reading *The Bell Jar* for that English project, but I can't seem to focus. Maybe it's because a pair of vampires are making out—fangs and all—at the table next to me. How do they not impale each other's tongues with those teeth? It's impressive.

My phone rings; it's Charlie. "Hey," I answer, closing my book for good. "What's up?"

"Nothing much." He pauses. "Where are you? It sounds like there's hyenas mauling each other in the background."

"Nah, just a couple of vamps hooking up."

"Oh. So you're in a bordello?"

"Yup. Just a regular Monday night."

"Cool, cool."

"But really I'm at the Black Phoenix."

"Again?" he says, voice rising in surprise.

"Yeah, I had to tell Amani about Vincent, and she was chomping at the bit to meet him," I say. "As a matchmaker, I couldn't deny her that right."

"Sure. So, you're just hanging by yourself?"

"I guess, playing chaperone to a lovefest."

"Do you need backup?"

"Not really."

"Let me rephrase," he says. "Would you like company? I'm right down the street."

I bite my lip to keep from smiling, not that he can see my reaction. What to do, what to say? I don't want to encourage this, but I am kind of bored right now, and who knows how long those two will float in their love bubble. So I do my best to play blasé. "I mean, if you're not busy."

"I'll have my assistant move some things around," he jokes.

"You do that." I hang up and finish my cherries. Not long after, Charlie shows up, still rocking a tie at 10:30 p.m.

"Do you always dress so fancy?" I ask as he sits next to me. He looks down at his shirt. "What do you mean?"

"You always look so proper and gentlemanly, like you could

spontaneously time-travel to the nineteen twenties and blend right in."

He considers this. "Except for the earrings. I don't think a lot of guys went for that back then."

"Right! You have so many accessories! What with the tie clips and suspenders . . . I think I own maybe two necklaces, and even they are probably borrowed from Windy City Magic."

He shrugs. "I like clothes." He waits a beat. "Is that weird?"

"No, it's not weird, it's just not very common."

"Isn't that the definition of weird?"

"I'm not saying you look bad—"

"So you're saying . . . I look good?" He looks down shyly at the table, his volume dropping in equal proportion to the swelling joy on his face. I'm surprised by his sheepishness, given that girls are routinely throwing themselves at him at school. You'd think a guy would take that as a surefire sign of his attractiveness, but he's acting like some kind of bashful doe, astonished that anyone would give him a second look. I mean, there's no way I'm the first girl to vocalize Charlie's visual appeal, right? Or is this just the first time he's truly hearing it?

I give him a small punch on the arm, just so he doesn't get too carried away. "Quiet, you." He does as I ask, his smile brightening in the absence of conversation. Just then Amani dives into the booth, burrowing her face into my shoulder. She mutters a muffled "Oh my Gods."

"So, how's your beau?" I ask. "Do I know how to match 'em or what?"

She pops up, and her expression is more confused than I'd expect. I thought by this point she'd have trouble keeping her head on her body from pure excitement, but instead, she looks like her brain is going to leak out of her ears. "Amber . . ." she says with furrowed eyebrows. "I can't stand that guy."

I blink a few times, unable to process. "Huh?"

"He's awful!" she exclaims. "All he did was talk about the most boring garbage, and the whole time, I felt absolutely nothing toward him. No fireworks, no chemistry whatsoever. Are you sure he's my match?"

I look up at the kitchen, where Vincent has gone back to perfecting plates for his clientele. Of all the matches I've ever made, none of them have been as clearly defined as Vincent; I'm surprised I haven't visualized his driver's license and bank account numbers by now. How could Amani not be into him, even just a little bit? I mean, it's not like I expected him to get down on one knee during their first meeting, but I assumed at the very least she'd be filled with butterflies.

"Amani, he is your match. I'm sure of it."

"And you're never wrong?" Charlie chimes in at the worst possible time. I shoot him a look of death, which makes him actually flinch. "Sorry! Just wondering."

"No, I'm NEVER wrong," I say with emphasis. "How could I be? Why would I be envisioning some random vampire chef every single time I've hung out with Amani for the past seven years if they weren't meant to be together?"

Charlie juts his lip to the side, in a "don't ask me" kind of way.

I look back at Amani, who is equally perplexed. "Amber." She shakes her head. "I could never see myself with that guy."

"But . . . but . . . *I've* seen it! The two of you! Dancing till midnight and taking trips to Spain and—"

Amani grabs my leg under the table to make me shut up, as Vincent is approaching with a tray of appetizers we did not order.

"On the house, my friends," he says proudly. He sets down the mozzarella sticks that I hope are filled with cheese and not bone marrow or something, and he's unable to peel his eyes away from Amani. Well, at least one of them is smitten.

"Do you have any sriracha?" Amani asks. Her request for something hot has brought a smile to his face, causing her to sink down further.

"Anything for you, *chérie*," he replies. Then, turning to Charlie, "Ah, the young Mr. Blitzman," Vincent says as he offers us napkins. "How does it feel coming back here after your heroic victory?"

"Well, I'm not having war flashbacks, so that's a good sign," Charlie says to Vincent's laughter.

"Good, good, I'm glad you both came in tonight, and not just because you brought this beautiful lady with you." Amani forces an awkward smile. "That goblin you two were chatting with the other day, Mr. Hollister? He had some more of his kind meet up with him after you left. I was bringing them a round of drinks and overheard one of them say Cassandra's name."

Charlie and I both sit up straighter.

Vincent continues. "Now, goblins aren't exactly the most cheerful folk, but they were definitely working on some kind of scheme. When I was cleaning up for the night, I found this under their table." He hands Charlie a scrap of paper.

Written in insanely tiny block lettering is an address and date.

Michigan and Jackson 8 Pm Thursday

"That's only a few days away," Charlie says. "What do you think this means?" He continues looking at it, as if prolonged staring will make the printed letters reveal different information.

"It's hard to say exactly, but I think Cassandra is mixed up with a bad crew," Vincent says with sympathy.

"Let me see it," Amani demands, hand outstretched. "Maybe I can get a glimpse of what's going on."

Charlie starts to pass it to her, but I grab his hand to stop him. "Amani, you don't have to do that."

She snatches the paper anyway. "Please. He saved your life. It's the least I can do." She takes a seat and holds the paper in both hands, centering her stare. We all sit in silence as she tries to conjure up a vision. I'm surprised, honestly, that she's willing to do this, especially after her blackout the other night. She hasn't used her magic regularly in years, and now she's trying twice in the same week? I'm simultaneously proud of her progress and nervous of how it will affect her.

It takes a while, but eventually something inside her clicks, and her eyes start doing that wild thing, like they're spinning tops in oval sockets. Charlie turns to me, clearly disturbed, but my focus is on Amani, making sure she doesn't go catatonic again. Luckily, she stops herself just in time, dropping the paper and burying her face in her hands. Quiet sobs slip through her fingers, but when she finally sits back up, her face is dry. If my mom were here (and I'm glad she's not), she'd call that progress.

"Vincent, can you get her something to calm her?" I ask. He nods and dashes off to the bar, bringing back a damp towel. He applies it gently to her forehead before moving to rub her back, but she inches away before he can reach her skin.

Her entire demeanor has changed, and not just because of the vision. She was SO EXCITED to come here tonight, and now she's slumped against the booth like all the air has been let out of her heart. I want to say something—there's just no way I'm wrong about Vincent—but I can't do anything with him still standing here.

Charlie turns back and forth between Amani and me, looking like he just witnessed an alien abduction.

"What just happened?" he half-asks, half-yells.

"Amani had a vision." He looks at me like I'm speaking Greek. "Didn't I tell you she's a precog?"

He rubs his eyes behind his glasses. "No, I think I missed that bullet point. So you two are like . . . wonder twins, or something?"

Amani chokes out a laugh and I smile. Sometimes our talents seem so mundane to us, so it's funny to view them through fresh eyes.

"We're amazing, clearly," I say, sniggering.

"The best of the best," Amani responds with a mocking tone.

"Okay, but seriously, guys, did you really just see the future?" Charlie asks earnestly.

She clears her throat. "Well, I cut it off before it got too poltergeisty, but I got a definite sense of danger. Cass will be at this meeting, but she doesn't know what's coming." She turns to me. "I think we need to call for backup."

"I have plenty of people we could use for muscle," Vincent offers.

"Thanks, but what I mean is, we should tell Charlie's dad. This could be the last time anyone sees Cass, and he deserves to know what's going on."

"We are talking about goblins, right?" I say with suspicion. "I mean, how much trouble could they cause? They're so . . . pint-size."

"You'd be surprised," Vincent says. "They can be pretty ruthless."

"You're right," Charlie says. "It's time to tell my dad what we've been doing."

"Wait a minute. How can we bring parents into the loop without divulging certain incriminating facts?" I ask. "My mom will ground me, literally—as in, cast a spell to attach my feet to the floor of our apartment—if she finds out I've come here not once, but twice."

"We don't have to tell your mom—" Charlie starts, but I hold up a hand to his face.

"Trust me. If your dad knows, my mom will know. Those two couldn't keep a secret from each other if their lives depended on it."

"But, Amber, you've been trying to help John, and he's your mom's oldest friend. I'm sure she'll understand," Amani adds.

"I'm sorry, have you met my mom?" I ask. "And we're not exactly on the best of terms, remember?" But regardless of where Mom and I stand, I'm now in an uncomfortable spot. What can I do? I don't know this Cass chick, but unless she feasts on the flesh of unicorn carcasses, we can't just leave her to some potentially gruesome ending. Of course, whether or not *I* am about to meet a gruesome ending remains to be seen. The last thing I want to do is go to my mom for help, but if I don't, a person's life could be in danger. Argh! Why can't I just exist without a moral compass? Life would be so much easier.

Eighteen

I DECIDED TO PROLONG MY STAY AT AMANI'S, EVEN THOUGH space is limited and mornings at the Sharmas are slightly insane. With so many boys running around, bathroom time is at a premium. Amani and I manage to snag the room before the crazy kiddos, and I lock the door behind us just as I overhear Mrs. Sharma talking on the phone with my mom, reassuring her that I'm okay. Oh yeah, I'm super; I never knew grooming could be an extreme sport. Thanks for asking *me*, Mom.

Amani and I are crammed in together, alternating mirror time. Even though it sounds like a pack of wild dogs is scratching at the door for us to get out, Amani is making no effort to hurry; in fact, she's been brushing the same section of hair for the past several minutes, her eyes unfocused in the pane of glass we're sharing. The edges of her mouth are weighed down by whatever's troubling her.

"Think they're performing an animal sacrifice out there?" I ask as the boys howl to come in.

"Hmm?"

"You're not hearing the stampede?"

"Oh, sure," she says in a daze.

"Are you always this spacey before coffee?"

She looks at me as if she's just realizing she's not alone in the bathroom. "What? No, it's not that."

"Then what?"

Her face scrunches. "I can't tell you."

"Of course you can; you can tell me anything." I sit on the edge of the bathtub, opening my eyes wide for my best "I'm listening" face.

Amani sets down the brush and slumps over the sink, her pained exhale audible over her brothers' cacophony.

"C'mon, it can't be that bad," I coax.

"It's about . . . Vincent."

Well, I knew this was coming. She was quiet last night after the Black Phoenix, wanting to go straight to bed rather than gossip. I know their first encounter didn't go exactly as she'd hoped, but this is a little melodramatic, even for her.

"It's just . . . you build something up in your head, you know? You fantasize about what it will be like when something you've dreamed about actually comes true." She frowns. "Then to have it be so . . . wrong . . ."

"Whoa, who said it was wrong?" I ask. "I mean, just because he turned out different than you expected doesn't mean it's wrong."

"Amber—"

"He's your match!"

She shakes her head. "No. There's no way. I didn't feel anything—no, I take that back. I felt . . . repulsion."

"Well, that's a pretty strong word," I say, crossing my arms.

"It was a pretty strong feeling!"

"Was it because he's a vampire?"

"No! Of course not," she says, offended. "He was all sleaze-ball, underworld slime, pulling out every gross line in the book. Do you know he actually asked me if it hurt when I fell from heaven?"

"I didn't think he was sleazy," I say.

"Well then, you date him," she fires back.

"He's not MY match." Amani rolls her eyes, and I continue. "Okay, so maybe a rainbow of light didn't shine down and encircle the two of you, but I'm sure lots of couples don't fall head over heels on their first meeting."

She bites her lip. "I just think . . . you missed the mark on this one."

Like a dagger to my heart. Never in a billion years did I think my best friend would be added to my long list of unhappy customers. It stings, and I struggle to find the words.

"You really think that?"

Amani twists her face, trying hard to land on a sympathetic expression. "I know it's not your fault. I know you wouldn't purposely lead me astray. It's probably the Fates trying to mess with us."

Now I'm getting annoyed. "It's not the Fates and you know it. This is you questioning my matchmaking abilities."

"No!"

"Yes! You're pissed because you weren't instantly smitten within the first thirty seconds of meeting your match, and now you're looking for someone to blame. Well, go ahead: fire away!" I yell, hands up over my head.

"It's not like that," she says quietly.

"Isn't it?"

Amani sighs. "This is why I didn't want to say anything. I'm not angry with you, just surprised. And yeah, disappointed at how it played out. I'm not trying to attack you, I'm only bringing up the possibility that maybe—MAYBE—your match-making isn't one hundred percent."

The pain, THE PAIN. "Like that's any better?" I huff.

She sits down next to me on the tub. "I know what you're thinking. *He's her destiny, I'm never wrong.*"

"Exactly. I'm never wrong."

"You've never been wrong . . . yet. There's a first time for everything."

"Wow, thanks," I say, burying my face in my hands so I

don't have to look at her. "Have you ever had an incorrect vision?"

"No . . . Well, I don't know. Maybe I have. I haven't pursued every single vision to see if it's played out exactly the way it did in my head."

This is too much. I can handle randoms hating me, but my best friend? Questioning me? And all before my morning pastry? NOPE. Insecurities are natural, but in all my life, I've never doubted my matchmaking skills. Never, not even when they were just emerging and I was the complete worst at communicating them. Even if the words came out wrong, even if I delivered them in the most socially unacceptable way possible, I've never questioned them. When I see a match, I don't just see it; I feel it, a temporary bubbling up of love that is so powerful, all I can do is let it out and hope the couple finds each other. If what I see isn't foolproof, if what I feel for these matches isn't real, then what the hell is the point? What am I doing with myself?

"Maybe I shouldn't have told you," I say, the words bitter on my tongue.

"What?"

"Maybe I shouldn't have told you about Vincent. Stuck to our pact, like we'd promised. Every time I gave you a sneak peek, I thought I was doing you a favor, helping you get excited. But now I see."

"See what?" Amani asks.

"That what I was really doing was setting unreasonable expectations." This tone is usually reserved for the masses, especially those who throw a fit over my matches. I never imagined it would emerge around my best friend. I don't like it, yet I can't stop it. "You took every clue and used it to create some perfect mental image, something no one in the history of ever could live up to."

"Amber . . ."

"So you're right: this is all my fault. Another ruined pairing, another broken heart." I quickly stand and open the bathroom door, causing three of her brothers to tumble into the room. I step over their intrusive pile, grab my book bag, and head out the front.

I am in a mood. A mood that is not made better when we arrive at Manchester and are immediately shuffled into yet another senior assembly. The thing about attending private school is the administrators expect you to do something BIG and IMPORTANT with yourself so they can sell the school as a launching pad to parents of middle-schoolers. There are lots of expectations crammed within these stone walls. It seems like the closer we get to college application deadlines, the more frequently we're being serenaded by motivational speakers. I wonder who's going to tell us to reach for the stars today.

The auditorium is filling up, and while I'd normally grab a seat next to Amani, I need some space after our conversation. I know she wasn't trying to hurt me, but the possibility of being wrong in my matchmaking is making me sick. Even if 1 percent of the matches I've seen over the years were off the mark, how many people may I have led astray? How many misled couples have trekked down the aisle on my blessing? I'm trying to do the math when Charlie sits down next to me.

"You ready to be inspired?" he asks.

"Excuse me, who said you could sit here?" I tease. Now this is a welcome distraction.

"I did." He smirks. "So are you?"

"Oh yeah. We are the future, after all."

"No doubt. Where are you planning on going to college anyway?"

"The Chicago Culinary Institute. To be a pastry chef," I say, smiling at the thought.

"Really? That's awesome."

"Yeah, I can't wait. I'll open my shop and spend every day covered in frosting."

Charlie raises his eyebrows in amusement. "I like that visual. I'm just going to linger on that for a moment. . . ." He stares off dreamily, but I hit him on the shoulder to bring him back. "You must have filled out your application a hundred times by now."

I shake my head. "I haven't even started."

"Why not?"

"Because if I fill it out, then I have to send it in. And if

I send it in, there's a chance for rejection. I have no backups; rejection is not an option," I say.

"They won't reject you," he says.

"Oh, and I suppose you're a precog now?" I ask.

"If I was, then I'd know where I'm supposed to go to college."

I clap my hands on my cheeks and give an exaggerated gasp. "You mean, you haven't already been accepted to your dad's alma mater?"

"Well, sure, if I want to go to Notre Dame," he admits. "But I want to stay in Chicago."

I do everything in my power to not show pleasure in this. For some reason, Charlie is looking infinitely cuter and smelling infinitely better than he ever has before. "That would be good," I say.

"Would it?"

"I mean, I'm sure your dad would be happy to have you home."

"Anyone else?" he asks.

"As a matchmaker, I can assure you your presence would be missed by many a female."

"Any particular females?" he presses.

I wag a finger in his direction. "I charge by the minute for that kind of intel."

He laughs. "I'll check the vault."

The auditorium lights start to dim, and thank the Gods,

because I cannot keep my face at its regular coloration any longer. I'm trying—I really am—to keep it together around Charlie, but every time he's near, my insides feel all warm and glowy, and I'm unable to pull my eyes away from his hands: hands that cradled my hips, that pulled me close to him. Ahh, I'm doing it again! STOP IT, AMBER.

Dean Adams takes the stage, immediately jumping into her routine spiel about Manchester pride and achieving our dreams. We have all heard this so many times by now that I think this string of words could automatically put the entire senior class to sleep. Sometimes it pains me to know that my future bakery success will reflect positively on this hellhole, but that can't be helped. While doing things out of spite is a perfectly fine motivator in my opinion, it doesn't apply when a girl's got stuff to accomplish.

Charlie leans over to me as the Dean rattles on. "My dad's speaking today," he says quietly.

"Oh, that's cool."

"He was practicing his speech over Count Chocula this morning."

"Now I like *that* visual," I snort. "Chicago Bears legend psyching himself up with monster-shaped marshmallows."

John Blitzman is introduced, and he enters the auditorium to enthusiastic applause. He's dressed very classy, in a full suit— Charlie definitely takes wardrobe cues from his dad. But even though his appearance is nice and crisp, his essence is all off; he's not the confident giant who commands attention on the field and in the pressroom. He's trying to mask it, but even from the back row, I can see the same sadness in his eyes as that day he came to my mom for help.

"How is he doing?" I whisper to Charlie as John begins his speech.

Charlie frowns. "I don't know. He seemed encouraged over our goblin lead, but it's making him crazy that we have to wait for this meeting to take place."

"He didn't say anything to my mom, did he?" I panic.

"No, he's keeping quiet." Well, that's a relief. Charlie continues. "Dad's a man of action, and right now, he's not himself. He's all mopey and listening to soft rock. It's gross."

"Love's a bitch," I say.

"I guess. I'm just not convinced it's actually love between them."

"You really don't like her."

"I barely know her. She's so secretive and closed off. They've been dating for a year, yet she makes no attempts to ever spend time with us as a family. Now, I'm not dying to hang out with a money-hungry leech or anything, but if she really loved my dad, don't you think she'd take a minute to get to know his kid?"

I nod. "You make an excellent point."

"And I don't like the way my dad is around her. He's the freaking mayor, but he's like a declawed lion around her, cowering and doing whatever she wants. That's not love; that's submission," he huffs, adjusting his glasses.

"Maybe it's just a side effect of being bit by the lovebug," I say, playing devil's advocate.

He groans. "You speak from experience?"

"No. It's just a possibility."

"So you've never been in love?"

"Not yet," I say. "You?"

"Not yet." Everyone is clapping and John is taking a bow; I guess we missed his inspirational nuggets. Oh well. Our mayor waves to the crowd, his Super Bowl ring sparkling in the spotlight. As the lights come back on, Charlie asks, "Hey, what are you doing after school?"

"Why? Do you have more Cassandra stuff to go over?"

"No . . . I was thinking we could hang."

"Oh," I say, trying to be cool. "I'm technically supposed to work, but I was going to blow that off to see my friend Ella at her bakery. I'm itching to get my hands on some fondant."

"That sounds fun. Can I meet you there?"

"That depends. Do you have an addictive personality? Because MarshmElla's is like a crack den for sugar lovers," I advise.

"I do like sweet things," he says.

We're both smiling at each other like idiots as we walk out into the halls, which is why we don't notice a sea snake crossing our path. Ivy stares at us, visibly offended at the sight of us together. Something wretched is swirling in that brain of hers, and I watch her blue eyes turn to green.

"Amber, have you finished our English assignment yet?" she asks.

"Oh yes, I've just been the busiest of bees, working to serve my queen," I say with an exaggerated bow.

Ivy scowls. "Charlie," she starts, asserting herself where she doesn't belong. "Is this girl bothering you?"

"Do I look bothered?" he answers with a grin. He turns back to me. "I should probably go say hi to my dad so he doesn't think I'm embarrassed by him. I'll see you later, okay?"

"Okay." I watch him head back to the auditorium; he throws me a smile over his shoulder that makes Ivy's jaw hit the floor.

"You two are not hooking up later," she says, more like a question than a statement.

"Seems that way," I respond. "Don't tell me a siren is jealous of a lowly matchmaker."

I've rendered her speechless, which is pretty much the best way to end any conversation.

After school, I make a quick stop at the apartment to get fresh socks and unmentionables, knowing full well Mom will be occupied at Windy City. I haven't been home for a couple days and even though she knows I'm with the Sharmas, I find it extremely negligent of her to just let me roam wild without calling or texting me to check in. I mean for Gods' sakes, I could be getting myself in a lot of trouble, and not just the typical kinds of teenage trouble, like drugs and whatnot. Even if I'm not up to her supernatural standards, I still know lots of ways to stir up the paranormal underworld. The more I think about it, the angrier I get. Do I really need to go to her for help on the Cassandra case? It seems like I'm doing all right on my own. If she couldn't make any progress, maybe the Sand bloodline is not as great as she's made it out to be. Clearly not, if her genetics resulted in my complete magical failure. Maybe I don't need her help, for this or anything else.

Because I don't care what Amani says; Mom will NOT CARE that my motivations have been pure and will bring out the big hexes for this. Heaven forbid I keep a secret from her when she refuses to ever let me even remotely near her inner circle. This kind of cyclical thinking convinces me that we *don't* need my mom, and I won't share any of this with her until we have Cassandra back safe and sound. I'd rather her be informed of my disobedience, after all is said and done, in a "well, it worked out in the end! SUCK IT, MOM!" sort of way.

While riffling through my drawers, I come across my blank Chicago Culinary Institute application. I've been looking at it every couple days since my campus visit last spring. Gods that was a fun day. Mom couldn't close the shop to go with me, but my buddy Ella was able to have someone cover at her bakery so she could be my guide. It was Ella who suggested the school; while

I could just get going with my own business straight after graduation, Ella said getting a culinary degree would help me with stuff beyond the kitchen, like learning about sanitary codes and managing a staff. We had such a good time peeking in on classes such as Pastry Design and World Cuisine that I wanted to ditch Manchester right away and start my coursework. But since then, I haven't even made progress on the application.

I keep reading the questions over and over, wondering how my life will fit neatly into a series of empty boxes. Besides the basics of my name, birth date, and social security number, I'm really not sure how to capture the essence of Amber without looking like I'm applying for a creative writing degree.

Tell us about yourself

Well, I'm the only girl in my family to be born without the powers of witchcraft, but I am super-talented at helping other people fall in love. My best friend has the ability to see the future, but due to a pact we made in middle school, I have no idea what lies ahead other than I will eventually escape high school. I'm currently working on finding a family friend who was most likely kidnapped by goblins.

No.

What are your extracurricular activities?

I don't participate in any school functions, partly because everyone at school hates me, but mostly because I work at my mom's magic shop five days a week. I can't play sports, sing, act, or do anything that would garner me a position in any club or team.

Cool.

Why do you want to attend the Chicago Culinary Institute?

Here's the big one, the question that actually means something and won't make me seem like a lunatic. This is the one that counts. But how can I put my reasons into words and convincingly convey how important this is to me? How can I make them understand how walking through those doors on my campus tour made me feel like I belong? How I never know what to wear but that a white chef's coat will fit me just perfectly? How baking is something I discovered on my own—not a talent bestowed on me by ancient mystical bloodlines but a skill I built myself from the ground up. Baking is something that's entirely mine, outside of the crazy world where I've always struggled to find my place.

And now that my match-reading for Amani completely blew up in my face, getting into school is even more important. I've always been confident in my supernatural skills, but now I'm plagued with doubt. I know I can make a kick-ass pumpkin pie, but do I know FOR SURE that I can make a match? I keep trying to convince myself that what happened with Amani and Vincent has to be a fluke; maybe I built him up too much or maybe she expected some sort of crazy, unobtainably romantic first meeting that could never match her ideal. I can't understand why I would've messed it up. I've always seen love as black and white: someone's either your match or he's not. But this stuff with Amani (and let's be real, Charlie) is throwing in shades of gray I can't process. Why would the powers that be even allow matchmakers to exist if our magic isn't a surefire thing?

Although . . . *although* . . . if there is an error in my match processor, it does open up some possibilities—possibilities that I shouldn't find any solace in, but that would definitely make my current conundrum less troublesome. Because if my matches may be questionable, that means maybe the girl who keeps taunting me from behind a certain young man's eyes may not be as big a concern and . . .

Stop it, Amber. Focus on something that's real, not crazy hypotheticals. I've started this college essay a billion times, but the words never come out right. It's always too cheesy, too schmaltzy, too melodramatic. Why do I have to prove I can write anyway? Shouldn't my admission be based on something more pertinent, like a perfect pineapple upside-down cake? Who cares if I can craft a moving essay if my pies can blow people's minds? Although I guess it would be difficult for an admissions counselor to eat his way through daily submissions of sugar.

ARGH!

I put it away and head to MarshmElla's, where I spend

the evening helping Ella prep tomorrow morning's batch of cinnamon buns and teaching Charlie the proper icing-to-pastry ratio.

Delicious.

Nineteen

THE NEXT MORNING, I WAKE UP AT DAWN TO MAKE BLUEBERRY muffins from scratch. There's something calming about being awake before much of the world, and though I haven't caught many sunrises in my day, I decide today will be a good one. Though it takes some time to acclimate to the Sharmas' kitchen (who puts a sifter next to a pizza stone?), I eventually find my rhythm, mixing in flour and brown sugar. The batter comes together nicely, and I carefully grease the muffin tin. As I work, I don't have to think about schoolwork or supernaturals; don't have to worry about the intricacies of love or heartbreak. I only need to fold in the berries and bake for twenty minutes. If only everything else in life was so easy (and delicious). I pull them out before they're completely done and add a sugar crumble to the golden tops. The batch cools on a butcher block while I finish getting ready for school; being up this early means I won't have to endure another bathroom confessional with Amani.

I decide to take a break from public transit and walk to school. I can roam the Chicago streets, taking in all the morning rush while sipping a nice overpriced coffee and enjoying the fruits of my labor.

A few blocks away from Manchester, I spot a familiar face coming toward me: resident adorable elderly person, Wendy Pumple. She sees me and panics. Physically unable to make a run for it and fully aware it would be rude to turn around and walk away, she stands frozen, nervously fumbling with her handbag as if she purposely stopped in the middle of the street to find something.

"Oh. Well hello, dear," she says, her voice quivering, and not in a cute old lady way.

"Hey, Mrs. P., are you sure you should be talking to me? I mean, I wouldn't want you to belittle your magical standing," I say. A little sassy, but whatever.

"Oh, Amber, I feel terrible about what happened the other night," she says sadly. "You have every right to be upset. The conversation elevated so quickly and I . . . wanted to say something, but I didn't want to rock the boat."

"Well, you weren't the only one. Seems like the whole group was content in sending me off to drift." Saying the words aloud only confirms how much their dismissal hurt me. I know I was never really part of the coven, but I felt like I belonged, like a spirited mascot or something. Instead, I was just some random who occasionally provided snacks.

"It's not like that, dear," Wendy tries to assure me, but I cross my arms to let her know I don't buy it. "The group is just going through some changes, that's all."

"And how's that going, hmm?"

Wendy looks nervous, like a hunted animal backed into a corner. I can see her mentally cycling through a series of statements, trying to decide which would be the less incriminating. "It has been interesting. Victoria has brought a different energy to Dawning Day."

Now there's a politically correct response if I ever heard one. "I don't trust her. I don't think Mom does either."

"Oh, well, I wouldn't know about that. Your mother has such a nurturing soul, what with taking in Bob and opening her shop to the mystical community. She's always been so welcoming to others."

Except to her own daughter. "I guess," I huff.

"Try not to be too hard on her, dear," Wendy insists. "Your mom loves you very much. Even though it may not seem like it, I know she doesn't act without reason." Whatever. This is witchy "give yourself over to the Fates" talk, and I'm not having it right now. If Mom had a reason for casting me out, she could have told me at any time. There shouldn't be a need for secrecy among the Sands.

"Give her my love, will you, dear?" she asks.

Sure, if I ever speak to her again.

A few minutes late to school, I've missed the opening rituals of a morning pep rally. Darn this school and its constant onslaught of organized student gatherings! I never know what to do with myself at these things. I mean, I wouldn't immediately land on "peppy" as an adjective for myself, so how am I supposed to conjure it for a group of my peers who are only being celebrated because they happen to show a slight advantage in athleticism? So you can take an air-filled shape and put it through another shape—so what? Didn't we get applause for that sort of thing as toddlers? Is this really something we have to cheer for?

The whole school is seated on wooden bleachers in the gym, watching the dopes from the football team wave from center court. There is a blanket of green and orange—our school colors—covering the bleachers, making me nauseous. I'm not a graphic designer, but I'm pretty sure those colors do not belong in such close proximity. Neil Foster, the school mascot, skips around in a copper fox suit, stopping to shake his bushy tail at random intervals. And of course, Ivy and the rest of the cheerleading squad are down there, dancing to some pumped-in beat, their skirts dangerously short. Sometimes I think these things are solely organized by the siren herself, forgetting that there's even a team to recognize and giving her an excuse to be "foxy" (vomit).

Well, at least it's getting me out of gym class.

Everyone is now up on their feet, singing the school song, but I stay put, a sea of butts in my face. It's uncomfortable, to say the least. The crowd starts yelling louder, spelling out f-o-x over and over.

After suffering through a final call-and-response cheer led by Ivy, I notice one boy in the crowd who's not completely hypnotized by her hip gyrations and is actually looking my way instead: Charlie. From across the gym, he gives me a little wave, and I wave back, my heart desperately trying to claw its way out of its current funk. He wraps his hands around his neck and pantomimes choking himself, which makes me laugh and catches the attention of Queen Ivy, who's not used to having her subjects disobey her command. Out of the corner of my eye, I see her watching Charlie's and my exchange, and even though she still wears a smile for the audience, I can sense jealousy in her eyes. Good.

Once we're finally dismissed, everyone starts to disperse, and I look for Charlie in the masses. One significant disadvantage to school uniforms is trying to find someone when we're all mashed together; forgive the cliché, but it really is like picking a needle out of a haystack. Physical discrepancies sort of disappear when all you see is plaid, plaid, plaid.

Of course I easily find Ivy, who's already claiming her next victim, climbing up on some sad, needy boy whose blond bombshell fantasies have gotten the best of him. Sucker. As everyone continues to exit the gym, I watch as she slithers up against him, a python squeezing her willing prey, hiding his features from view as she consumes him. It's messed up. I've seen it time and again and usually turn away before my gag reflex kicks in, but for some reason, I can't stop watching this boy happily and willingly be a part of her power trip.

Until I see why. She's doing this snake-charming performance just for me. Because when she's finished writhing, it's clear the boy is not some random choice.

It's Charlie.

I feel myself break into a thousand pieces. Sensing me behind her, she playfully pulls Charlie's hand from her hip and looks back at me, her lip gloss smudged with satisfaction. Once she's released her siren grip, Charlie shakes his head, as if he's just awoken from a bad dream. His eyes lock on mine, and his lips form a horrified "oh." He tries to push himself away from her, but there's so many people still exiting the gym, they keep knocking him back into her, much to Ivy's delight.

"Amber," he calls, panicked. "This isn't what it looks like."

"Charlie?" Even though it was only a whisper, a crowd starts to gather around us, sensing blood in the water. I hear giggling and hushed gossip, but my pounding heart drowns it all out.

"I was waiting for you, and she threw herself at me."

"Yeah, and he caught me. With his lips." She wipes some of her cherry-red lip gloss from his mouth.

"Stop." He winces.

"Stop what, Charlie? She saw you; *everyone* saw you." She gestures like a game show host. "We've been doing this dance for years."

Charlie looks at me, desperation behind his frames. "It's not like that."

"Sure seems that way," Ivy says, relishing the moment. "And it's about time." She snuggles up next to him, but he squirms away. By this time, Amani has pushed through the horde to be by my side.

"What's going on?" she asks.

"He . . . she . . ." I can't find the words. I can't feel my face. I'm completely numb, like I'm having open-heart surgery in front of the whole school. Everyone's humming and buzzing around me, but I can't move, paralyzed by an unresponsive organ.

"Amber?"

"Amani, let me explain," Charlie begs.

Despite our recent friendship chill, she immediately goes into a protective stance. She sees Ivy's victorious gloating and quickly connects the dots.

"Let's go," Amani says to me. She grabs my arm, pulling me into the crowd, hurrying toward the nearest girls' restroom. The echoes of whoops and hollers ring in my ears.

"Are you okay?" she asks as we duck into an accessible stall.

She grabs a fistful of toilet paper, and the words that escaped me finally start vomiting out through intermittent choking.

"I . . . I don't even know why I'm upset. It's not like he owes me anything. I'm not his girlfriend; I'm not his match. He can kiss whoever he wants," I say, forcing the building tears to stay put in their ducts. And it's true: I have no claim over Charlie Blitzman. I have no right to even be here, on the verge of tears over someone who isn't mine.

"Well, it doesn't always work out nice and neat, does it?" Amani says gently. She pulls me toward her, wrapping her arms around me. I wipe a few escapees on her uniform, leaving a trail of splotches on her shoulder.

"This is so stupid! Why am I crying?"

"Because . . . you like him, whether he's your match or not. The heart wants what it wants."

And suddenly I'm in the shoes of every client whose dreams I've dashed, whose hearts have broken right before my eyes as I've told them their love is not meant to be. I've never under-stood why they get so upset; isn't my advice a blessing? A warn-ing not to go down a path that leads to a dead end? But now I know: the heart, for all its strength, beats blindly.

The bell echoes through the bathroom; the four-minute passing period of pain is over.

"Want to just stay here?" Amani offers. "We can stand on the toilet seats if anyone comes looking."

"No, I don't want to give anyone, most of all Ivy, the

satisfaction of knowing I'm broken in the bathroom," I say, wiping my face clean. Amani gives a weak smile. She takes my hand as we head off to English together through the empty hallways. The problem with suffering a personal tragedy at school is that no matter the outcome, you're still *at school.* Your insides can be bleeding, but you're still expected to turn in your homework and take notes on the wars of our ancestors, when all you really can focus on is the war within yourself. It's an isolated battle, fought in silence at an ancient desk, one exceedingly pointless class after another. There's no escape, no place to hide, the only mercy being the final bell.

I hold my head high as we walk in late to class, ignoring the whispers and mocking gestures as I take my seat. I stare straight ahead, tuning out everything around me. I can't control if my classmates talk, but I can control whether or not I show I care.

"Amber, Amani, you're tardy." Ms. Dell states the obvious. "Our first group has already started, and now you're interrupting their presentation on Jane Austen." I look at the three suckers squirming in full Regency costume. They seem almost grateful for the intermission. "Explanation now."

"I was attacked by a sea snake," I say. "I'm bleeding internally." (Overdramatic? Sure. But you gotta know your audience. A teacher who forces her students to dress in nineteenth-century formal wear enjoys theatrics.)

Ms. Dell's face twists in confusion as Ivy groans, "Oh please. Don't be such an attention whore."

"Takes one to know one," Amani retorts.

"Girls, that's enough," Ms. Dell says to deaf ears.

"You act like it's some big surprise. I know you thought you and Charlie had this little flirtation going, but honestly, hon, don't you think that's a little bit sad? I mean, why would he go for a peacock-haired freak when he could have a woman like me?" Ivy says, twisting the ends of her golden hair like a mustachioed villain.

And I realize, this whole thing is just a game. Even if Charlie is not my boyfriend, he would never kiss Ivy, not without a healthy helping of siren powers manipulating him. Evil is not his type. Ivy hates coming in second, and it must have been eating her alive to know there was a Manchester boy who wasn't worshipping at her feet.

"What's sad is being so jealous of a peacock-haired freak that you have to force yourself on innocent victims," I say. There's a small smattering of gasps and snickers; the Mr. Darcy up front shifts uncomfortably in his codpiece.

Ivy stands up, incensed. "You are such a bitch!"

And before I can stop it, my fist is connecting with Ivy's nose.

Twenty

HOLY HELL, MY KNUCKLES FEEL LIKE THEY'VE SHATTERED INTO A million razor-sharp shards. No one tells you how much pain is inflicted on the one who throws the punch. While it was totally satisfying to watch blood drip down Ivy's pearly whites, I'm not sure my immediate suffering was worth it.

I'm sitting in Mr. Boger's office, ice pack resting atop my throbbing hand. I'm pretty sure he and the dean are in the other room discussing whether or not I should be suspended. I've been in plenty of fights before, but I've never thrown a punch. It's usually been your basic girl-fight combo of scratching and hair pulling, but since I never start it, I can always play the good ol' self-defense card. Not this time. Too bad I can't use one of my mom's super-sensitive listening charms to hear what they're saying, but she'll be here soon enough to end my life, so it really doesn't matter what they decide.

Condensation drips on my thigh, and I mentally replay the morning. How did I get here? Somewhere, the Fates are laughing, pointing their spectral fingers at the silly matchmaker who is clearly veering off course. I bet they're having a real good time at my expense. But you know what? Screw those bastards. They may have a looking glass into past, present, and future, but they're just bystanders, absently watching while life happens around them. It's easy to be high and mighty when you never have to take a chance.

Mr. Boger comes back through the door, wearing his usual "oh, Amber" face. I wonder if other students have gotten to see this winning combination of disappointment and pity, or if I'm just special.

"Well," he starts, grunting as he takes the seat across from me. "I wish I could say I'm surprised this happened."

"I'm surprised it didn't happen earlier," I say, trying to add some levity. "I mean, it's not like she didn't have it coming."

He is not amused. He leans his elbows on his desk, burying his face in his hands. A sigh leaks through his meaty fingers. "Let the record show that I do not condone violence."

"Noted."

"I will agree that Ivy is a repeated bully, but you're smarter than this, Amber. I wish you could've risen above her level."

I swish the melting ice around the bag. A quiet "I know" escapes me.

"I tried to advocate for you, showing how you've been a target for bullying, but the dean is really cracking down on fighting, so it's a three-day suspension."

I say nothing.

"I called your mother. She should be here soon to pick you up."

"Good Gods," I whisper.

"I'm sorry, my hands are tied," Mr. Boger says with a frown. "I think it would be best if you put Ivy Chamberlain out of your mind."

Not likely. She seems to be a permanent stain on my existence.

"The dean was going to come in here and have you issue a statement, but I held her off, as I assume you do not regret your actions."

"No, I don't."

"That's what I thought." A short knock at the door makes him stir, but before he can get up to answer, Mom is walking through. It's not the first time she's been here, but it's definitely her first time picking up a guilty offender.

"What happened?" she asks Mr. Boger.

"Ms. Sand, please take a seat." He gestures toward the empty chair beside me. Mom eyes me like a bomb ready to detonate as she sits.

"Amber threw a punch at a classmate, Ivy Chamberlain, during their second-period English class. She caught Ivy kissing her—boyfriend?—Charlie Blitzman, after a pep rally." Mom's eyes grow wide at the succession of "boyfriend" and "Charlie Blitzman" but says nothing. Mr. Boger continues relaying the facts. "Ivy taunted her afterward, and in front of the class, Amber threw a punch."

"Charlie's not my boyfriend," I say, as if it matters.

Mr. Boger nods. "Still, Amber assaulted a student on school grounds. She's been suspended for three days."

Mom sighs, but not her usual fire-breathing dragon sigh. The air comes out softer, more like a cloud than a flame. She frowns, and I almost see a touch of sadness in her eyes. Where's the fire and brimstone, the crackling cauldron of pain? What's going on?

"I understand," Mom says. "I will handle this at home. Let's go, Amber."

Water trickles down my leg as we exit the office, and I dump the leaky ice pack in a trash can. We walk down the empty halls in silence, occasional curious eyes peeking out from classroom doors. I smear a smile on my face for anyone who catches a glimpse: an unapologetic criminal happy with her offense.

When we get outside, I see Mom has borrowed Bob's giant Hummer, the only car large enough to accommodate his mountainous body. We're pretty much never alone in a car together, so the discomfort of the situation skyrockets.

We drive a few blocks before she finally asks, "So what do you have to say for yourself?"

I think before speaking, watching the city landscape roll by. I know I must choose the best explanation if I want to survive. If I turn it back to witchcraft—emphasize how I'm having an existential matchmaking crisis—maybe she'll spare me. "Things have been really hard with the love stuff lately, and—"

"You're dating Charlie?" she interrupts.

"No. Well, not really."

"Why didn't you tell me?" She stares straight ahead, but even in profile, I detect hurt feelings. Telling my mom about Charlie would have been awkward no matter how you sliced it, and this delightful revelation is not made any easier thanks to our days spent in mutual stubborn silence.

"Oh. I don't know. There's not really anything to tell. . . ." I trail off.

Mom takes her right hand off the wheel and reaches for mine. Her grasp is firm, almost pinching, echoing the pained expression on her face. "When I watched you two together that day at the shop, I had my suspicions. Your combined auras just seemed so . . . light. I'm sorry this happened."

Her sympathy is surprising but not unwelcome. "So, you're not mad?"

"Well, I'm not happy my daughter is suspended. But from my perspective, some actions are justified. And sticking it to a siren is one of them."

Ha! How about that? I smile to myself, but am honestly confused by this gentle, almost understanding reaction. How am I getting off this easily?

"Mom, I don't want to sound ungrateful here, but what's going on? The first time you see me in days is me getting kicked out of school, and you're all chill? Did you take some sort of witch Quaaludes before picking me up?"

She neither cracks a smile nor a grimace. She just keeps her eyes on the road. "What happened the other day with the coven . . . I was . . . wrong to shut you out." The word "wrong" comes out slightly mangled, like she's speaking a foreign language. I don't think I've ever heard her apologize for something, especially anything magic related. "Everything with Dawning Day has been changing; I don't have the same authority within the group lately and . . . I was embarrassed for you to see it."

My mom, embarrassed? What the what? "It's not anything to be embarrassed about; they're the ones being jerks. Anyone who listens to anything Victoria says is clearly deranged."

She tilts her head to acknowledge what I've said, but I can tell she doesn't completely believe it. "Still, you shouldn't have to worry about your mother's social problems."

"But that's the thing Mom: I do. You're my mom, and I actually give a crap what happens to you." This makes her smile a bit. "You don't have to shield me from everything."

She looks over at me quickly, her dark eyes starting to warm. "Okay. I'll try to remember that."

Mom drops me at home and goes to relieve Bob from his solo shop management (being left alone with so much magical merchandise is often a recipe for madness for a recovering addict). When I get upstairs and check my phone, I have a bazillion text messages from Charlie waiting for me.

Amber, I'm so sorry about today

You have to know I would NEVER kiss her

Just the thought of her lips on mine is making me nauseous

In fact, is penicillin over the counter? I should get some

Or is there a bacteria-killing potion your mom sells?

Please text back

Holy crap, did you punch Ivy?

I heard you got suspended

Now I'm extra sad

Greetings from the outside, I type back. It's lunch break at school, and I get a response right away.

OMG! You're alive!

Of course I am, I'm not the one who got punched in the face

I can't believe you did that. So badass

She deserved it

Yes she did

You know it was her, right? She put some sort of spell on me

Well, that's her MO

It was gross

I bet

I'm sorry

You don't have to apologize to me

Don't I?

I pause before typing back. It makes me nervous, having my thoughts captured for potentially all of eternity. It's easy to refute words you've said, but it's hard to deny the digital proof. Anything I type will be carried around not only in his head but in his pocket, so I feel like I have to be extra careful with every response. My reaction to the scene probably already gave away my true feelings for him, but it still doesn't change that he's not my match, and I need to steer clear.

You're a free agent

Technically

But I hope not for long

Better change the subject before I say anything too incriminating.

You ready for our big adventure tomorrow night?

Which adventure would that be?

OMG the one where we save your stepmom??

Oh right, that

Yeah, I told Dad the plan

And he's cool?

As in, not gonna tell my mom?

I told him not to

Thanks

I'm already on thin ice. Don't want any more punishment

Me too. Don't want you locked up

That would be a travesty for society

Or at least for me ;)

My chest swells with a fluttery feeling—bubbling around in what I used to think was a dark empty chamber—but I still can't let that out. Charlie doesn't seem to have a problem expressing his feelings, but then again, he's not burdened with the same obligation to cosmic forces as I am.

Ignorance is bliss, no?

Twenty-one

THE NEXT DAY, I HAD TO FAKE MENSTRUAL CRAMPS TO GET out of my last two hours at Windy City so I could make the goblin hoedown on time. Mom seemed suspicious, but since cramps come with the silver lining of not having any outwardly disprovable symptoms, she let Bob finish out the night without me. This performance was only really a half lie, because while I wasn't having any side effects of my monthly cycle, the idea of deceiving my mom does make me physically ill. I hope it's worth it, and I can show her once and for all that my magic doesn't belong at the bottom of the mystical pile. That I can swim in the deeper waters of witchcraft without floaties.

Now I'm waiting just west of the designated address, at a Starbucks across the street. Mr. Hollister's instructions were to meet at Michigan and Jackson, which is right by the Art Institute downtown. I'm surprised he'd pick such a public, touristy meeting spot to conduct his goblin business, but maybe he likes to stick to easily recognizable landmarks. Still, even at this late hour, there are people milling around the stone steps to the museum; I can't see how he'll pull anything shady with so many potential witnesses, which I guess is to our advantage.

I'm really embracing this whole covert affairs thing, wearing a black trench coat that's way too warm for the season, and oversized black sunglasses, even though the sun has already set and it's so dark I can barely see my macchiato. If I were really a secret agent, I'd probably have a tiny handgun strapped to my inner thigh and a lipstick case that's actually filled with poison, but since I'm a matchmaker, all I've got on me is my phone, a candy bar wrapper (the contents of which I meant to save for later, but . . .), and a small bag of contraband from the shop, including a stupefying powder that when blown into an opponent's face, will give you a ten-second head start at running away while they temporarily forget where they're standing. That may not seem like a lot, but every second counts when you're making a getaway. Watch out, supernatural element!

Charlie and John show up just as I've finished my overly sugared drink, and between my kickass outfit and caffeine, I'm buzzing to get started.

"Alpha, alpha, one, two, three," I say into an imaginary wristwatch. "Do you read me?"

"Sorry, my walkie-talkie's in the shop," Charlie jumps in right on cue. He's dressed in regular, non-spy attire. Lame. "Guess we'll have to communicate by homing pigeon."

"Fine," I sigh. "But I'm sending you the dry cleaning bills."

"Are you implying my birds are crappy?"

I open my mouth to respond, but John holds up a massive, football-size hand to silence our banter. I can see why he wouldn't be in the mood for spy games; the stakes are high for him.

"Guys, please," he says, his voice heavy and low. He sounds like someone who's battling a migraine, wanting to shut out all sensory input. He too is wearing an unnecessary coat, but I'm sure his is more about keeping the general public—not goblins—away. The Blitz is the most recognizable figure in the city, and drawing attention to himself is the last thing he needs right now. The hood of his coat is pulled down over his forehead, but I can still see the tension in his brows. "Amber, I'm concerned you haven't mentioned this to your mother. I appreciate your helping Charlie and me, but don't you think she'd be of assistance here? I don't exactly know how to handle"—he lowers his voice—"goblins."

"Well, you've probably worked with them before but just didn't realize it," I say. "It's not like they'd print 'goblin' on a business card. It doesn't exactly have the best connotation. But the good thing about goblins is they're tiny. With all your football prowess, you could probably fling a lot of them aside like a pair of dirty socks."

He shakes his head. "The mayor of Chicago can't go around flinging his constituents."

"Right, of course not. Which is why I brought these." I pull out a Ziploc baggie filled with a scoop of gold shavings. I snuck them from the shop when Bob wasn't looking, from the bulk-size "mystical properties" section. Customers can fill up pouches with rose petals, feathers, assorted bones, and other miscellaneously magical elements for only $5.99/quarter pound to make their own "potions." While the stuff we sell can legitimately be used in real spells, most people just buy combinations that look pretty enough to put on a shelf. The gold shavings are generally overlooked, probably because when they're piled together they kind of look like dirt, and also people assume they aren't real. Of course they're real, though, because while my mom is a lot of things, a con artist she ain't.

"What are those, pencil shavings?" Charlie asks, stepping closer to examine my haul. (See?)

"Yes, exactly. We're going to rub tiny wood fragments into their skin until they get splinters." He scrunches his face in confusion. "They're *gold* shavings," I say, shaking the bag so the fluorescent light shows off the shimmer. "Goblins are helpless in the presence of treasure. It's a documented fact."

"So, we'll make a trade?" John asks. "Cassandra for the gold?"

"Seems civil enough." Charlie nods approvingly.

"Keeps us off the evening news," I say. "I mean, I've never met Cassandra, and I'm sure she's one in a million, but unless she's gold-plated, I don't see how those little guys could resist." I pass the stash to John, who handles it delicately, like a water balloon you don't want to burst. "You should make the trade. Goblins are businessmen. They won't be able to pass on a deal from someone like you."

John looks at his Rolex. "How much time do we have?"

"The note said eight o'clock, but you should probably lie low until they show up."

We sit at our table, staring out the coffee shop window, waiting for our target. Charlie's sitting across from me, with his dad in between us. Poor John looks like a wreck, biting his nails, barely able to keep his knees from bouncing against the table. I guess if I hadn't seen my partner in weeks, I'd be anxious too.

But to be honest, I'm too distracted to even think about being nervous. I'm all revved up from my venti pre-gaming, leading me to believe that coffee is not the best choice for a stakeout. My eyes refuse to stay still, checking out everything but the window I'm supposed to be studying. Somehow the stainless steel milk frothers and giant pumps filled with gooey syrups seem much more important, and I watch as a parade of customers order drinks in mind-boggling combinations. *Grande non-fat non-whip mocha . . . Triple venti soy no-foam latte . . . Quad grande extra-hot caramel macchiato.* It's kind of insane, and yet, it's what I love about food. Take one simple ingredient, and an endless amount of transformations spill out. Talk about magic.

Just as I start daydreaming about what kind of coffee-flavored desserts I could whip up when this is over, I feel a small kick under the table. For a second, I think it's John, who's all jittery himself, but no, it's Charlie, playing with my foot. Turns out he's barely on Cassandra watch either. In fact, he appears to be more on Amber watch. With his chin propped up by his palm, a shy smile peeks out from his curled fingers, like the sun eclipsing the moon. I can only see the edges, yet I still feel its warmth; it radiates through me, and when combined with the caffeine, I have to literally hold on to my chair to keep from falling off. I nudge him back, and his expression brightens, more so in the eyes than lips. It's the kind of look you cannot fake; I've seen it plenty of times during joint matchmaking sessions, when a couple comes together to confirm their impending union. Once I give my seal of approval, they turn to each other full of love, pupils turning into stars. You can almost hear their inner string quartets swelling. It's pretty gushy, straight-from-the-movies kind of stuff. . . . I've never had anyone look at *me* that way. It's a little unnerving, and yet, I don't want it to stop.

I'm feeling all tingly, until I foolishly take a deep look into his eyes, causing my matchmaker visions to activate. There she is again, Charlie's future wife, all adorable with her wide, toothy smile and funky fashion flair. I try to fast-forward, but I can't; I watch her come up from behind him with an overflowing popcorn bowl, then snuggle down next to him on a couch. He kisses the top of her head, and she sighs, leaning into his chest: another sickeningly sweet scene among the many I've witnessed so far. Only this time, right before the happy ending fades to black, I'm given another snippet, a final detail I truly hoped would keep itself concealed.

A name floats up from the depths of his heart, percolating to the surface of my consciousness. Kim—it's official, the name of the girl who will be his bride. I've become quite familiar with her face and the love they'll grow to share, but somehow knowing her name makes her more real, an actual person and not some spectral buzzkill interrupting my time with Charlie. I thought it would take longer for me to learn this concrete fact—the only other match name I've ever learned is Vincent—but I guess time flies when you're falling for someone who isn't yours. Up until now, I've been haunted by the idea of this girl, knowing I was encroaching on someone else's turf, but she was still just a vision, a vague notion of his coming attractions. But a name—Kim—is inescapable, something I can't ignore. I can't unsee it, I can't unknow it, and the guilt is overwhelming.

Suddenly, I'm burning up, angry at myself for letting things get this far, for letting myself get so attached to someone who's already matched. Why didn't I distance myself, put up the walls that have worked so well in the past? What was I thinking spending so much time with him? I ignored my logic, letting my feelings take the wheel: stupid, messy emotions overriding my screwed-up matchmaker judgment.

"Are you okay?" Charlie asks, clearly sensing my self-flagellation.

"Yeah . . . just . . . too much caffeine," I lie.

"There she is," John says, causing us all to look toward the window. I'm momentarily disorientated, taking a moment to refocus on the task at hand. It's very dark now, streetlamps casting pocketed spotlights of sidewalk and green space. Just across Michigan Avenue she waits, in a small park south of the museum. All alone, swinging her wild wavy hair, she's clearly nervous as the meeting time draws near.

The three of us stand in unison, but John sets his hands on our shoulders. "You two stay here," he commands. He never takes his eyes off Cassandra, causing him to stumble and bump into the Starbucks clientele as he makes his way to the door. As we watch him jog away outside, Charlie slides over to the seat next to mine, his eyes still trained on his dad.

"So, now that we're rescuing Cass from a seemingly shady fate and we know she'll be safe, you're going to break the news to my dad, right?"

My stomach sinks, churning with my own frustration over being attached to someone who's not mine. Suddenly, the idea of spreading this horrible feeling fills me with dread.

"Right?" he asks again.

"Right, yeah," I say weakly.

"What's with the hesitation?"

"Nothing, I just . . . hope everything goes okay."

"What do you think is gonna happen?" he asks, his face suddenly much closer to mine. I feel my ears starting to burn, so I shake my hair over them.

"Um . . . I . . . really don't know."

"He'll be fine, though, right?"

Charlie's proximity is causing my brain to scramble, like words floating randomly in a bowl of alphabet soup. The thoughts are there, yet articulating them is proving frustratingly difficult. "Um . . ."

"You know, once this is over, I'd like us to still hang out," he says, giving me a small, hopeful smile that turns my insides into pudding. He notices my right hand resting on the table, and slowly moves his left to join the two together. What was just an empty palm is now a tangle of fingers, united in a gesture unlike any I've ever experienced. Every day at the shop, I take the hands of strangers, and all I ever notice is clamminess or a severe need for lotion. But this, with Charlie, is entirely new, like I can feel his entire body chemistry just from a small patch of skin. It's humming inside me, rushing like a waterfall, so loud I almost don't hear him ask, "Would that be okay?"

My brain and my body are both fighting for my full attention, and I can't decide who deserves it. While holding Charlie's hand feels so, so nice, my brain is screaming *KIM KIM KIM*. I start to regain use of my jaw just when something pulls Charlie's attention outside.

"Hey, look, he's got her."

I turn to see John and Cass reunited under a streetlamp, but for someone who's been missing for a while, she sure doesn't look happy to be found. They're not embracing like I'd expect; they're not even standing that close to each other. It wouldn't take a lip-reader to see that they're fighting; Cassandra's arms are crossed firmly over her chest, while John is making sharp, firm gestures to indicate that they need to leave. We watch their angry pantomime in silence, unsure of what to make of their strange greeting.

The couple is so consumed by their bickering, they don't notice the circle of goblins that has quietly surrounded them. Dressed all in black, child-size suit jackets and bowler hats, their tiny bodies blend into the night, almost undetectable as they stand just outside the artificial light. They assembled so quickly, but there have to be at least twenty of them, standing each about five feet apart. My heart starts to race as I realize what's going on. I know an incantation circle when I see one.

"Charlie, get up," I say in a voice that instantly shifts his expression from dream to nightmare. His hand still clutched to mine, I yank him upward, our chairs toppling over as we make a hasty exit.

"What's going on?" Charlie asks as we start running.

"We've got to get them out of that circle!"

"What circle?"

Good Gods. While any other girl would probably be over the moon if Charlie Blitzman was so enraptured by her presence that he had no awareness of his surroundings, that kind of swooning does not help me right now. Goblins have fairy blood in their lineage, and fairies have a long and confusing history; they aren't all Tinker Bell. For every Zen, Mother Earth worshipper with wings, you've got a spiteful, pissed-off little sprite who hates being a pixie. No matter what, their magic is strong, and they can stir up trouble in a blink.

There's a reason why witches and other magically inclined beings do their business in a circle formation. While sorcery may be in their DNA, it still takes a decent amount of energy to get the juices flowing; circles keep that effort from spilling out and being wasted. But there's also a reason why no one ever stands in the middle. The center is the focal point; it's where magical folk place the token, which will either aid in manipulation or *be* manipulated. And since John and Cass have no idea they've just entered a mystical cage match, I have a bad feeling I know which kind of token they are.

We run down Michigan as it starts to drizzle, keeping the oblivious duo in our sights. Even though most of the goblin clan's backs are to me, I know they won't take their time getting stuff done. With the traffic roaring by on the always-busy street, my warning cries would go unheard; I need to break the circle before the spell is complete.

We get to the corner, but there's too many cars to just bolt across. I try to mind-meld with the traffic signal to make it change, but the only response I'm given is a quick flash of white light. It bursts in and out, like a visual shock wave, disappearing before it can fully register. Too bright to be lightning, I blink it away, thinking it was one of those traffic cameras catching a lead-footed driver, but when my eyes refocus, it's clear the light had nothing to do with modern advances in law enforcement. Because our mark—our whole reason for this pseudo spy mission— has disappeared, along with the man who loves her and the supernatural element that clearly has something against her.

As the rain picks up, we finally get the go-ahead from a white-lit stick man, yet now we have no need to cross.

Charlie blinks in disbelief, unable to process the scene—or lack of scene—before us. The walking man trades places with a red warning hand as Charlie's words fill the now empty space.

"Um, Amber? Where's my dad?"

Twenty-two

THE RAIN IS COMING DOWN HARDER; I DIDN'T REALIZE MY trench coat would be so practical when I grabbed it earlier tonight. While Charlie's plaid button-down looks like he just pulled it from the wash, my clothes are dry under the coat's water-wicking fabric. But I still feel damp, my insides heavy and soaked with guilt. I'd never proclaim to be the most selfless person, but I never knew I could be so selfish.

We've crossed the street, standing under one of the stone lions that guard the entrance to the museum. Both of us stare at the empty park, as if we could make them reappear simply by wishing it.

"Amber, what the hell just happened?" Charlie asks. A valid question, and while I can explain the magic behind it, I cannot justify my negligence here. What was I thinking? How could I be so stupid? Did I really think a baggie of mystical crap would save the day?

"Charlie, I'm . . . so sorry," I choke out. I rub my palms into the rough stone (he's since let go of my hand), the texture grating on my skin.

"What are you sorry for? Where's my dad?" he repeats.

"I . . . don't know."

He walks around the grassy area where his father stood moments before, looking for clues he won't find. I don't know exactly what happened, but I do know a goblin would never leave evidence. The rain has already washed away their tiny footprints.

I shake my head. "I should've known better. I should've told my mom and brought her here. She could've stopped those goblins and whatever they were up to with a flick of her wrist, but I was too stubborn. I didn't want to admit I needed her help. I'm such a jerk."

It's hard to see his face through the sheets of icy rain, but I can't imagine anything positive is resting there. "You didn't know what would happen," he says flatly.

"You put your trust in me, and I completely and utterly failed. I didn't want to get in trouble, and now your dad has been vaporized."

"Vaporized?"

"Well, probably transported. But who knows to where!"

Charlie takes off his rain-speckled frames and tries drying them on his sopping wet shirt. The droplets smudge the lenses, so he wipes them on his bare forearm instead. The dragon's flames are unable to make a difference.

"I get the guilt trip," he says, anger creeping in his tone, "but that doesn't help anything at all. My dad is GONE, Amber. Gone! I don't even know if he's dead or alive! What are we supposed to do?"

"We?" I ask incredulously. "There's not going to be any more 'we.' I've mucked this up enough for you, Charlie, so it's time I pass you off to someone who can actually play in the big leagues."

He turns to me for the first time, his face shiny with rain. If he were to shed a tear over his disappeared dad, the weather would be a great cover. "What do you mean? You're bailing?"

"Uh, in case you haven't noticed, I have no magical qualifications for this. I can't see the future or throw a mystical wrench into anyone's cauldron. I am totally powerless, and my only real skill is just making this partnership worse."

"And what does *that* mean?"

I look into his green eyes, deep and lovely, but turn away before I have to endure another clip of him and Kim. I've made so, so many mistakes here, I can't even rank which is worse. "It means . . . that our pairing is completely pointless in every conceivable way."

"Amber, stop." He moves to take my hand, but I shove it

behind my back, scraping it on the brick. "You can't do this. Not right now."

"No, you stop. I'm really glad you came to me for help, but I'm no good for you. I care about you too much to keep leading you astray."

"But—"

"I'm going to tell my mom everything. I'll have her call you from now on. She'll be able to get your dad back, I'm sure of it." I see a bus sloshing up the street, so I dig through my deep coat pockets for my bus pass. I hustle over to the corner stop just as the bus sprays the sidewalk with water.

"Wait!" Charlie runs after me. "You can't just leave me like this!"

"And why on earth would you want me to stay?" I cry out. The bus doors swing open, but Charlie grabs my shoulders, his grip firm despite the slipperiness of my coat.

"How can you ask me that?" he cries back with accusing eyes. "I need you, Amber. What am I going to do without my dad? And not just me, but the city? What am I supposed to say when the mayor stops showing up for work?"

The bus driver, impatient at listening to us squabble, shuts the door and presses on.

"I don't know!" I say, arms swinging wildly against his grip. "I don't have the answers—clearly!"

He grits his teeth, either from frustration or freezing in the rain. "I'm not asking you to have all the answers. I'm just asking you to stay with me. As a friend. As . . ." I watch the rain muddle the anger and fear on his face, as longing emerges as well. I know what he's thinking, and it kills me to continue kicking him when he's down.

"I can't do that for you, Charlie. I want to . . . you have no idea. But I can't."

"I don't understand." His voice is low. "There is something here, I know it. But you're pushing me away when I need you the most."

Another bus is rumbling up the street, and I'm so cold I feel like I'm drowning: in the rain, in my desire to wrap my arms around him and tell him it's going to be okay. In knowing that I'm trapped in a reality where that can't be. The weight of not being able to act on what I want is unbearable, and watching him stand there, soaked to the bone and completely defeated, is making it hard to stay afloat. "It's too hard!" I spit out, almost strangling on the words. "Okay? Being around you . . . it's too much."

He lets go, setting me free as the weight of my words hits him. Even through the deluge, I can almost see his realization, understanding what my confession means.

Embarrassed and exposed, I climb on the second bus, giving him one last "sorry" as the door closes behind me. I refuse to look back through the window as we pull away, knowing full well Charlie's disappointed face would be forever burned in my brain. I take a seat near the back, checking my phone as the bus rumbles north. I have several missed texts from Amani, wanting the status of our rescue mission, but I leave them unanswered. My fingers cannot be trusted to communicate right now. It would be a fury of caps-locks and sad emoji, and no one wants to be on the receiving end of that.

The bus ride lasts for a lifetime, yet I find myself at my apartment doorstep much quicker than I'd like. I fill my lungs with fresh Chicago air, unsure of when I'll get another opportunity once my mom is through with me. My keys in the lock sound like prison bars slamming shut, and while I thoroughly deserve any punishment I receive, it's not any more comforting.

As soon as my foot crosses the threshold, Mom's in my face, rightfully ranting about my lies to get out of work. I stand in the doorway, my coat dripping a puddle of shame around me, and see the makings of a locator spell on the floor; Mom must have been on the verge of chanting. This is the reaction I expected after I punched Ivy. She's already pissed, so I might as well keep the fire burning.

"Mom," I say when she eventually stops to take a breath. "There's more." I give her a play-by-play of the last several days, leaving no detail untold. Pagan religions don't partake in this kind of ritual, but I imagine it being like Catholic confession, asking forgiveness for all my sins. Only I doubt my mom will be a very benevolent deity.

Oddly, though, the longer I talk, the quieter she becomes. I expected unbridled rage, hands and lips shooting lightning bolts at the bull's-eye painted on my forehead. But instead of conjuring an electrical storm, she's placid, currents swirling under the surface. I've only seen her react this way once or twice, and never toward me, and honestly, the lack of fury is even more terrifying.

She doesn't reply at first, her hands lying neatly in her lap. She looks like she could be meditating, and maybe she is, repeating the mantra: "Murdering one's own child is wrong."

"Amber," she starts, her voice icy but measured, "it goes without saying I am beyond disappointed in you. You are aware of your magical deficiencies, yet you chose to engage with forces beyond your range." The word "deficiencies" stings, like I'm some kind of deformed mutation, but I'm in no position to bring this up. "Your pride put people dear to us in danger, all because you couldn't admit you are not a witch."

Record scratch. "Um, that's not it at all. I never pretended to be a witch; I told Charlie from the start that this whole thing was outside my wheelhouse—"

"Yet you kept going with it. Why?"

Okay, so maybe I didn't tell her *everything*, like how holding Charlie's hand lit up a part of me I wasn't even sure existed. Of course I kept it going because I liked being with him. But I keep those nuggets for myself.

"I don't know, I guess I thought I could figure it out. It was vaguely love related after all and—"

"Amber, you need to accept your mystical limitations."

Now I'm pissed. "Limitations? Mom, I know I'm not a witch and will never be one. I happen to like being a matchmaker. I've accepted it, but clearly you haven't."

Her head jerks in reverse, a literal taking aback. "Excuse me?"

"You're always reminding me of how I don't fit into the Sand family genetic code. Sometimes I think you have a bigger problem with it than I do." Mom sits frozen, stunned by my words. I don't usually talk this way with her, but I'm on the verge of punishment anyway, so I might as well unleash. "I'm sorry I'm not the daughter you hoped for, the one who could use your grimoires for more than dusty old bookends. I'm sorry I'm not a witch, not for my sake, but for yours."

Tears I'd rather not shed are building up, so I start to storm off, but she snaps her fingers and says, *"Congelasco,"* and I'm stopped in my tracks. Great. A holding spell.

"Don't you dare flip this back around on me," Mom growls. "You've put me in a very difficult position, and I should not have to defend my disappointment." She walks around to face me, her long skirt flowing behind her like an angry, anthropomorphic cape. "I don't have time to deal with you right now; I have to go clean up your mess. You will stay right here until I return." She raises her palms and chants, *"Manete resideo,"* and while I'm able to move my feet again, I know she's performed a binding spell, keeping me within the confines of this building. Which honestly is fine. It could've gone way worse. Now I can just sleep away my soul-crushing guilt.

Mom slams the door behind her, and I head to my room to get out of my wet clothes. I leave the trench in a mushy pile, and I pull on a fresh cotton tee and jersey pajama pants. After standing in the rain for so long, the dry fabric feels practically indulgent. I flop back on my twin bed, looking up at the glow-in-the-dark solar system I adhered to my ceiling when I was five. Even though most of the stars have lost their luster, I keep them up there to remember a simpler time, when I could look at things with my own eyes and not have to worry about performing a magic trick upon meeting a stranger.

The rain has really picked up. Being on the top floor, I can hear it pounding on the roof. It's always nice to experience a storm from indoors, watching it rage all around you from the safety of a blanket. I remember I never texted Amani back and realize she's probably freaking by now, so I get up to dig through my coat pockets just as the apartment buzzer sounds.

At first I ignore it—people are always hitting the wrong buttons downstairs—but the obnoxious buzzing persists, rattling my nervous system with every incremental tone. It's like a swarm of cracked-out bees, completely destroying the rainy misery I was just starting to sink into, so I stomp over to the receiver, pounding my fist into the answer button with a frustrated "What?!"

"It's Charlie," the speaker crackles. I'm so surprised to hear his voice in my apartment, I accidentally release the call button. I take a beat before I reply, "What are you doing here?"

"I need to talk to you," he says, voice distorted by the ancient communication system. "Can you buzz me up?"

"I'll be right down." I slip on some mismatched flip-flops and head down the three story staircase. When I get to the telephone booth–size entry, I see him through the glass door, shivering. Yet when I try to usher him in, he stays in the downpour.

"No, I need to say something first," he says through chattering teeth. "I like you, Amber."

"Charlie—"

"No. I *like* you. And you like me too; I know it. But you're keeping me at a distance, and I want to know why."

I want to refute him, to say some snarky little comeback to cover my true feelings, but I think it's too late for that.

"Please," he adds. "I'd like some answers before I die of hypothermia." The rain is so intense, it's like one aggravated cloud is hovering directly over Charlie, unleashing its pent-up wrath. "Why don't you want to be close to me?"

I don't respond at first, but he gestures to the rain like an impatient person tapping on a watch. "Because. It's . . . pointless," I eventually admit.

"Why is it pointless? Is it because you know my match?"

He's going to make me say it, crystallize his fate by declaring the identity of his future partner. But even though it's what I was born to do, I can't bring myself to say her name.

"I want you to do it," he demands.

"Excuse me?"

"Do it, matchmaker. Work your magic; tell me my match. You should be able to see her, right?"

I look down at my bare toes, unable to face him as I say, "Yes."

He's silent for so long, I'm afraid the rain has washed him away, but when I look up, he's smiling. Genuinely smiling.

"I see her too," he says, joyful. "Because she's not out there; she's right here, in front of me. She's the only one who treats me like a person and not a prize. She doesn't say what she thinks I want to hear just to get me to like her; she doesn't even care if I like her at all. But I do. So much."

I hold on to the doorframe, reeling from his response, unsure if I should categorize him as romantic or certifiable. "Charlie, that's . . . very sweet, but . . . that's not the way it works."

"People aren't allowed to follow their hearts, to make their own decisions?" he challenges.

"Sure, but . . . people don't always make the best decisions for themselves. That's why I have a job. And thanks to my job, I know that I'm not your match."

"Yeah, well, I know what I feel."

His determination floors me, and not just because he's confessing his affection for me. It's so rare to see someone so confident in his feelings, throwing caution to the wind even after official confirmation that it's the wrong choice. "How can you be so sure? People follow their hearts all the time and get led astray; they end up with the wrong person, break up, fall apart, get divorced, disappear."

"Yeah, and that sucks!" he says, causing me to choke out a laugh. "But I don't want to spend my life worrying about what could happen in the future. This girl that you've planned for me . . . I don't know her. She's not the one I think about at night; she's not the one I look forward to seeing in the morning. Hell, she may not be the one at all!" He throws his arms out to his sides, spraying water everywhere. "Think about it, Amber. You matched Amani incorrectly; you could be wrong here too. All I know is what I want right now, and I won't deny myself that."

Maybe he's right. Maybe Kim isn't the girl for him. Maybe I'm a complete hack who has no right to meddle in other people's love lives. Or maybe she is, but he's right; she's not here right now. She could show up tomorrow or in ten years; either way, if they are truly meant to be, they will be, and nothing that happens now can change that. Right? Suddenly, there's a window, a peek into a possibility I've yet to let myself fully consider. Maybe . . . I can let myself have this, for now, and maybe, that's okay. The storm continues to rage, but for the first time since Charlie asked for my help, there's a lightness in my heart, pulsing warmth to every inch of my being.

I'm almost afraid to ask the question, but I can't keep the words inside. "So, what do you want?"

In one swift movement, he walks through the door, wrapping me in his arms and pressing my back against the wall of metal mailboxes. The rain from his shirt bleeds into mine, sticking us together as our lips meet. His skin is cold, but his mouth is warm; the kiss is soft yet passionate all once, like a sweet and salty cupcake that satisfies your every craving.

I press my hands into his chest to push him back, and he looks worried, like he's done something wrong. But the kiss was so unexpectedly electric, I just need a second to catch my breath, to let the moment properly register.

"Sorry," he says quietly, as I notice the raindrops dotting my arms and legs. I push his storm-tossed hair off his forehead, admiring the close-up view of his face.

"I'm not sorry," I say, and I grab his tie, pulling him back to me for more.

I've kissed boys before, don't get me wrong, but it's always felt like more of a chore, like an obligation of adolescence. Since it's always been crystal clear that none of them were the one for me, making out has seemed like preparation, coasting on training wheels before the real run. I don't know if it's my feelings for Charlie or his feelings for me, but this is the first time the ride has been a thrill.

His arms hold me tight, and I press myself as close to him as possible. We stay like that for a few blissful minutes, before I realize how incredibly public the foyer is. So I slowly pull away and take his hand to lead him up the stairs, stopping every few steps to kiss, touch, and be close to each other. It takes a while to get to the third floor; I'm out of breath and sufficiently soaked when we make it to the top. I run my finger over his smiling wet lips as I turn the doorknob to my apartment.

Yet after all that stairway action, when we make it inside, we simply lie on the couch, my face pressed close to his chest, listening to his heart as he runs his fingers through my choppy hair. It's nice. More than nice; it's the closest I've ever felt to a boy.

"So, can we just accept this as a possibility for a while? Defy the stars and just be?" Charlie asks softly.

I can feel my matchmaker ancestors shaking their stubborn fists at me, but I ignore them all by answering, "Okay."

Twenty-three

CHARLIE STAYED FOR AN HOUR OR SO, BUT WE BOTH AGREED
it would be best if my mom returned to a boy-free apartment,
what with the punishment and all. As we said good night, he
kissed my forehead, our hands entwined at our sides.

Of course I had to call Amani as soon as Charlie disappeared
down the steps. I think our conversation can be recapped thusly:
!!!

I've never been a girly girl and doubt I ever will be, but I'd
be lying if I didn't say it was fun to share all the swoony details
with my best friend.

Mom didn't come home until 2:00 a.m. I'd fallen asleep
watching the Food Network, but sprang to life when she came
through the door.

"Can I get you anything?" I asked, noticing the dark circles under her eyes.

"Tea." She collapsed onto the couch, pushing her gray hair back with ring-covered fingers. I set the kettle on the stove and settled down on the cushion next to her.

"Any luck?" I asked.

She sat staring at the ceiling, eyes heavy with regret as she answered, "I went to see Victoria."

"What? Why her?"

She looked at me with one of those stern, "I'm still pissed at you so don't push it" faces. "She's going to aid me with a more powerful locator spell," she said in a reluctant tone.

"Really? I wouldn't peg her as the charitable type."

"It's not charity. I offered to supply her craft for six months."

I could not believe the horribleness of such an arrangement. "Mom! I don't know if you've noticed, but Victoria has been trying to single-white-female you ever since she moved here: relocating coven meetings, sitting in *your* circle spot. She's slowly weaving her way into everything you've worked so hard to create. If you give her an opening, she'll take it all."

She kept looking up as she said quietly, "You don't think I know that?"

"If you do, then why are you doing this? Why go to her?"

Suddenly, her volume knob spun to max. "Why do you think, Amber? These goblins have obviously found some mass power source, and I'm not strong enough on my own. Not only is John my dearest friend, but he's the mayor, and his absence won't go unnoticed for long. And Charlie, he can't be left alone. I need help and I need it now, and the only way I can get it is with other powerful witches."

"But why not just use the coven?"

"All of their power combined does not compare to what Victoria wields," she said bitterly. This revelation surprised me, but I held my tongue. I tried to picture Victoria doing anything besides getting an eyebrow wax, but somehow, the image of her bundling a sage stick with acrylic nails would not compute.

"Good Gods, are you serious?" I asked.

"Victoria is not a stranger; I've known her for years," Mom confessed. "She's not someone you want on your bad side. It's why I silenced you at that meeting."

What? "And that's the kind of person you let into Dawning Day?"

"*Let* is a generous term. More like, made room to avoid repercussions."

I can't even. All this time, Mom has been battling with a frenemy all on her own. And now I've put her in a position that gives Victoria the upper hand. Just the thought of Mom standing before that smug she-devil, all vulnerable and small, makes me want a lobotomy so I don't have to visualize it anymore.

"Witches aren't the only ones with magic," I pleaded. "This city is crawling with ancient bloodlines that can conjure up some trouble."

"What do you suggest, then, huh? Stand on Michigan Ave with a sign that reads 'Will work for magic'? Where do you think you'll find all these supernatural allies just waiting to jump into a potentially dangerous situation that has nothing to do with them?"

The answer came to me immediately, but I knew the suggestion would be rubbing salt in a wound. "The Black Phoenix," I said with caution.

"Excuse me?"

"The Black Phoenix. When I was there, I had a . . . situation with a vamp, but everyone there jumped in to help. They barely knew me, but they all stood up to that bloodsucker."

She circled her pointer fingers at her temples. "Funny how you failed to mention that part before."

Crap. "Oh. Um, sorry. But it was okay! There are good people and creatures there."

She considered this, sleep deprivation dulling her decision-making abilities. "Fine. But if we don't find help there tomorrow night, it's Victoria."

Now I'm sitting at Windy City, mind turning to mush as I listen to a pair of preteens debate over which color of stardust (a.k.a. glitter) would make their boobs look bigger. The correct answer is none, since they're both flat as boards and shouldn't be worrying over superficial stuff like that, but hey, who am I to derail the strange and twisted path toward self-acceptance. I want them to hurry up so I can dig into a massively oversize cupcake I bought a few doors down.

I've been here all day, and for a Friday, it's been painfully slow. I've had enough time to dust and sweep every square inch of the shop, and even alphabetize the essential oils. I'm hoping things will pick up now that it's late afternoon, because if not, I'm going to stab myself with a raven feather.

I ring up the boob twins (who chose pink, by the way) to find Charlie as the next customer in line. He's dressed slightly more casual than I'm used to, missing his usual button-down and tie, so I know he's struggling today. He's been trying to put on a brave face about his dad, but when a dapper dude shows up in a T-shirt, that's a pain you can't dismiss.

I'm just about to give him a comforting kiss when Mom walks in, looking as tired as she did when I left her. "Charlie," she starts, instantly wrapping him in a hug. "How are you?"

"Well, I've been better. It was really weird being in the apartment by myself last night. But thank you for calling and checking on me," he says.

She nods. "I sent Bob by your place in the middle of the night; he laid some crushed citrine at your doorway as a precaution. It wards off wickedness."

"I appreciate that," he says with a sad smile. "You know, I

didn't mean for any of this to happen when I came to Amber for help."

Mom works to untangle her hair from her scarf, then sighs in futility. "Don't even worry about that. I know that both of you were only trying to help John, and unfortunately, you can never predict how those in the community will conduct themselves. Even still, we'll find a way around this. Goblins are not the nicest of fellows, but they often stay under the radar for fear of drawing attention to their schemes. Kidnapping—especially a celebrity—is not their usual MO."

"Yeah, they usually just sneer and look at you like you killed a puppy," I say.

"What do you think they want with my dad?" Charlie asks.

"Based on Amber's retelling, I suspect they only wanted Cassandra, but took John as a two-for-one transaction. If she tried to back out of any sort of deal with them, they wouldn't stop until they received their end of the bargain."

"Like a goblin mafia," Charlie says.

"Only less machine guns, more magic wands," I add.

Mom looks like she's about to scold me for making light of a serious situation, but then the unholy pile of pink sugar sitting near the register catches her eye. "Is that yours?" she asks me, pointing at my cupcake.

"Um, actually, it's yours," I offer, sliding the confection her way. She doesn't question it, simply picks up the cake and says, "Thank you," before ducking behind her velvet curtain.

"That was very generous," Charlie says.

"Strategy, my friend. Sugar makes people happy, and happy people put an end to punishments." I tap at my temple to emphasize my inherent brilliance.

He smiles, but there's no warmth in his eyes. He's so worried about his dad, and although there's plenty of supplies in the shop that could temporarily take his pain away, it gives me a sense of purpose to know that for once, *I* am the magical thing most likely to give him any comfort. I take his face in my hands; he closes his eyes and leans his cheek into my palm, clasping my wrist in his hand. "It's going to be okay," I whisper. I lean in to gently kiss his lips, when I hear a voice near the shop's entrance.

"Amber Sand, getting physical." I look over Charlie's shoulder to see Ivy, weaving around our display of vintage apothecary bottles. Her nose is still bandaged and slightly bruised from where I hit her, which fills me with more pleasure than it should. With her are two random harpies, standing just far enough away so as not to upstage their leader but close enough to prove she's got a posse. I don't know the names of the other two and don't care to; I'd rather they all be sucked back to hell than engage in conversation.

"Ivy Chamberlain, as I live and breathe toxic fumes," I reply.

"Must be the contents of this alleged 'business,'" she says, pinching her arms and hands close to her chest, as if coming in contact with our merchandise would burn her. Though, who knows, maybe it might. I wouldn't be against finding out.

"How does your family survive selling slimy blobs?" she asks, nodding at our selection of mosses.

"Thanks for your concern, but we do just fine," I say. "This banter is fun and all, but why don't you just tell me why you're here."

"Our English assignment, hello? Why else would I come all the way to this tourist trap?"

"Calm yourself. It's not due till next week."

"Yeah, well, since you were suspended and seem to think that physical violence is an acceptable interaction, I wanted to make sure you still remembered our agreement."

"Aww, did you miss me?" I pout.

"I'll tell you who I do miss." She sets her baby blues on Charlie, who squirms in response. "This beautiful man right here." Her manicured hand rubs his shoulder before she rests her chin on top. Long lashes flutter like something out of a romance novel how-to guide.

I take a deep breath, trying to keep my aura in the blue. I know this is Ivy's thing; as a siren, she almost can't stop herself from going after something that's not hers. She feeds on that energy and needs constant attention to survive. But now that Charlie is specifically mine, I feel that primal protective rage building inside me, and if she doesn't back up soon, there's going to be a very big mess at Windy City Magic.

"I'm not sure why you'd miss me." Charlie steps aside. "Ivy, don't you have other things you could be doing?"

She crosses her arms as her cronies cluck in disapproval. I want to high-five that boy but dig my hands into my pockets instead.

"So are you two, like, official now?" Ivy asks. She eyes me up and down with a disgusted expression before turning back to him. Charlie puts his arm over my shoulder, and I lean into him as confirmation. I really like the view from here, as she seems on the verge of vomiting. "I'm surprised at you, Amber."

"Oh yeah? Why is that?"

"I just thought a matchmaker would have better common sense and use her magic with a side of logic."

"Right, because sirening people to make them like you is so logical?" I say.

Ivy lets my words roll right off her. "At least I'm a realist. I know what it takes to survive. I know you live in a land of fairy tales, but believing in love not only makes you stupid; it makes you weak."

Five seconds ago, I planned on keeping my mouth shut and zoning out until she crawled back into the sea, but dammit, my integrity as a matchmaker is being challenged, and that is one thing I'll always defend.

"You know what, Ivy? I shouldn't have to justify myself to you, but this is about more than just me. Wanting to find love does not make someone weak; it's not a character flaw. Life is hard, and grueling, and having someone root for you and travel beside you is a gift that anyone in this world would be lucky to have. I'm not saying that people can't be happy or fulfilled on their own; of course they can. But being open to the possibility of love doesn't make you weak; it actually makes you strong."

I'm out of breath after my random soapboxing, but I feel amazing, especially because Ivy is neither clever nor quick enough to come up with a response. Blond curls swing in my face as she and her groupies leave, but just before she exits out to the pier, she calls back, "Well, good luck to you both; you're gonna need it."

Charlie has to grab my arms to keep me from going animal kingdom on her.

"Whoa, tiger," he says, spinning me around when the shrews have left the shop. "Let's relax."

"Just because she's a siren doesn't mean she has to give in to the worst possible stereotypes of her kind. She's *choosing* to be that wretched. Like, way to give your ancestors a bad rep. It makes me crazy."

"You're right. She clearly gets off on it."

"And what about you?" I ask. "You seem to be the only guy who doesn't get off on her." There's a tinge of insecurity in my voice that I neither like nor recognize.

"Listen, she's obviously gorgeous, but she's also a ridiculously terrible person. Even before you told me about her skewing supernatural, I could see right through her twisted mind games. She goes after easy prey: guys who let themselves be manipulated."

"She seems to keep going after you."

"Well"—he adjusts his glasses—"that's because I come with an extra gold surprise. A lot of girls come at me for only that reason."

"Not me," I joke. "I could take ya or leave ya."

He pulls me closer, squeezing a gasp from my chest. "Good thing for you, then"—his smile returns to full wattage—"I'm already taken."

Twenty-four

AFTER HOURS AT NAVY PIER IS A WEIRD PLACE TO FIND oneself. The shops are closed, but the lights are on, giving it a simultaneously enchanted and eerie vibe. The neon-outlined Ferris wheel against the inky Lake Michigan water is legitimately cool when there aren't thousands of meandering tourists spilling overfilled popcorn tubs and making out on sidewalk benches. There are no screaming babies, no looped carnival music, just water, light, and cool night air.

Unfortunately, the people who do witness this fleetingly peaceful scene don't appreciate it at all, because we're here every damn day and want to get home as soon as possible. It's not like we're going to hang out and soak in the scenery of the place we've been trying to escape for the past twelve hours. I imagine it'd be the same for the after-hours crews at a place like Disneyland; while the die-hard fans would kill to get a peek of the park when the gates close, the mechanics who ensure the tiki room birds still sing just want to be binge-watching TV at home.

But tonight Mom and I are sitting at the west end of the pier, right between Bubba Gump Shrimp and Giordano's Pizza. We're waiting for Charlie, who said he'd send a car to take us to the Black Phoenix. Mom, who pretty much never accepts help from anyone, didn't even resist his offer, saying his thought-fulness was "much appreciated." While Charlie certainly is thoughtful, I couldn't help but feel her comment was somehow aimed at me, like I am the total opposite of thoughtful. I know she's mad and has a right to be, but it's not like I meant for any of this to happen, and let's not forget how she never refuted my points on her regretting my lack of witchiness. It still stings.

So we're sitting in silence, taking in the weirdness that is an empty amusement center. I pop up at the sight of a shiny black Town Car, but instead of a Converse stepping out the door, there's a snakeskin stiletto. With a smooth shimmy emerges Victoria, who is so overdressed it's almost comical. She probably blasted her own personal hole in the ozone with all the hair spray holding her dyed tresses.

"I didn't realize the pier turned into a red-light district after dark," I say from the side of my mouth.

Mom is not amused. "Amber, do not say another word."

"C'mon, you know that was funny."

"Zip. It," she says through clenched teeth.

Victoria catwalks straight toward us. "Luciiiiiiille," she cries, as if they haven't seen each other in ages. With outstretched arms, her mink stole falls around her elbows. I try to imagine how she and Mom originally met; was it a high school rivalry? Bridesmaids at a yeti wedding? Or is it possible that at one point they could have been—gulp—friends? "Darling."

Mom stands slowly, taking the spray-tanned hands. "Victoria." I can't believe this air-kissing banshee has as much power as Mom says. Nothing about her reads "mighty Wicca"—more like "sad wannabe." I mean, I'm sure the chicks at Salem weren't running around in pleather. But Mom clearly knows something I don't.

"Is there a reason you're here?" Mom asks. "We're not scheduled to meet until tomorrow."

"I came to check the merchandise, of course," Victoria says. "I can't very well offer my services without verifying payment."

Mom is so over this. "Are you questioning my inventory?"

"No, no . . . not yet, anyway."

Mom's about to spit nails. "I'll have you know that Windy City Magic upholds the finest—"

"Oh, Lucille, relax." Victoria waves. "I don't doubt your integrity. You've always been very devoted to your principles. Detrimentally so. I just need to take a closer look at your selection."

"The store is closed." Mom crosses her arms.

"Of course it is," Victoria laughs. "But you are the owner, aren't you? I don't commonly shop with riffraff. Surely you can offer me a private session, no?"

I hate this woman. I hate her for acting so high and mighty. How could her showy persona not be a cloak for a lack of talent? What kind of magic does she have access to that Mom doesn't? I can't imagine. I've seen Mom in action, and there's nothing she can't handle; she only stays away from the darker stuff, and that's by choice, not from lack of skill. She could go all dark side in a second if she needed, but she always tries to find another way. But Victoria, who knows what she's into? Maybe Mom has come to her because she'll cross any line without thinking twice. Whatever the reason, I HATE that she can lord her authority over Mom and make her feel like less of a witch. If anyone's gonna make my mom feel bad, it's me, and I've earned that right by being her daughter.

"Fine," Mom relents, slouching as if granting this request is causing a growth on her back. "But we only have a few minutes."

"That's all I need." Victoria flips her animal carcass over her shoulder. "Ta-ta, Amber. Pleasure seeing you."

I raise my eyebrows to acknowledge I'm not deaf, then turn around without response. Maybe Mom will trap Victoria inside the shop in a tiny glass vial where we can laugh at her all day. That would be fun.

I sit and watch a parade of buses and cabs pull by, until I'm the only one left standing in the plaza. Finally, Charlie's Town Car pulls up, and I smile in relief.

"Good Gods, am I glad you're not a forty-year-old prostitute," I say as he approaches.

"Um, likewise?" he answers.

"My mom's meeting with one now."

"Really?"

"Not really."

"Okay." He pauses. "I don't get it."

I proceed to fill him in on covens and witchcraft hierarchy.

"Your mom should just kick her out of the coven," he says when I'm finished. "Screw that witch."

"Yeah, I know. But Mom doesn't see herself as the leader. She's a big part of Dawning Day, but really, organized practice is not her style. She's more of a lone wolf," I say, then add, "I guess that's where I get it."

"Nothing wrong with that," Charlie says, taking a seat on a bench. "I'd rather be alone then spend time with people who don't value me."

"Is that why you cruise the halls like you're too cool for school?" I ask, sitting beside him.

"First of all, I am too cool for school. Obviously." He laughs. "Second, I just haven't met many people at Manchester I connect with. I have friends outside of school, but I don't know. I don't mesh with anyone in class."

"But then you started talking to me and your whole world turned upside down," I say with jazz hands.

"Well, my dad never disappeared into a secret goblin ring before I met you, so yeah, that's accurate," he says with a forced smile.

Ouch. I will never not feel guilty about this. I turn away and fixate on a spot on the sidewalk, unsure of how to respond. He reaches for my hand and gives it a light squeeze to bring me back.

"Still, there have been perks."

"Such as?" I ask innocently.

He runs his fingers through my hair, stopping behind my ear to pull me in for a kiss. It's slow and gentle to start, a roller coaster climbing its first hill, but then builds momentum, plunging forward with speed. I move to his lap, his hands running up and down my back. I've never had this before; I've always hit the brakes before I could let myself feel a thrill. But with my eyes squeezed tight, there's only me and Charlie, nothing to stop us . . . and neither of us wants to stop.

Except my Spidey sense is warning me I should probably cool down before Mom and the wicked witch return.

"Valid points, sir," I say, pulling back nearly breathless. I hover just above his nose. "Let's continue this discussion later."

His fingers dig into my waist. "Yes, ma'am," he mumbles, nuzzling my neck. A vibration in my pocket causes him to jerk back. "Hey there," he winks.

"Quiet, you, it's my phone." I pick up. "Hey, Amani."

"Hey, I'm at the club. I thought you'd be here by now," she says, with Black Phoenix ambience in the background.

"Yeah, well, there was a wench in our plan."

"Don't you mean *wrench*?"

"I'll explain later."

"Okay. Just hurry up. I asked Vincent for some help rounding up some of the regulars for Operation Blitzman, but I don't know how long they can stay."

"Look at you, event coordinator for the undead," I say.

She is not amused. "Amber, Vincent won't leave me alone. You need to get here already and rescue me."

"Ooh, I see my mom. Be there soon." I peel myself from Charlie's lap and spring up before she sees me in that position. I'm sure the topic of us dating will come up eventually, but I'd rather it not be while I'm straddling him.

"Where's Her Royal Highness?" I ask when Mom shows up alone.

"Her driver pulled around to the north entrance. I guess it was too far for her to walk in those shoes," Mom says with an eye roll.

"I still can't believe you even considered asking her for help," I say.

"Yes, well, hopefully we won't have to use her services after all."

"My car's ready, Ms. Sand." Charlie gestures.

"Thank you, Charlie, but you know you can call me Lucille."

I shake my head violently behind her back, warning him that even though she said it's okay, really she'd rather he use formalities.

"Thank you, Ms. Sand," he says on cue.

She beams. "You are your father's son."

"I appreciate that. I can't wait to tell him you think so."

"Same here," she says.

The drive to Black Phoenix is brief but cozy, sitting pretty on the plush leather seats. I'm not sure if I'll ever get used to my mode of transportation coming sans cranky commuters and eau d'urine. If there is a perk to having money, it's getting to travel with the luxury of solitude.

Pulling up to the club, Amani is waiting outside, fidgeting under a dim yellow streetlight. She's biting her thumb, her eyes unfocused and worried.

"What's up?" I ask, stepping to her side.

She reaches into her dress pocket, pulling out a cream-colored envelope sealed with wax. She hesitates before handing it to me.

"There's been a development."

Twenty-five

"I DON'T UNDERSTAND," I SAY. "I JUST TALKED TO YOU A MINUTE AGO."

"Yeah, and this arrived a minute after that," Amani says. Charlie, Mom, and I all huddle around to read the same tiny handwriting we encountered before:

To the matchmaker and her young friend,

We are quite aware of your efforts to track us down. While we do not appreciate interference in our personal business, we do acknowledge your possession has been wrongfully acquired in the cross fire. We are fully prepared to return the esteemed mayor without harm, provided our dealings with the leprechaun go undisturbed. If you agree to these conditions, please meet me at the eighteenth floor of the Merchandise Mart at midnight tomorrow. I will leave one door unlocked for you. Backup will not be necessary, lest you plan to breach this contract.

Sincerely,

Mr. James Thadamus Hollister, Esq.

"This is like the worst treasure hunt ever," I say after reading the note several times.

"So, when he says *leprechaun*, is he referring to . . . Cassandra?" Amani asks.

We all look at Charlie. "Don't ask me!" He throws his hands up. "I only found out magic was real, like, yesterday."

"Mom?" I ask.

She shrugs as if it's not a totally weird revelation. "It is possible. Leprechauns, while not as common as fairies, are from a similar heritage. They don't possess much magic, and therefore are usually quite resentful of their social standing, often turning to trickery to get ahead. To say they're green with envy is an understatement." She pauses. "I am surprised, though, how easily John could let himself be ensnared by one. He's usually much more perceptive about when he's being manipulated."

"Wait a minute, wait a minute!" Charlie waves his arms. "Do you mean to tell me that Cassandra—the woman who is practically my stepmom—who I accused of being a gold digger, is an ACTUAL gold digger?"

No one speaks. Amani hides her face in her hands. My cheeks are so full of laughter I could burst.

"SERIOUSLY?!" he yells.

"It does add up," Mom admits. "What was it her pendant said?"

"*Felicitas ubi lux tangit,*" Amani recites. "It's seared in my brain from that session. Though I don't know what it means."

We do a quick translation on my phone to find it means "happiness is where the light touches."

I snicker, though I don't mean to. "As in, at the end of the rainbow?"

"Why didn't we look this up before?" Amani laughs.

"Even if we did, I'm not sure I would have connected the dots," my mother says.

Charlie sits down on the sidewalk, the weight of the discovery too much to handle.

"It's okay, buddy," I say, patting the top of his head like a puppy. "It could be worse. Your dad could be dating a banshee."

"Or a mermaid," Amani suggests.

"Oh yeah, that'd be no fun. You'd have to live underwater, and I doubt the lake has very nice views. Think of how wrinkly your fingers would always be. And your clothes!" I hear a sound that could be a laugh, or maybe a sob. "Leprechauns ain't no thing. They're even less magical than matchmakers, and that's saying something."

"Really?" He looks up.

"Yup. So don't worry."

He gives a wan smile. "It just seems so random."

"Welcome to my world."

"Although," he says, tipping his head to the left, "I guess it is slightly satisfying that I was so on the money."

"That's the spirit!" I cheer.

"So, do we go in with help or not?" Amani asks. "I've assembled quite a team in there; it's like a supernatural Avengers." She nods back to the club.

"How did you manage that?" Mom asks.

"Actually, it was super-easy." Amani grins. "All I had to do was mention the Sand name and creatures were lining up to help. A werewolf, another witch, a shape-shifter, and . . . Vincent is demanding he be included."

"Well, that's nice of him," I coax. She just rolls her eyes.

"Thank you, Amani," Mom says, blushing a little. "I would definitely prefer their assistance over Victoria's. But perhaps we should follow the goblin's instructions. They seem pretty determined to hold on to Cassandra for whatever she owes them, and I'm not sure what we could do to remedy that. Unfortunately, that will mean John will lose her too." She turns to Charlie. "Do you think he could handle that?"

"He's not going to like it," Charlie says. "But I mean, he doesn't like being lied to either. So . . . I don't know. This whole thing is crazy."

"I say we go in alone, grab John, reveal he's dating Lucky Charms, and then go from there," I offer. "Maybe he won't care that she's a rainbow worshipper and will want to fight for her, but since she's not his match, I think we can convince him otherwise."

"Agreed." Mom nods.

Amani looks deflated. "So I spent the past hour spurning

Vincent's advances for nothing? I guess I'll tell the others they're not needed."

"Mom, maybe you can buy them all a round of drinks, to say thanks?" I suggest. She eyes me suspiciously. "Only for the volunteers who are of age, of course."

There's a hint of a grimace, but deep down, she knows I'm right. Lucille Sand would rather burn at the stake than forgo proper etiquette. "It is the least I can do. I'll be back shortly."

Amani starts to follow her, but I grab her arm. "I appreciate all your help, BFF. You continue to be the greatest, you know that, right?"

She sighs. "Duh."

"Do you want to come with us to track down a four-foot-high villain?" I ask.

"I'm not sure if I'm up for the challenge." She looks at Charlie, who is still sitting on the sidewalk, staring off. "What about him?" she whispers. "Is he gonna be okay?"

"I'll take care of him."

Amani smirks. "Sure you will." She turns, but I grab her arm again.

Love you, I sign.

Love you too.

I push her away and take a spot next to my guy. "Everything okay here?"

"Yeah, it's just . . . I kind of can't believe all this is happening." He rubs his hand over his tattooed forearm. "When I was a kid, I had this dorky hope that maybe dragons could be real. It was just stupid fun, but now, I don't know; it seems like a possibility. And that's just . . . surreal."

There's a worry in his eyes that concerns me. "So are you still glad you came to me for help? I mean, it's kind of my fault your worldview has been shattered."

He takes my hands immediately. "Oh geez, I didn't mean to imply that. Of course I'm glad. In fact, I kick myself for not making knowing you a priority earlier. I just think it's crazy how life can change so quickly, how everything you thought you knew can be challenged."

I rub my thumb over his. "I know what you mean," I say softly.

"You do?"

"Yeah, well . . ." I stumble for a second, trying to find the right words. "I'm a matchmaker, right? I should be an expert on everything to do with love: a one-stop shop of romantic knowledge. And for a long time, I really thought I was. But now that I'm with you . . ." He looks at me hopefully. "Look, it kills me to say this and I will deny it to my grave, but there's a lot of stuff I still don't understand. Like, I used to think people were stupid for opening their hearts without surefire confirmation that they'd made the right decision. How could you just throw your heart out there like a Frisbee on merely the hope that someone will catch it? What if they don't? What if it falls to the ground, gets all cracked and muddy, and never flies again? I didn't want to take that chance unless I knew I'd land safely. I've always been more of a boomerang, my feelings circling back before they even left, and yet, here I am, flinging myself into the unknown . . . with you."

Good Gods, I can't believe I said that out loud. For a second, I wish I could take it all back, suck up my words like an invisible vacuum. I don't think I've ever—EVER—spoken so openly about my fears about love, not even with Amani. You'd think he slipped me some truth serum, but no, this was all on my own. All this crap I've been holding on to, so afraid to share because of who I am and what I do.

But he doesn't laugh or judge. He simply kisses my forehead, clutches my hands tight, and says, "Don't worry, Amber Sand; I'll catch you."

Twenty-six

MERCHANDISE MART IS SO GINORMOUS, IT USED TO HAVE ITS
own zip code. If it seems imposing during the day, at night it
reaches a whole new level, with the highest floors lit bright
yellow. It looks kind of like a castle, with torch-armed guards sur-
veying the top perimeter. Add to that the fact of goblins congre-
gating somewhere in its bowels, and it pretty much makes it the
last place I'd like to be right now (other than school, of course).

Mom, Charlie, and I are standing at one of the many locked
entrances, trying to find the one promised to be unlocked. It's
very slow going and slightly embarrassing; we look more like
inept burglars than supernatural forces of nature.

"It would've been nice had they specified which door,"
Charlie huffs.

"Yeah, this feels way less badass than I imagined," I say.

"How did you imagine it?"

"Well, I figured Mom and the crew from Black Phoenix would summon some sort of powerful menace and use it to the storm the barricade, green and silver sparks shooting everywhere, and then we'd rush in on unicornback and save your dad."

Charlie pinches back a smile. "Unicorns? Again?"

"Uh, yes, really. They are majestic creatures: the utter embodiment of magic itself. Just finding one would be amazing enough, but riding one to victory? Are you kidding me?"

He shakes his head to the soundtrack of light laughter. "You're too much." He nudges me with his shoulder, and the combination of his sunny eyes and warm denim shirt rubbing against my bare arm makes me want to grab his tie and pull him over to me, but I stop myself, hitting the pause button on my instincts. I need to focus on the task at hand.

We've stopped circling the block; Mom is watching us from an open doorway. She's got that look on her face, that freaky sixth-sense expression that all moms (not just witches) get when they know their offspring is up to something. While she's not officially a mind reader, she always seems to know when one of my plot lines has advanced.

"You two ready?" she asks, peppered with a sweetness that's not the norm.

"We were born ready," I say with a fist pump.

She gives a verbal eye roll. "Mmm-hmm."

The mart's lobby is as you'd expect for such a grand building: towering ceilings, glossy tiled floors, a varied collection of paintings and sculptures. The physical space is fine; it's what's *not* here that's unsettling. For a place that usually houses a non-stop cycle of busy people, its emptiness is palpable. There are no security guards, no trace of additional life; it's the kind of eerie setting that'd be right at home in a horror movie. Like a merry-go-round without any kids or water park without any H_2O, it's just wrong, and I don't like it. Just when I feel like it couldn't be any more uncomfortable, all the lights go out, save for one overhead fluorescent, beaming the path to the staircase.

"Proceed," says a disembodied voice from an invisible PA system.

"Well, this is straight from my nightmares," Charlie says in the darkness.

"Right there with ya," I reply, shaken.

"If I ask you to hold my hand, will they take my man card away?"

"I'm sure you could make an appeal."

"Okay then." He moves to link his fingers with mine, and I don't hesitate; there's a security in his touch that a girl could really get used to.

"Mom?" I call out, extending my other hand. "Safety in numbers."

"Good idea." She takes my hand, and it's instantly apparent

how long it's been since we shared contact in this way. Her skin feels thinner, less taut, and while the strength in her grasp remains, it's definitely different from when I was a little girl. It takes me by surprise, the change in something I once knew so well. All the problems and drama between us has never shaken my belief that she can take on the world, and I don't like this tangible reminder that even though she is a witch, she's still a mortal.

Our eyes adjust to the darkness as Mom pulls a handful of something from her bag. Some of the powder slips through her fingers, but most is tossed just above our heads, and with one word—*"lucem"*—the specks light up like a caravan of fireflies. They flitter and dance in a disorganized yet contained cloud, guiding us with a golden glow.

"Amazing!" Charlie exclaims like a kid watching fireworks.

"Thank you," Mom says with an appreciative nod. We make our way forward, our footsteps echoing through the empty space. The goblins have led us to the service staircase, all dark and concrete, the only light coming from the emergency exit signs and our magical floating "bugs." Since I'm not exactly a regular on the stair machine, this ascent to the eighteenth floor might get ugly.

"Now," Mom starts as we begin our climb, "I understand you both have made acquaintance with this Mr. Hollister fellow, but I think it's best if I handle the proceedings. Goblins expect their business partners to uphold their promises, but that doesn't always mean they reciprocate. I will need to act if they try to pull anything shady."

"Fine with me," Charlie says.

"Yup. You know best, Mom," I say with chagrin.

"We'll see."

We continue upward, stepping on what seems like a million stairs. I try to keep it together, but around floor ten, I start breathing so heavily I *almost* wish I put a little effort in during gym.

"These guys can leave the door open yet can't power the elevator?" I say in between pants. "Rude."

"Between this and my dad's kidnapping, I've decided goblins are my least favorite magical being," Charlie says, struggling to catch his breath as well.

"And what would be your favorite?" I ask over my shoulder. "Dragons, right?"

He shakes his head, too tired to speak, but I catch him silently mouth, "You," in response. My already pumping heart does an extra flip.

Mercifully, we reach the freaking eighteenth floor, all taking some time to return to a normal breathing rate before continuing on. The fake fireflies continue to shimmer, mocking us with their effortless bounce. Mom seems to be doing better than Charlie and me, and I wait for her to comment on our generation's deterioration of physical fitness due to constant screen time, but she doesn't. She must be conserving her strength for whatever lies ahead.

Once again, it's so dark we can hardly see our surroundings. There's a single light at the end of the hallway, beckoning us forward. The whole charade is getting a little old, and instead of building fear, it's starting to brew annoyance. If the goblin gang wants this to go down peacefully, couldn't we have met somewhere less foreboding, like a Baskin-Robbins? Who doesn't like a celebratory ice-cream cone after a successful rescue?

As we get closer, it's clear our final destination is a run-of-the-mill conference room. Through a glass-paneled wall we see them: eight almost-identical goblins sitting on opposite sides of a rectangular table, with John perched like a prize at the head.

"Dad!" Charlie yells, causing John to turn. He tries to move from his chair, but it looks like invisible ropes have bound him. Charlie starts to run toward him, but Mom catches his arm, pulling him back. "Dad, are you okay?" Charlie calls out.

"I'm okay," John says reassuringly. "But, Charlie, what are you doing here?"

Before he can respond, the goblins rise in unison like they share the same brain (good Gods, maybe they do?!), continuing their efforts to disarm us. Instead of using the room's overhead recessed lights, two uniform rows of candles sit on the table, giving the manila walls an ominous glow. It's not exactly the dungeon I envisioned this going down in, but this is still the weirdest thing I've done in a while.

Our old buddy Mr. Hollister sits closest to his capture. He gestures to the two empty seats nearest us, a tinge of frustration creasing his brow. "We were not expecting three," he says coldly.

"This is my mom, Lucille Sand," I say, trying to affect an authoritative tone.

"Yes, we've met before," he reveals, unimpressed. Mom nods in acknowledgement, and I grit my teeth in frustration. Was this not important information to share with the class? I know Mom used to have more supernatural associations back in her younger days, and that she doesn't like revisiting those magical blasts from the past now, but I don't see why she chose to make this omission. If I withheld details like that, she'd go off the broom handle. Annoying. She motions for Charlie and I to sit, and stands over us like a queen holding court.

"Lucy, what's going on?" John asks. "These men won't tell me anything."

"We've come to take you home," Mom answers evenly.

"But what about Cass? I know she's here too, but they won't let me see her." He is seething, unaccustomed to not getting his way.

"Cassandra is no longer your concern," Mr. Hollister answers in a monotone.

"Of course she's my concern!" John pounds a fist on the table, but the goblin doesn't flinch. "She's my . . ." He pauses, unnerved at sharing something personal in such an absurd setting. "She's about to be my wife."

"That will no longer be happening."

John tries to reach for the goblin's throat but is still restrained.

Through his clenched jaw, he growls, "How dare you? I do not take orders from you."

"Certainly not, Mr. Mayor. But unfortunately for you, she does." Mr. Hollister adjusts his button-down vest, picking at a piece of lint.

"What are you talking about?" John yells. "I'm tired of all this!"

"John," Mom says softly. "There's something you should know."

"What? What is it?" he cries, his anger turning into panic.

Mom puts her hand on my shoulder. "Amber, tell him."

Twenty-two eyes turn to me, but only two are filled with desperation, waiting for a revelation only I can give. Being a family friend, John knows all about the Sand talents. He's passed by my matchmaker table countless times, and I'm sure Mom's entertained him with stories of my early attempts at Cupidism. He knows what I can do, so I hope he knows I take no pleasure in delivering this kind of news.

I swallow hard. "Mr. Blitzman, I'm so sorry, but Cassandra is not your match."

The room is so quiet I feel like my words are darts bouncing off the walls, pinging around until they lodge themselves in his heart.

"Are . . . are you sure?"

"Yes. I'm really sorry. I would've warned you earlier, but I didn't know until Charlie showed me a picture of who you were

dating; she didn't line up with the woman I see in your future."
John breaks eye contact, staring at the floor. His fist loosens flat,
anger releasing into a puddle. With a few words, I've managed
to destroy the most powerful man in Chicago, my legacy as a
heartbreaker confirmed. I love being right but not at the price of
someone's happiness. And anyway, am I really sure? Can I really
say with 100 percent accuracy whether or not my matches are
right? Until recently, I would've said yes without a doubt, but
with the weirdness with Amani and all my drama with Charlie,
who's to say whether or not there's a glitch in the system? This
doesn't seem like the right time to waver, though, and yet, I
can't let someone I care about wallow without hope. "There is
someone waiting for you out there, Mr. B. I've seen her, the two
of you, and you're going to be so happy. Sunday brunches, trips
to Paris, late-night movie sessions: you'll have it all. I know it's
hard now, but something better, something you deserve, is just
around the corner. It just won't be with Cassandra."

Mom squeezes my shoulder as John looks back up,
glassy-eyed.

"Dad, I hate to see you like this, but Cass has been lying
to you . . . to both of us." Charlie slowly approaches his dad,
waiting for a goblin to stop him, but when no one does, he
kneels beside his crushed father. "Dad, she's a . . . leprechaun.
She was after your money."

I still can't believe how ridiculous it sounds, and that's
coming from someone who's well versed in the paranormal.

John shakes his head in disbelief, and Charlie looks back at me, slightly panicked, unsure of how to elaborate. Fortunately, Mr. Hollister steps in with some much-needed puzzle pieces.

"I can confirm that Cassandra is of leprechaun descent, and unfortunately for her, her species' worst traits run strong in her veins. She came to us, desperate to climb the social ladder by skipping a few rungs, and promised our assistance would pay us back handsomely. She did not follow through on that arrangement." Mr. Hollister licks the roof of his mouth in distaste.

"No, no, I won't believe it," John spits. "Amber, I appreciate your input, but all this leprechaun business is crazy. I want to hear it from her."

"That is impossible," one of the other goblins says.

John gives him a look of death. "Well, make it possible. Or else I'm going to report to the Chicago board of trade how you conduct business in this city."

The goblins murmur to each other, lips barely moving but somehow conveying information. After a few seconds of incomprehensible speech, Mr. Hollister declares, "Fine. We will bring her in so she can tell you herself."

The goblin closest to me disappears from the room, and we sit in awkward silence in the candlelight. This Cassandra . . . we've been looking for her for so long, she's almost like a mythological beast, ripping apart the hearts of men wherever she goes. Will she be as intimidating a force in person?

The goblin returns with Cassandra. She's not a wild-haired

beast, but there is a palpable savagery pulsing through her veins. Just like in her picture, she wears a crown of strawberry-blond curls and drips with designer jewels. I envisioned a tiger, a man-eating animal, and looking at her now, those descriptions feel accurate. Her wicked smile displays a weird sense of pride, as if being put on trial by goblins was all by design, just part of the plan. As she passes me by, we lock eyes for a second, and there he is, clear as day: her match, a man who is certainly not Charlie's dad. She walks by too quickly for me to get a full profile, but it's not like I need further confirmation. The only one who does is John.

"Cassandra," he says breathlessly, like he's just popped his head out of deep waters. He reaches for a stray curl of her hair, but she backs away, keeping herself just out of reach. "Is it true what they're telling me?"

She tilts her head. "John, I'm sorry things had to end this way. I had a nice future planned for us."

"Don't you mean, planned for *yourself*?" Charlie asks, arms crossed.

"Charlie, that's enough," John demands. "Please let her finish."

Cass takes John's hands in hers, her fingers running over his Super Bowl ring. "You have to understand, when I moved to Chicago, I had nothing. No family, no real home, stuck in a minimum-wage job, going nowhere. I went to the goblins to help me get ahead; they promised they'd make me some connections, if I made them some connections in return. It was Hollister who got me into that charity ball where we met. . . ." She looks off in a corner, her face glowing with the memory. "You looked so handsome in that dark blue suit, and then you asked me to dance. . . ." A smile peeks through her severe facade, softening her. "I knew I'd hit the jackpot. Only a man like you could give me the kind of life I'd always imagined."

"But then you refused to hold up your end of the bargain, which is how we've arrived at this point," Mr. Hollister interjects.

"I was getting to that," she says with an angry look that inspires goose bumps. I make a mental note never to double-cross a leprechaun. "I knew what I had promised, but the more I got to know you . . . the harder it got to . . . so I tried to disappear for a while, lie low and hope the goblins would forget. But as it turns out, they never do." She frowns.

John is beyond shocked, visibly recounting all their past interactions and trying to spot the deceit. "But I did fall in love with you. How did you do it?"

She laughs, a weary, weighted sound tinged with regret that chills my heart. "A magician never reveals her secrets."

John shakes his head, not finding the humor. "You lied to me, to my son. I wanted to make you my wife."

At this statement, Cass's tough exterior cracks, and she covers her face with her hands to hide it. Since she stepped foot in the room, she's tried to put on an unapologetic swagger, but

John's heartfelt words put a dent in her bravado. I'm not sure if she's suffering the loss of becoming the first lady of Chicago or if it's truly hitting her what she's actually lost. Clearly her plan backfired, but perhaps not in the way she thought. Maybe along the way, she developed actual feelings for him.

But whereas Cass is looking like she's losing her strength, John is slowly becoming emboldened, his face growing hard before our eyes. "You owe me the truth," he bellows.

Cass takes his hand, though he tries to recoil, and removes his Super Bowl ring. As the jewelry leaves his finger, a stream of tiny red spots trails off it, revealing a spell it must have encased. The spots flicker like pinpricks of light, until they burn out, the magic complete. Just as the last spot fades away, John rubs his eyes, as if the little lights were somehow blinding him. And clearly they were, because when he looks back up at Cass, there is no more love in his eyes; any positive feeling he carried for her has been replaced with anger.

"You put a spell on me?"

Cass puts her hands on her hips, trying to regain some of her confidence. "Technically the goblins did, but yes, I had them do it."

"You couldn't just take the chance that maybe I'd love you on my own?" John asks. This is the final straw for Cass; her head hangs low, unruly red curls cascading to hide her face. A faint sniffling comes from her corner of the room, and the tension is becoming unbearable. Both of them are broken. Witnessing the end of a relationship is never easy, even when you want it to happen. It's still two lives coming apart, something that was whole being split into pieces. Even though neither should end up with each other, it's still hard to witness the dissolution.

Though you wouldn't know it from watching the goblins, who seem to have no emotion at all. Cass and John are both crying quietly, but their captors stand there stone-faced. Charlie sits back down next to me, allowing them some space. I can tell he's hurting on his dad's behalf, despite this being his desired endgame. I feel like I should do something, offer him some comfort somehow, but with the creepo goblins and seriously intense energy in the room, nothing seems appropriate.

"What did you promise them?" John asks eventually.

"What?" Cass responds, wiping her face.

"The deal. What was it for? Money?"

She shakes her head. "No. That would have been easy to get."

"Then what?"

"Power," Mr. Hollister interrupts. "Like everyone in the magical community, we are tired of being treated like second-class citizens, having to keep our diverse lineage and talents under wraps. This city would be much more vibrant if magic could be out in the open."

"You don't speak for the entire magical community," Mom interjects.

"Don't I?" he retorts. "Lucille, as a witch, you would benefit from magical equality more than anyone. Your shop profits would soar."

"That's not what magic is about. And you know exactly why we keep it hidden."

The goblins share a look of frustration, obviously aware of Mom's objections but not in agreement with her warning.

"Why do you?" Charlie asks innocently. It takes great self-control to keep myself from pinching his adorable face.

"Because magic, just like money, brings out the worst in people. Greed, jealousy, violence: it's a gift, not a right, that is easily abused," Mom says. "John knows this. You cannot keep him hostage, regardless of what Cassandra promised you."

Mr. Hollister raises his chin, perhaps in effort to make himself look taller. "Perhaps not. But that doesn't mean this is over. Especially for Cassandra, who will need to repay us regardless. We will release him as long as you all agree not to further interfere."

Cass flings herself into John's arms, sobbing. "I'm sorry. For all of this. You deserve someone worthy of your love."

John pats her back carefully as if her clothes are made of gum. "What will you do with her?" he asks.

"She will be cared for; she will just be working. Constantly. Like a personal assistant that never sleeps," Hollister says with a grotesque grin, making him quite possibly the first creature that looks worse with a smile. The goblins stand to leave, and Mr. Hollister snaps, freeing John from his chair. Cass quickly surveys the scene, taking stock of her captors and the future before her. There's a fierceness in her eyes that says she won't disappear to a sentence of servitude, and just like that, she takes off running into the dark hallways. The goblins begin shouting, and it strikes me as ridiculous that they made the effort to secure John, who only wanted to see his girl, but not Cass, who only wants to survive. Even more surprisingly, the newly freed Mr. Blitzman takes off running after her.

"Dad!" Charlie yells, bolting out of the room. Mom and I are left alone, staring at each other in the candlelight.

"We can't let John or Charlie get stuck in the cross fire," Mom says, instantly in action mode. "C'mon, I need your help."

She needs my *help?* I wonder as we take off into the shadows. *What can I possibly do?* Nothing in my arsenal of tricks could contribute to solving this bonkers situation. Still, I keep pace at her side, trying not to run into corners or random furniture lining the halls.

The goblins are using some sort of teleportation charm to move around, similar to how they whisked John and Cass away in the first place. Their little legs are not suitable for a chase, so they continuously keep popping up and disappearing in the dark, searching for their lost leprechaun. At one point, one materializes right in front of me, causing me to trip over him, but he disappears again before hitting the floor. Too bad they don't have time to pull their ring-around-the-rosy trick with Cass, because then they could just bind her up with a snap. But outside of formation, their powers are not as strong. Mom pulls me back up and takes a pause to gather some supplies from her bag.

"Clearly we're not going to find them like this in the dark," she says. She takes out two magnolia flowers and places one in my hand. "Each of us has a strong connection to the Blitzmans: my friendship with John, your feelings for Charlie. These flowers will help take us to them." She grasps my other hand and closes her eyes, chanting something indeterminable under her breath. I've never done any sort of teleportation before and wince in anticipation over what will happen next. Will it hurt? Will it make me sick? Or more important, will it even work since I'm not a witch?

Luckily, Mom is powerful enough for the both of us, because suddenly we're outside, standing on the roof of the Merchandise Mart. After flailing around inside the pitch-black building, seeing the glittering Chicago skyline takes my breath away. We find our bearings, and see John and Charlie, who have Cass cornered on the ledge. Her hair blows wildly in the wind, her dress whipping at her ankles. The two ex-lovers are quarreling again.

"You can't do this!" John yells, struggling to be heard against the howling wind.

"Why would you even come after me, after what I did to you?" she yells back. Mom and I slowly make our way over to them; the goblins seemingly haven't found their way here yet. Charlie looks at me, eyes filled with fright. I know he never liked Cassandra, but her standing so close to the edge of this behemoth is the last thing he'd want. My heart is throbbing, propelling me to do something—ANYTHING—that would make this better, but I'm paralyzed, unable to help.

John tries to inch closer to Cass. "Because you're still . . ." He trails off. Magic or no magic, Cass left an impression on him that can't be wiped away with a simple abracadabra. "I don't wish you harm." He frowns, looking down at the city landscape.

"You can't save me," she says sadly. "They'll never stop coming after me."

"Maybe not, but at least we can try," he says, extending his hand. As he reaches out to the woman who manipulated him and played him like a fool, all I can think is, damn, the heart is a hell of a machine. Even when it's broken, it still finds a way to carry on.

Cass looks as if she's ready to consider his offer, but just then, Mr. Hollister and crew appear on the roof, looking incredibly creepy in their frustration. They huddle together like a pack of pissed-off mutant toddlers, ready to cause hell.

"Enough of this!" Mr. Hollister yells, at a volume I didn't think could come from such a tiny being. "You belong to us!" His bony finger points at Cass as the rest of the goblins link arms, undoubtedly uniting to give their leader more strength. But Cassandra doesn't wait to witness the results of their efforts; in one turbulent motion, she turns and leaps off the building, falling from our sight. I scream in shock, and we all rush to the edge, but in that split second, she seems to have disappeared. There's no body on the concrete, no evidence of her fall. It's like she took a leap of faith and was caught by a migrating rainbow that carried her to safety.

Mr. Hollister grumbles—something about never doing business with leprechauns again—as he rallies his troops. Mom, John, Charlie, and I continue standing there, staring out into the mysterious night. I can't think of a single appropriate thing to say, so I focus instead on meeting Charlie's eye.

"That was . . ." he starts, but fails to complete the thought.

"Totally," I respond.

"Thank you all for coming for me," John says, looking out onto the city that loves him so. The night's events seemed to have aged him five years. "I'm sorry to have put you all through this."

"I'm sorry you had to go through this," Mom says sympathetically.

John shakes his head. "I'm not. It's disappointing, not to mention extremely bizarre, but given the chance, I'd do it again." He sounds like a wise old soothsayer as he says, "You never know what you're getting into when you fall in love, but that doesn't mean you avoid the jump."

Twenty-seven

THE NEXT MORNING, MOM DECIDES WE DESERVE A DAY OFF. FOR a woman who believes federal holidays are a chance to stay open and make extra cash, this is a major reversal. She puts Bob in charge, who's probably having a panic attack at the thought; I'm sure he's rubbing that rabbit's foot bald. I make a batch of cinnamon rolls with double cream cheese frosting, Mom brews a strong Italian roast, and we sit in our jammies and slippers out on the back porch. Our building backs up to a cluster of other apartment buildings, and while it may not be the most majestic of views, it makes for good people watching.

"Looks like someone's doing a walk of shame," I say, pointing to a guy heading down the alley with only one shoe. "Must have been some night."

Mom chuckles. "Not compared to ours."

"That's the truth. You know, Cassandra wasn't as awful as I thought she'd be. I mean, clearly she has some issues, but I think she actually cared for John. I almost felt kind of bad for her."

"In all the times John described her to me, no alarms ever fired. It didn't seem like she had ulterior motives, but I guess people can surprise you."

"Do you think he'll be okay?"

Mom nods thoughtfully. "I'm going to meet him for dinner later to talk everything through. But if he survived the death of his wife, he can survive this." She takes a long sip of coffee. "What about Charlie? Will he be upset?"

"Nah, I mean, he came to me with the hopes of breaking them up, so I'm sure he'll be having his own private celebration."

She eyes me from the rim of her mug. "You two seem . . . close."

I reach for another cinnamon roll to draw attention from my blushing cheeks. "Yeah, well, I'm not really sure what's happening with that."

"The two of you used to play when you were toddlers."

"What? Really?"

"Back before John was mayor and Windy City was just an idea of mine. We both had more time to get together then."

"But what happened? I don't remember any Sand-Blitzman family picnics or anything," I say.

Mom shrugs. "Life happened. Your dad left; the store

opened. They were always traveling. It gets harder to stay in touch when you get older."

I try to wrap my head around the vision of little Charlie, running around our apartment in diapers, but all I see is a miniature version of him: a tattooed baby with hipster glasses.

Mom puts down her coffee mug, the one I bought her two years ago at a Renaissance fair Amani dragged me to. It says "witchy woman" in a Gothic font. "Amber, I need to tell you how proud I am of how you handled last night." I almost choke on a glob of frosting. "You were compassionate, delivering painful news with care and grace. I've watched you share difficult information in the past, but I've never seen you give so much hope alongside something so unpleasant. You've come so far with your gift; it was beautiful to witness."

I can count the times Mom's complimented me on one hand. Since her applause comes so infrequently, I never know how to react. I'm happy, for sure, but it's like having a spotlight suddenly flashed in my face. The light makes it hard to focus.

"Wow, um, thanks, Mom," I manage to say.

"What you said a few days ago, about me regretting your not being a witch . . . you know that's not true, right?" Her face is creased in concern.

"Honestly, Mom . . . I don't."

She holds my gaze, tears building. "I never meant to make you feel that way," she says softly, looking down. "Did I expect that a child of mine would not follow the Sand family tradition?

No, I did not. But, Amber, you have your own magic." Shiny eyes glance up at me. "You've worked harder than I ever did to hone it; my talents came naturally, but you strived to make yourself better, stronger. You turned an unexpected surprise into something powerful. If that's not witchcraft, I don't know what is."

I didn't expect an early morning pajama party to turn into a confessional, but without sounding too corny, it does make the pastries taste sweeter. I wipe the crumbs from my lips and move toward her, sitting in her lap like when I was little. I wrap my arms around her neck, getting tangled in her scent as the arms of her pink sleep shirt tuck around my waist.

Neither of us says anything more; we don't have to.

After a day spent watching infomercials and sitcom reruns, Mom hops in the shower to get ready for her dinner with John. Usually I'd take the opportunity of an empty apartment to have some quality time in the kitchen, but the laziness of the afternoon has transformed me into a sloth, moving only to change the channel or take bites of Nutella. I'm pretty much never this lethargic, constantly bustling back and forth between school and the shop, so the heaviness in my bones is a welcome stranger. I know people say you should live every day like it's your last, but sometimes it's nice to do absolutely nothing; the lack of activity recharges you for whatever lies ahead.

A knock at the door interrupts my fifth straight episode of *Friends*. I don't move at first—movement of any significant kind has not been achieved in hours—but the insistent pounding forces my feet to hit the floor. Who the hell could be out there? I'm not expecting anyone except a Lou Malnati's delivery guy, and he'd need to be buzzed in.

My socks slip on the hardwood as I lurch over; my right leg is completely asleep. When I open the door, I wish I'd just stayed on the couch.

It's Victoria.

NOOOOOOOOOOOOOOOOOOOOOO!

"How did you get past the buzzer?" I ask.

"Amber, darling," she says in that deep voice that doesn't match her face. She takes in my faded purple tee and ripped sweatpants. "You look . . . rested. I'm here to pick up your mother."

"Huh?"

"For our arrangement? I'm ready to help the Sands find their missing friend." Her smile is so smug that I'm instantly super-excited to wipe it from her face. "Aren't you going to ask me in?"

"Actually no. You and your leopard-print miniskirt can stay right there," I say in the bitchy tone I reserve for the truly wretched. I've been craving a moment like this, and I'm going to savor it like the key lime pie you only get to have in summer. "We don't need you anymore."

"Excuse me?" Her jaw twists to the side like she's been punched.

"You heard me. Get your second-rate witchcraft off our welcome mat."

"What is the meaning of this? How dare you speak to me that way, you disgraceful little matchmaker!"

I step forward, my cotton-covered toe encroaching on her stiletto. "I may be a matchmaker, but I'm not a disgrace. I don't know why you came to Chicago, but ever since you got here, you've been trying to intimidate her, I'm guessing because you know despite your power, you'll always be standing in her shadow. *That's* disgraceful."

Victoria's fuming, her fake chest rising and falling in anger. She reaches into her black Birkin bag and pulls out a bottle of something green. She raises the putrid liquid above her head, chanting, *"Suffocat,"* but just before she smashes the glass on the ground, the bottle starts levitating, and flies past my head, into my apartment. I whip around to see Mom in her bathrobe, fingers perched like a claw, drawing the nearly detonated spell toward her. She takes the bottle in her hand and charges forward, pushing me out of the doorway. In a swift movement, she completes the spell Victoria intended for me, causing the liquid to turn into an asparagus-colored steam that swirls around the hag's neck. Victoria's angry huffs turn into strangled gasps as the green cloud closes off her airways.

Mom watches her struggle to breathe, stepping closer to feel the tortured cries against her skin. There's a vacancy in her eyes that's truly terrifying; I get the feeling Mom could snap Victoria's neck and then just turn around and get dressed like nothing had happened. She's calm—serene even—as her nemesis labors to stay alive. It's the scariest thing I've ever seen.

"If you ever—EVER—try to use magic against my daughter again, I will end you," Mom says coolly. She tilts her head, giving Victoria one more moment to let this sink in. "Do you understand?"

Victoria nods her purple head, unable to speak. Tears stream down her collagen-pumped cheeks, creating streaks of what I am sure is extremely overpriced mascara. Mom snaps, and the choking cloud dissipates, causing Victoria to fall to the floor. Her pained gasps fill the hallway; her acrylic nails claw at the carpet. While she most definitely brought this on herself, it's still unnerving to watch someone fight for her life.

"The deal is off. I don't need your help." Mom steps back, slamming the door in Victoria's face. I can still hear her wheezing on the other side.

Mom walks into her office and lights a candle. She sits on the floor, cross-legged, and closes her eyes. I'm sure she needs to reset her chi or something, but I can't stay quiet.

"Um, holy crap, Mom, that was terrifying!" I exclaim. "You were straight up torturing her!"

"She was about to do that to you," she replies calmly.

"I know but . . . wow! I didn't know you had that in you!"

"There's a lot about magic—about me—that I'd rather you not know."

"Like how you already knew the head goblin man?"

"Yes, exactly that. Just as you fought to manage your match-making, I too had a journey." I wait for elaboration, but it seems like that vault is staying shut.

"Well . . . besides almost committing homicide, it was cool to see that witch get knocked down off her silicone pedestal," I say.

A tiny, very un-Wicca smile wiggles onto Mom's face. "I wouldn't have let her die. Just suffer."

I run out of the room before my laughter adds to the weight of her aura.

Twenty-eight

WEEKDAY MORNINGS USED TO BE A NEVER-ENDING TANGO BETWEEN me and my alarm, its repeated chimes reminding me of my inability to perform a time-bending spell. I'd hit the snooze until the last conceivable moment, when I'd pull on my plaid skirt and begrudgingly head to school. Now I find myself waking up without digital assistance, just so I can get to school early. Yes—EARLY. Today is my first day back from suspension, and I'm weirdly itching to get back to it all. Charlie and I don't have any classes together, so passing periods are our only chance to see each other during the day. We have to maximize what we've got.

Dating Charlie has not increased my popularity; in fact, I'm probably even more hated now than I was before. I've been a bottom-feeder for most of my life, and I'm comfortable in the muck; let us not forget what happens to those who throw their hearts in the ring for the wrong reasons (good luck to you, Cass, wherever you are). I'm not sure if his gaggle of admirers hate me because of me or if it's just because I've secured the position of "Charlie's girlfriend," effectively taking him off the market, but either way, it's hilarious and I love it. The looks we get range from mild confusion to blind rage, and I can't help but relish the tears of those who witness our affection.

"So, what do you hope to take away from your educational experience today, Miss Sand?" Charlie asks as we wait for the morning bell to ring. We're standing outside my English class, my back up against a case of trophies, Charlie leaning his chest into mine. I'm twirling the little golden fox pinned on his tie, appreciating for the first time how good a Manchester Prep uniform can look on the right guy.

"Well, sir, I'm planning to reach for the stars and go for the gold and any other possible academic cliché."

"Sounds like you'll be busy." He bends closer. "I'm glad you could squeeze me in."

"I'm an overachiever." I smile before he kisses me. The bell rings, three loud monotone bongs, and when he pulls back, I notice Ivy glaring at us from the classroom's doorway. There's a delicious mix of envy and disgust on her face; just the right recipe I like to inspire in my enemies. And is it me, or has her nose healed in a less flattering shape than its original? I resist the urge to rub my romance in her face, deciding it's better to focus on my boyfriend than some spiteful siren.

"See you after class?" he asks, picking his bag up off the floor.

"I'll pencil you in," I say. He heads off, giving Amani a wave as she rushes into class just in time.

"Whew, almost didn't make it," she wheezes.

"But here you are. Ready to be dazzled by my Sylvia Plath presentation?" I ask. One of the benefits of my brief suspension was having the time to finish this project, since I've been a little preoccupied otherwise.

"Oh yeah, can't wait."

I'm feeling good—so good that not even having to talk about a famously depressed woman can get me down. For the first time in the history of ever, sitting next to Ivy does not turn my insides to ice. She glares at me in her usual awful way, but I just smile, relishing Charlie's scent on my skin. It's moments like these that I wish I could somehow bottle, capturing the magical goodness to use in times of future unhappiness. Now that's a spell Mom should manufacture: happiness in a bottle.

I'm pulling my notes out of my bag while Ms. Dell makes a few boring announcements. I'm not really listening as I shuffle my note cards, but her last few words trickle in to my awareness.

". . . new exchange student all the way from Tokyo. I know you all will give her a warm Manchester welcome. Why don't you come on up here, Kim?"

All the air is sucked from my lungs as the girl I've envisioned for weeks materializes in the front of the room. Kim. In the flesh. Politely waving and looking adorable with multicolored barrettes in her jet-black hair. I rub my eyes to ensure she's not a mirage, but no, she's still there, looking just as I pictured . . . though I never envisioned her in Manchester plaid. What is she doing here? Why is this happening now?

"Jesus, Amber, you look like you've seen a ghost," Ivy whispers in mock concern. "I hope you puke."

But her ill wishes barely register, as I'm laser-focused on Kim. The beautiful, bright, future Mrs. Blitzman.

"Hi, everyone, I'm Kim," she says in a voice that could easily have come from an animated princess. "This is my first time in Chicago, though in addition to being born in Japan, I've also lived in San Francisco, Paris, and New York."

"How exciting!" Ms. Dell exclaims. I really hate her right now.

"We've moved a lot, but I'm hoping this city becomes home." Kim smiles as she takes a seat. I feel chunks starting to rise in my throat. Chicago WILL become her home! She'll meet her perfect man and start a perfect life in this perfect city and AHHHHHHHH!!!!!!! I whip back to Amani and start frantically signing a spew of craziness, which she struggles to catch. Either my hands are too shaky or I'm so overwhelmed I've forgotten how to sign, but all Amani signs back is *What?*

"Would anyone care to show Kim around for the day? Take

her to her classes and get her acquainted with campus?" Ms. Dell asks.

My hand shoots up like it's under demon possession, a move that shocks not only me, but my teacher as well.

"Amber . . . really?" Ms. Dell looks concerned at my uncharacteristic display of school spirit, but since no one else has volunteered, she's forced to relent. "All right, then. And since you're so full of enthusiasm, why doesn't your group kick off today's presentations."

Ivy, Brendan, and I head to the front of the class, looking like a very sad lot compared to the other groups. We aren't dressed in costumes; we don't have any props. What would we bring anyway? Since Ivy declared from the start that she would be contributing absolutely nothing to this effort, it's up to Brendan and me to get it done, but between his visible shaking and my sudden shock, I doubt this will go very well.

"Sylvia Plath was a brilliant, troubled mind who is forever remembered for her exit from this world," I begin. "The words that swirled within her were a gift she shared, but she was unable to let their vividness brighten her worldview. Her suicide was a tragedy, especially because it painted a darker cast on everything that came before that afternoon of pain. Somehow, her ending became just as significant as her life as a woman, mother, and talented writer."

Just over the tops of my note cards is Kim's face, watching me with genuine interest. Seeing her makes my vision go wonky, and though I know I should avoid it at all costs, I can't help but lock eyes with her momentarily. It's a mistake, an irreversible mistake, because suddenly Charlie is swimming in my thoughts, only not with me, but with her. Honey-covered episodes of their love start playing before me, and even my high sugar tolerance cannot handle it. I force myself to look back at my notes, but they seem to be written in another language, and I struggle to continue.

"This got me thinking about endings and how the final moments of a story can color our entire perception of a narrative. But endings aren't the epitome of a story; they are just how it stops. The real story is the middle: the ups and downs, the lefts and rights. There are so many directions a story can go, and it's that meaty middle that gives us insight into what is truly going on."

My brain is turning to Jell-O; I can't feel my face. These words I wrote in the thrall of love are taunting me now. I recite them like a robot, trying to separate the sentiment from the delivery, but the irony of it all is making me sick.

"I used to think stories had only one trajectory: up. That the people you meet and challenges you face are just collateral damage until you reach your final destination. But studying Sylvia helped me realize that a life—and story—cannot be defined simply by the way one says good-bye. It's the introductions, the mistakes, and the triumphs that create a clear picture of who we are and where we're going.

"Appreciate the journey, because when you get to the end, you'll only be able to look back and hope you don't regret what you see."

Then Brendan takes over, and for the first and probably last time, I'm thankful for Ivy's siren powers, as she's clearly whispered something into Brendan's ear that has turned him into a human Wikipedia page on the life of Ms. Plath. I stand there, dazed, as he recites her timeline and notable achievements, and it's all I can do not to melt into the floor. At some point, the presentation ends, but I don't remember walking back to my seat or sitting through Amani's group presentation on Maya Angelou. Suddenly, the bell is ringing, and Amani is shaking me.

"What is going on? Are you okay? Why are you so clammy?" she asks in rapid fire.

"Kim . . . it's her. Charlie's match." I almost choke on the words. Amani clutches her gut like she's been sliced by a sword, but there's no time to assess the wound because Kim's approaching.

"Hi . . . Amber?" she asks shyly.

I feel like an alien, unable to communicate with other lifeforms. Slowly, my brain comes back into focus. "Uh, yes." I cough, rubbing the sweat from my palms on my shirt. "Yup, I'm Amber."

"Thanks for helping me out. At my last school, I was put through weeks of hazing before anyone would speak to me, and even then it was in French, so . . ." She shrugs off the pain of the past, looking to me with hope. What on earth made me volunteer to take this girl around? I'm probably the last person at Manchester who should be her guide, and yet I willfully accepted the challenge. Why? Does she harbor a kind of dark magic I can't detect? Is she some sort of black widow hybrid, luring me into a trap so she can devour me whole before claiming her prize? She looks normal enough, but who knows if she's hiding a stinger under her skirt. I have to find out.

"I wouldn't expect most people at Manchester to roll out a welcome mat for you either," I say. "Ninety-nine percent of the student body has been infected with *horriblepersonitis*."

"Seems to be an epidemic across several high schools, then," Kim says. Hmph, that was kind of funny. Dammit.

"This is Amani Sharma. She's one of the immune."

"Nice to meet you," Amani says with caution, and I don't blame her; how do you greet someone who is most likely going to take away your best friend's happiness? "I have to run, but maybe I'll catch up with you girls at lunch?" she says through gritted teeth.

"Sure, we'll be fine," I assure her.

Text me ASAP, she signs as she walks away.

"She seems nice," Kim says. "Was that sign language?"

"Yes, to both." We walk down the halls in silence. I truly am the worst tour guide, but I have no idea what to say. *Here's the bay of lockers a senior girl shoved me into last year after I told her her boyfriend was a dud, and here's the gym, where your self-esteem will plummet once you don the terry-cloth shorts. Also, what are you doing here, and why are you ruining my life?* None of it sounds particularly welcoming, so instead I ask, "So what's your next class?"

Kim pulls out her schedule. "Chemistry. With Mr. Longhorn."

Of course it is because the Fates hate me today. I am now literally leading her to Charlie, who also has that class, because naturally the first time these two future lovebirds should meet is in CHEMISTRY. Of all the subjects. I can see them giving a toast at their rehearsal dinner now . . . "Tra, la, and to think it all started in chemistry!" UGH.

But really, this moment was unavoidable, right? I'm doing exactly what I'm supposed to. A matchmaker, bringing a couple together. I stressed over my feelings for Charlie potentially disrupting his happily ever after, but from the looks of it, everything's still running on course. I foolishly hoped my error with Amani and Vincent would bleed over into my life, giving me the possibility of a future with Charlie. But no, I am just a bump along the road, a detour from the final destination.

"I'll take you there," I say. I wish I could do something magical—actual magic—like temporarily blind her or transform her into a frog I could cram in my pocket, but before I know it, we're rounding a corner, and there's Charlie, leaning against the chemistry doorframe, waiting to meet up with me. His class is on the way to my calculus class, so we like to meet up for sixty seconds of kissing and whatnot. He sees me and perks up, repositioning his bag to his back so I can snuggle up appropriately.

He greets me with a kiss on my forehead, then asks, "Who's your friend?"

I resist the urge to wrap my arms around him and stake my territory. *Be cool, Amber.* "This is Kim. She just transferred here. She'll be joining you for chem."

"Ah. Be sure not to sit in the front row. Mr. Longhorn starts sweating when he talks about solvents."

"Thanks for the tip." She laughs.

"I'm Charlie," he says, offering his hand, and as they shake, I watch him closely for any type of reaction. Did he feel something when they touched? An electric current running from his fingers to his heart? Did she? His expression seems normal, and yet I'm imagining him pulling her toward him and swooping her into his arms for a Hollywood-style kiss. Nothing even remotely close to that happens, but I can't help but wonder if the seeds of romance have been planted.

"Nice to meet you, Charlie, and thanks for the help, Amber. I should be okay now. I'm glad we met," Kim says with a smile so sincere it almost makes me sick. There's no evidence of her being a two-faced miscreant; in fact, she seems like a rare breed of decent human being. I can't fault her for that.

I feel weird, beyond weird, and barely reciprocate when Charlie presses his lips to mine. He pulls back, confused at kissing a mannequin.

"Everything okay?" he asks, tucking my hair behind my ear.

"Hmm? Yeah. Fine." But I'm not fine; I'm the opposite of

fine. There's no way I'm going to survive a whole day under this roof where Charlie and Kim could potentially be falling in love. No. I need to get some clarity, and nothing in these textbooks will provide me the answers I need.

It's taking me five times longer than normal to process every word. My heart is beating so loud I may as well be listening to death metal with noise-canceling headphones.

Charlie looks at me like he's worried I'm having a stroke. "Okay . . . but will *you* be fine, partner? You seem a little . . . unhinged."

Oh, it's nothing. I've faced goblins and vampires and more, but it's adorable transfer students that have me shaking in my knee socks.

When the bell rings, I walk past Calculus and right out the back door. I walk all the way home, in fact, my thoughts playing on an unhelpful, psychotic loop.

I like him. I like him so much. It's kind of unreal how fast and hard I've fallen for Charlie. My work has always prepared me for the worst; for every happy ending I've witnessed, there have been ten more train wrecks piled behind them, the dust of their wreckage clouding my vision. That sediment started clogging my arteries, making me feel like love would never truly course through my veins. And now, after I JUST opened myself up to romantic possibilities, I feel like it's all being taken away from me. It's not fair, the timing is insane: soul mates meeting in high school? What are the odds of that? Like, 1 percent of the population?! They couldn't have met in college, or through some horrible online dating app like normal people? GAH!

And yet . . . I brought this on myself. I let myself be swayed by Charlie sans warranty, and now here I am, with a relationship set to expire. What am I supposed to do? Step aside gracefully and just let the inevitability of Charlie and Kim happen? Or keep on moving forward, letting myself grow more and more attached to him until his fated departure would truly be heart-breaking?

I go straight home and hide in my bed, ignoring my phone and doing everything in my power to turn off my head. Suddenly, I'm struck with an idea. A stupid idea, to be sure, but since I'm home alone and have no one around to stop me, I act before I can talk myself out of it. I charge into Mom's office, grabbing the jar of white incantation sand off one of the many shelves. I open the lid and start hastily making a circle on the floor. It comes out lopsided—more of an ellipse than a circle—but it doesn't matter. I light whatever candles are within arm's reach and place them in the center.

I don't care if I'm not a witch. I've seen this done a hundred times; I know I can do it.

I'm going to conjure the Fates.

Twenty-nine

I SIT CROSS-LEGGED ON A PILLOW ON THE LINE OF SAND, breathing in the conflicting candle scents. If I weren't in such a messed-up state of mind, I'd probably think twice about asking one of the Fates into my home; *if* I can get one here, he or she will not be happy about being conjured by a lowly matchmaker. But so what? Only the Fates can explain to me why this is happening, so I don't give a crap what kind of mood I'm met with.

I close my eyes, running my lines internally before speaking aloud. I've heard the spiel before, but the words have never crossed my lips. There's no room for error if I want this to work.

"Divine Fates, watchers of this lowly realm, the Sand family calls upon you. Bless us with your wisdom, your eternal foresight, and share with us the secrets of our mortal coil." I take several deep breaths, envision the scene I wish to see before opening my eyes. If I can hold a proper image of the Fates in my head, they will know I'm worthy of their time, and grace me with their presence.

Slowly, I open my eyes, and to my satisfaction, a glowing pinprick of warm blue light is bobbing in the middle of the room. Quickly it grows, stretching vertically, until a humanlike shape begins to form. A head, limbs, and torso all come into focus, but no feet; the Fates look kind of like a genie without a lamp, just a wisp of curling light dangling down below. I guess you don't need feet when you can float into existence.

I'm so pleased with my victorious conjuring, I want to scream a battle cry of success, but I refrain from self-congratulation, as the male Fate is clearly not as pleased to see me as I am him.

"What's this?" he snips. "I thought I was being called by a Sand sorceress."

"Well, I am a Sand, but—"

"You're a matchmaker," he says, disgusted, as if he were addressing a leper.

"Yes I am," I say with my chin held high. I'm not going to let a spectral jerk add to my drama. "And I need some information."

The Fate laughs. "I don't answer to the likes of you!"

"Why not? I was able to get you here, even without being a witch. Don't you think that deserves at least a minute of your time?"

He raises a sky-blue eyebrow. "I suppose. . . ."

Great! Better make this quick before he changes his mind. "I need to know if a matchmaker is allowed to be in love."

There's another laugh, which is pretty rude if you ask me. "*This* is your concern?"

I nod.

The Fate swoops in closer, hovering like a cloud just above my head. "Little girl, do you realize what I deal with all day? War, destruction, disease . . . the absolute depths of human existence—"

"And you know what *I* deal with?" I cut him off. "Loneliness, betrayal, heartbreak. Every single day people come to me, looking for a sliver of hope, wanting to know that they won't go through this world all on their own. They come to me for answers about love, but what do I know? I've never been in love! I'll probably never . . ." I choke on my words.

"There is nothing in the stars that says a matchmaker can't fall in love," he says. His tone is more clinical than sympathetic, like he's reading from a supernatural textbook.

"But then why . . ." I whisper, my head hanging down so as not to reveal any potential tears. I cannot let myself cry in front of a Fate. "Why would someone I can't keep cross my path? Why even present me with an option that's not truly open?"

He sighs in frustration. "You went against your own advice, did you not? With your latest romantic entanglement?"

"I did."

"And if you were faced with the same set of circumstances, would you do it again?"

I consider this. If I knew Kim was about to enter our lives, would I still offer my heart to Charlie? Would I let down my guard, go against the self-imposed barriers I've built over the years? My knee-jerk reaction is no, I wouldn't; who would willingly throw her heart to the slaughter? But then, if I didn't, I wouldn't know what it felt like to be held by someone so tightly, to be looked at like I was the sun in someone's sky. I wouldn't have the memories of fingers and lips that warmed me, of smiles that lit me up inside. Even if he does get lured away, aren't the memories worth something? Does it all have to be swept under the rug of regret?

No. It doesn't. I don't regret falling for Charlie, no matter how spazzy my insides feel. I'm scared, yes, about what will happen next, but I'm still here. My heart aches, but it still beats. I've made tons of recipes that didn't come out right: too sweet, too bland, too gooey. But I don't regret trying them; they helped me figure out where I went wrong. I'd never stop baking after burning a batch of cookies, so I don't fault myself now.

"Yes," I finally admit. "I probably would."

The Fate rolls his eyes. "Well, there you go."

I know the Fates are notoriously obnoxious, but I thought I'd get something a little more substantial out of this. "Is there any chance there's a bug in the system?"

"Excuse me?"

"You know, like, a percentage of error? In my magic . . . in matchmaking in general?"

"In general, or in reference to your particular situation?" he eyes me suspiciously.

"Both! Either! What does it matter?" I exclaim.

"Do not get fussy with me, young lady."

Ugh. "Sorry. I just feel like I should know, you know? If there's a chance I'm leading people astray, maybe my match-making should come with a disclaimer. A 'follow at your own risk' or something?"

The Fate is looking around the room, clearly bored by this discussion. "You have yet to make a false match, if that's what you're asking."

I shake my head. "But what about Amani?"

"My previous comment stands."

"But she hates her match."

The Fate stays silent. Either he is over this, or he has no idea what I'm referencing. I mean, I'm sure the Fates don't sit around and gossip about the love lives of teenage mortals, unless we are oblivious stars of the weirdest interplanetary reality show of all time.

"And Charlie?"

"You know I can't reveal one's own future."

I take a deep breath, realizing this is my only chance for an answer. I have to try. "I know, but can't you just, like, point me in the right direction or something? Just this once? I know

I'm asking about myself here, but really this is about something bigger: about my magic as a whole. If what I'm feeling for him is somehow skewing who I see for his match, or if there's a love loophole I'm not aware of . . . I just feel like I need all the details to keep moving forward. Not only for myself, but for anyone who comes to me for help. I need to know that what I'm telling them is real. Please. Share your magical wisdom or whatever?"

Unmoved by my plea, his light starts to fade, undoubtedly heading off to deal with his next crisis. My time with him is up. But before he disappears completely, he says, "I already have."

I go to bed early and ditch school the next day. I just don't feel like dealing with the outside world. My phone keeps buzzing; Charlie has called me a hundred times. Well, maybe not a hundred. I know he's probably worried about me ditching school without a heads-up, but I need to be alone with my thoughts.

What did that Fate mean when he said that he'd already shared his wisdom? For someone who is "all knowing," he was pretty vague on the actual information. Did he mean his point about me not making a false match? Because that's obviously wrong, since Amani and Vincent are a total no go. Unless there's still a chance they'll end up together? Amani seems pretty adamant in her repulsion of him. Even though I have envisioned them together, it's hard to see her doing a 180 at this point.

If, for the sake of argument, I haven't made a false match, does Charlie fall under that umbrella? Technically, I haven't actually matched him; I've never revealed Kim's identity as his match, though I did introduce them yesterday. Does that count? In the times that I have physically brought couples together, it's usually been with the revelation of their destiny, not just a random meeting. Does that have to be shared? Do I have to say, "This is your match"? Or is the meeting enough? GAH.

I feel like everything I once knew is now muddled, and I just want to give up altogether.

I take a sadness nap, and when I wake up, Amani is sitting on the edge of my bed with her cosmetics bag.

"What are you doing?" I ask groggily, cheek adhered to my pillow with drool.

"I'm going to paint your toes with glitter polish," she says, searching for my feet under the piles of blankets and empty cookie bags.

"What? Why?"

"Just because you're having some sort of emotional breakdown doesn't mean you can't have cute toes. Rainbow or gold?" she asks, holding up the two bottles.

I love her train of thought sometimes, no matter how nonsensical it can be. So I submit. "Fine. Rainbow. But beware when you take off my socks."

"I'll breathe through my mouth." Friendship, ladies and gentlemen. "So, can I regale you with tales from the outside world?"

"Depends," I answer. "Are they filled with happiness?"

"No. Only pain and suffering."

"Okay then. Proceed."

She starts working on my right foot, filling me in on Manchester gossip I really don't care about. But then she segues into, "So . . . Kim."

"Yup. She's real."

"And now you're avoiding Charlie."

"Huh?"

"You're avoiding him. You haven't answered any of his texts or calls."

"How do you know?"

"He came up to me yesterday after you bailed. He's worried about you."

"He's not too busy falling for Kim?"

Amani scrunches up her nose and lips, but I doubt it's because of my stinky feet. "Listen, you know I love you, but don't you think you're being a little ridiculous? I mean, yes, it is stressful that Kim has magically arrived, and yes, I do understand your freak-out. But Charlie is with you. He chose *you*. You're acting like he dumped you the moment he laid eyes on her."

"It's inevitable, though."

"Yeah . . ." She twists the nail polish cap back on. "You don't know for sure what the future will bring."

"And you do? Are we having conflicting visions? Is this the classic matchmaker versus precog showdown here?"

She's biting her lip like there's more she wants to say but can't.

"What are you not telling me?" I sit up quickly, smearing sparkles on my sheets.

"Nothing! It's just . . . I think you need to relax. Don't cast Charlie off just yet. He's holding on to you. The whole thing deserves a closer look." The word launches off her tongue with extra pep, like a clue being flung airborne. Did she break our pact and have a vision, see a further future between Charlie and me?

"Okay, Sharma: spill."

She hangs her head like a dog caught using a rug as a restroom. "Look. I didn't mean to spy on your destiny. Charlie was sniffing around me, so I almost didn't have a choice."

"WHAT?!"

She fluffs the skirt of her uniform. "Something's going on with me. Ever since that séance, my visions have been coming back. And it's been getting easier, or at the very least, more involuntary. Like it used to be." She gives a small smile. "The other day, I envisioned a pop quiz in world history just by passing by Mr. Whittle in the hall."

"Amani, that's amazing!" I wrap her tight in a hug. "I can't believe it!"

"I know, it's weird. And I still have some work to do in learning to control it."

"I can help you!"

"Yes, and I'm going to hold you to that," she says. "But it doesn't change what I already know. I don't think it technically goes against our pact when I say, as a precog and your friend, I feel very strongly that there is more to your and Charlie's story, and I urge you to find out what it is."

A few days ago, I was only at the beginning; the ink had yet to dry on the introduction of our relationship. I certainly wasn't looking for a way out or a sudden plot twist. I was excited to see where the story was headed, what kind of adventures were chapters ahead. Was this event just a small diversion from the sunny days to come? Or am I destined for a depressing ending no matter what?

I really don't know.

"Just . . . think about it," Amani continues. "You better be back at school tomorrow. You can't just leave me there alone."

"Sorry," I say. "I'll get it together."

"Good. I have to be going; biology homework awaits." She stands and collects her things. "Call me if you need to talk."

I nod, and when she's gone, I return to my former vegetative state, this time with cuter toes.

Thirty

"CONGRATULATIONS, YOU ARE EACH OTHER'S MATCH." TWO twentysomething girls sit before me, our hands joined in a circle at my matchmaking booth. The minute they hear the news, they forget all about me, trading my fingers for each other's, sharing a kiss that could easily be the final shot of a romantic movie. One a partial fairy, the other just a boring ol' human, the two girls fit together so perfectly, I almost didn't bother putting them through my whole Cupid charade. Still, people like ceremonies. Even if they know the final outcome, it's the pageantry and traditions that cement those moments in reality. I let the lovebirds carry on for a bit; it's nice, comforting somehow, to see love with my own eyes.

After they've finished rejoicing in their bona fide romance, the pixie turns to me, blushing at her full-on public make-out session. "Oh my gosh, I'm so sorry for carrying on like that!" she says with a southern drawl. "We're both just so thrilled!" Her girlfriend grins in agreement.

"Don't worry about it. It's fine," I say, waving a hand in dismissal.

"You must be used to it, though, in your line of work, right?"

"I get a wide range of reactions, but trust me, your kind is my favorite."

They both giggle, each wearing the other's lipstick. They are bliss personified.

"What a romantic life you must lead!" the fairy exclaims.

Sigh. This happens sometimes. While the kids at school surely envision my life as one filled with torture and sadness, my clients here have often remarked on the seeming dreaminess I must float around in all day. Of course neither iteration is true; I exist somewhere in the middle, seeing other people's love lives so clearly but being completely dumbfounded by my own. No one wants to hear about that, though, especially two brides-to-be who just want to exist in their deserved fantasy state for as long as possible. And since they're paying customers, I do my best to uphold that magical image.

"Yes, well"—I smile coyly—"a lady never reveals her secrets."

This pleases them, and they leave a big tip before they go. Tips are certainly a perk of matching; happy couples tend to be more liberal with their dollars. You can't expect someone whose heart you just smashed to thank you with extra Benjamins.

"Time to lock up." Bob lumbers over. My clients were the last ones to enter the shop, and Bob was drilling holes in the backs of their heads the whole time, waiting for us to be done.

"Big plans tonight, Bob?" I ask as I straighten up my booth. The girls took the last of my business cards, so I pull out some extra from a box under the table.

"Yes. I'm going to my mother's. We're going to play chess and eat frogs' legs." He smiles dopily.

"Livin' the dream, my friend. Let me just grab my bag, and then we can go." I duck into the back room and pull off the Windy City Magic long-sleeved tee I wore for my shift, back from the literally one day when my mom thought we should have some kind of staff uniform. She could barely wear our cheesy logo across her chest for an hour before deciding it was a horrible idea. I still wear mine sometimes just to remind her she's not infallible. I change back into the black tank I wore under my Manchester getup today. When Bob and I walk out into the crisp October air, I realize I may have been warmer wearing that crazy shirt.

"You okay getting home?" Bob asks. Sometimes he gives me a ride when Mom doesn't close up, but from the way he's hopping between feet, I can tell he's anxious to get to his amphibian cuisine.

"I'll be fine. My public transit chariot awaits."

"Okay. Good night." He shuffles off toward the parking garage. I start heading toward the bus stop, but for some reason, find myself climbing the steps to the Pier Park area. I never go this way—it takes too long and my arms are cold—but my feet are defying logic. Orange and yellow Ferris wheel spokes guide me upward, until I'm standing alone under the neon ring.

Well, not completely alone. Because sitting at the start of the ride's queue is Charlie, elbows on his knees, staring at the sidewalk. I almost don't recognize him at first, because a smattering of stubble covers his always clean-shaven face. He could easily be a statue, or one of those street performers who pretend to be statues; everything about his person displays a frozen sadness. I wonder how long he's been sitting there.

"Hey," I call out, my voice breaking his trance. Citrus-colored specs reflect on his lenses, but even still, I see the pain that lies behind them.

"Hey," he echoes back, but with more melancholy. "Um, I hope this isn't weird." He approaches slowly, unsure of himself, so I meet him halfway to ease the struggle.

"It's not weird, per se. Though you do know the wheel stops turning at eight o'clock." I point up.

"Yeah." There's a long pause. "You've been avoiding me."

I take a deep breath but exhale in shivers. Upon seeing this, Charlie removes his cotton blazer and drapes it over my shoulders, leaving him in a heather T. rex tee. It's so rare to see him dressed so casual; something must really be wrong, and I'm pretty sure it's my fault.

"Thanks," I say, hugging the fabric close to me. My senses are suddenly overwhelmed by everything Charlie: his scent, his warmth, his touch. It catches me by surprise, how quickly these simple things take hold of me. My skin is covered in goose bumps but not because I'm cold. I was using my mini break-down to see how I feel, giving myself time to breathe and see if any strong emotion pulls me in either direction. I think I finally have my answer.

"So what's going on?" he asks. I wish that I could tell him, and maybe I should, but the truth stays locked inside me, a secret I shouldn't keep but can't release. If things are going to happen between him and Kim someday, I can't stop it, but I can exist here, in the moment, with him. Where I want to be.

"I missed you," I whisper.

"You did?" he gasps, eyebrows perched like ski slopes.

I nod. This gives him a shot of confidence, and he steps closer. "I missed you too." He reaches for my hand, and I let him take it. The goose bumps continue to spread. "Amber, I don't know what's going on in that head of yours, but I want you to know: every time I'm around you, I feel like a non-fatal firework is lit inside me. It's magic—actual magic—and you'll have to forgive the pun, but I don't want to be under anyone else's spell."

I try to be indifferent, but his admission is so honest, so unabashedly dorky and adorable, I'd have to be completely dead inside not to smile. Is this stupid, to keep moving forward? No, I don't think so. Stupid would be denying my heart something it wants just because it's afraid. I'm not going to live my life in fear just because of the unknown.

"Charlie," I say with a tender laugh.

"No, I'm not done, I—"

I put a finger over his lips. "It's okay," I say softly. "I feel the same."

Then he smiles—that majestic smile I know now is truly just for me—and picks me up, swinging me around and around until the blazer falls to the ground. The skyline and lake take turns spinning in my view, a flurry of twinkling lights, and then we stop as Charlie buries his face in the crook of my neck. A happy laugh tickles my skin as he wraps his arms around my waist, squeezing tight.

"Thank the Gods," he cries, and I couldn't agree more.

I'm not sure what will happen next. Maybe Charlie and I will end up together. Maybe my perception of his match is really the Fates trying to screw with me, preventing me from using my talent on myself. Maybe it's destiny, and we'll ride off into the sunset on the back of a rainbow-maned unicorn (shut up, it could happen).

Or maybe our paths will diverge someday, taking us in separate directions, making our relationship a brief but beautiful spot in a series of unforgettable encounters.

Either way, it will be a journey worth taking.

Either way, it will be a love story.

ACKNOWLEDGMENTS

Amber Sand came to me while I was on the treadmill. Since my main thought while running is usually "Please don't die," I figured this character must be pretty special to break through my gasps for air. Amber's adamant belief in love helped fuel me during a difficult time, and for that I will always be thankful.

I've always adored spellbinding stories, but seeing this book come to life was a magic all of its own. Every step of the way, I've been so touched by the support and encouragement I've received, and have been brought to happy tears many times.

To my agent, Jess, for picking Amber out of the slush and pushing her to be her best. You got this story right from the start and have been such a wonderful advocate. Thank you for believing in me and being a sympathetic ear to my endless, crazy questions.

To my editor, Kieran, for all the brilliant feedback and little smiley faces dotted throughout my drafts. Your insight has been invaluable, and I feel so lucky to have such a smart, thoughtful ally to help me bounce around ideas. Everyone at Hyperion has been so helpful and kind; the Fates were truly on my side in this partnership!

To all the sassy, flawed, amazing heroines (and the creative forces behind them) who have helped shape my world, thank you for fighting the good fight. Buffy Summers, Veronica Mars, Lizzie Bennet, Katniss Everdeen: I'm looking at you (to name just a few).

To all my friends and family who have encouraged my creative endeavors throughout the years, your support means everything to me. Meghan, thank you for giving me time to write, and fueling my fangirl tendencies. Cheryl, thank you for your endless supply of friendship, love, and milk shakes.

To Tiff and Chris, my life coaches who are so fiercely protective and loving; I couldn't ask for a better couple in my corner.

To Eleanor, for sitting by my side.

And to my mom, who somehow always knew I'd be a writer. Although you'll never read this story, you are infused in every word and exclamation point. The foundation you gave me is truly the best kind of magic, without which I would never be where I am today.

Turn the page for a sneak peek at the first two chapters
of the next *Windy City Magic* novel!

One

MOUNTING EVIDENCE SUGGESTS I MAY BE A MASOCHIST. I WOULDN'T have thought this until recently, with my previous top character descriptions being "sunny," "winning," and "eager to please" (jk, they'd be "misanthropic," "sarcastic," and "cantankerous"). I guess part of the human experience is to grow and change, though I didn't think it could happen all at once.

Why else, other than a deep-rooted desire to see myself suffer, would I be in my kitchen, elbow-deep in powdered sugar, making peach tarts for a girl who is predestined to ruin my life? If I'd been asked a few months ago what kind of social activity I'd be least interested in, pretty much all situations involving other people would have made the list, but a front-runner would definitely have been inviting over an alleged rival to sample my latest culinary endeavor. Yet here I am, carefully plating a masterpiece for someone who may someday cause me severe emotional pain. Am I deranged? Insane?

Don't answer that.

"Oh my goodness, these fruit-pie thingies are amazing," says Kim Li, licking the final crumbs of my legendary baking skills off her lips. An adorable pixie-size girl (though not of pixie descent), Kim has the poreless complexion face-wash commercials promise and a worldly style cultivated after living on several continents. She currently has an entire rainbow of barrettes clipped in her jet-black hair yet still manages to look sophisticated and not like a five-year-old gave her a makeover at Claire's.

She was invited by my best friend, Amani Sharma, who is also finishing up her dessert. Never to be outdone, Amani makes being a girl look easy, with a pink dress I wouldn't even know where to buy. Per usual, I am the least done up in the room, wearing jeans I picked up off the floor this morning, and my only accessories being peach flesh and flour. "Really, Amber, nicely done," Amani confirms.

They're both lounging on my couch like it's the most natural thing in the world and not some freak occurrence where I suddenly have more than one friend and we get together for girl time. Maybe, in addition to my being insane, a shape-shifter has stolen my body and taken over my social calendar?

"You both are too kind, and also correct," I say. "These tarts came out perfectly."

"What's next on the menu . . . humble pie?" Amani asks, with an exaggerated wink, wink.

"Ugh, humble pie takes way too long to bake; I don't bother with it."

"Clearly."

Kim laughs sweetly beside us. Even though we've been hanging out for a few months now, I think we're all trying to decide how she fits in. Especially me, since I'm the one with the potential roadblock. Kim is, after all, my alleged competition, based on nothing except the visions of her and my boyfriend, Charlie Blitzman, living happily ever after in my head. In fact, I knew her before I knew her, getting more and more peeks into her personality every time Charlie was near. So when she showed up at school two months ago, I handled it with my usual finesse and grace (i.e., I lost it). It would be easier to hate her. To prick a voodoo doll and put a curse on her children's children's children. But as the Fates would have it, Kim is actually a delightful, interesting person, making it nearly impossible to churn up negative feelings around her. And since she and Amani seem to have almost identical class schedules, they've been getting to know each other at a rapid pace, whether I like it or not. In an effort to be a Bigger Person, I've kept a running mental list of Kim's positive attributes to pull out whenever I feel myself having irrational feelings.

For example, reason number three: Kim is always ready with a compliment. I've never had to work so hard at maintaining a friendship, but then again, that may be why I don't have many friends.

The entrance buzzer goes off, though we aren't expecting any other guests to this already-out-of-the-ordinary gathering. I'm very comfortable buried under a pile of blankets and a plate of tarts, so I don't feel like moving if it's a solicitor or drunken neighbor punching the wrong button.

"Amani, should I bother to answer?" I ask my friend, who is slowly reemerging to the fortune-telling fold. For way too long, she kept her unique brand of magic under lock and key, but now she's welcoming it back in. Most of the time her visions come to her fast and furious without her control, but other times, for very mundane happenings, she can conjure up a visual or two. Her precog abilities are the extra cherry on the awesomesauce that is Amani, and I'm so happy she's opened up this part of herself again (not just because it works to my advantage from time to time).

She taps her chin thoughtfully, fluttering her ridiculously long lashes. "Hmm, let me see." The buzzer sounds again. "Yes, I'd say this visitor is worth your while."

"Scale of one to ten?"

"A solid nine. Maybe a nine point five, due to provisions."

"That sounds promising!"

Bzzzzzzzzz!

"All right! I'm coming!" I yell, although the mystery guest is two floors below. I almost drop a pastry in prying myself from the couch, but Kim manages to catch it (reason number twelve: has good priorities, and number thirteen: excellent reflexes). I pound the button to open the front door, and before long, there's a tap at our apartment entry. Our visitor is dressed in an orange gingham tie coordinated to his glasses, and holds an extra-large vanilla cupcake with a disproportionately large cake-to-frosting ratio that looks like something from a My Little Pony coloring book. It's Charlie.

"Well, there's a masculine treat," I say.

"Why, thank you," he says, putting his free hand over his heart and performing a small bow.

"I was referring to your pastry."

"Oh, this?" He turns it around, showing off the density of pink sprinkles. "Yeah, it's pretty freaking delicious."

"It's also pink."

"So? It could be a rainbow swirl topped with unicorn wings, and I'd love it just the same."

"Unicorns don't have wings. You're thinking of a Pegasus," I correct.

"You know what I mean."

"I've never seen a guy so devoted to buttercream," I say.

He leans in close, his lips hovering by my right ear. "Well, I got it for you, so what does that say about my devotion?" A plague of goose bumps covers my skin, and I have to playfully push him away before I grab his face and lay one on him.

"Can you guys, like, turn the cuteness down a notch?" Amani calls from behind us. "Some of us are trying to keep down our peach tarts."

"Yeah, all this adorable affection is making me nauseous," Kim chimes in.

Charlie grins at me, all white-toothed and proud, and I take a deep breath in preparation for his match reel. Looking into his dark green eyes, my matchmaking abilities activate, giving me an unfiltered view of his romantic future. This would be fine, of course, if I were his destined leading lady, but instead, I'm treated to scenes of him and Kim drinking piña coladas on a white-sand beach, and sipping coffee on a lazy Sunday. I work through them quickly, not eager to linger, and refocus on the actual boy in front of me.

"Hey, Amani. Hey, Kim." He waves. I try not to cringe when her name passes his lips.

"Hi, Charlie," they respond in a unified monotone, though I know their mocking disdain comes from a place of affection.

"What are you doing here?" I ask him.

"Oh, you know, I was in the neighborhood." He smirks. This is definitely not true, since Charlie and I are at completely different pinpoints on the Chicago map. Maybe, just maybe, he could spot my tiny Wicker Park apartment from the top of his Gold Coast penthouse if he had a set of quality binoculars. This is not the first time he's found himself so far from home; I expect it won't be the last. "I forgot you were having the girls over."

"Yeah, well . . ." In all honesty, I've about had my fill of female friendship for the night, as Amani and Kim are much better at finding acceptable conversation topics not involving witchcraft tangents and supernatural subplots. They can riff on deep conditioner treatments for longer than I thought possible. And yet, being a hostess with the mostest means suffering for the benefit of your guests. (I guess. I'm still not very familiar with this role.) "Can I call you later?"

"You better," he says, planting a small kiss on my forehead before calling out, "Bye, ladies!" I watch him disappear down to the second floor, and then I retreat to my living room, where Amani and Kim are hanging themselves on fake nooses of sweetness.

"All right, I get it," I concede, biting into the offensively pink cupcake. "Our undeniable chemistry makes you queasy."

"You guys are just perfect." Kim sighs. I tense at her praise, trying to focus instead on the swirling sugar on my tongue. "You make me simultaneously happy and jealous."

Amani, knowing my pulse will race at Kim's envy, quickly interjects, "Yeah, but mostly grossed out."

"Sorry, not sorry," I singsong just as there's another knock at the door. I thought Charlie had left by now, but maybe he's being oversentimental in his need to see me. "Geez, back for more already?" I call out, turning the knob.

Yet instead of being greeted by my delectable boyfriend, I'm met with something truly stomach turning: Ivy Chamberlain.

Two

"IVY? WHAT IN THE GODS' GOOD NAMES ARE YOU DOING HERE?" I ask, making a mental note to check on where Mom keeps her protection potions. Wherever they are, they need to be relocated to the front entry closet ASAP.

Ivy Chamberlain, resident teenage dream/nightmare (depending on how you look at it), crosses her arms across her ample chest and lets out the world record for longest, most exasperated sigh. You'd think I'd dragged her away from her usual Friday night football-player make-out session to be here, not that she came here of her own mysterious free will. Seeing most Manchester Prep students outside of school is an unpleasant experience, but interacting with Ivy when not absolutely forced to is the highest level of torture.

"Don't for one second think I didn't explore literally every other option in this world and beyond before coming to you," she sneers, her spun-from-gold locks falling over her shoulder. "I'm desperate."

I try to hold it in, but I can't. "Oh, Ivy, acknowledging the problem is the first step. Bravo." I do a slow clap.

"I knew this was a bad idea," she mutters as she starts walking down the apartment building stairs. I look back at Amani, completely flabbergasted, and use sign language to ask, *Do I stop her? What is happening?* Silent communication definitely comes in handy at times like this.

Amani shrugs, looking just as confused as I am. I definitely have zero desire to have my mortal enemy in my sacred space, though I am puzzled (and admittedly intrigued) by what could've brought her here.

"Ivy!" I call out. Damn curiosity! I hear her stop somewhere on the second floor. "C'mon, now. Tell Auntie Amber what's wrong."

She hesitates, then huffs dramatically as she makes her way back up, glaring at me as she enters.

"Please, come in." I gesture sarcastically.

She barely surveys our quaint apartment, not even peeping into my mom's office, which is right off the living room and filled to the brim with every supply needed to start a Wiccan apocalypse. Yup, just a totally normal home.

"So this is where you live," Ivy says, keeping her limbs

close, like she doesn't want to accidentally brush up against something.

"Obviously."

"And you have friends?"

"Yes. Shocking, I know." I wave at Amani and Kim, who are in stunned silence over the sudden vibe change to our gathering. "Say hi, friends."

They both wave robotically. The whole thing is going really great.

"So, um, what can we do you for, Ivy?" I ask, my thirst for knowledge waning. "I can whip up some poisoned brownies if you're hungry."

She gives me the evil eye, which in her case, is just her eyes. It must be hard, I guess, to be a siren and not have people fall all over you like normal. Since Amani and I are mystilogically inclined, Ivy can't pull her usual mental manipulation on us, and Kim's doing her best to blend into the background. We've mapped out a Manchester survival guide for Kim, with Ivy starring as Public Enemy Number One (we even drew her as an Ursula-esque sea urchin). Kim has transferred to many schools, so she's pretty street savvy on her own, but even having lived on different continents never alerted her to the presence of earthbound supernaturals. When she learned of our particular strains of magic, Kim opted to stay out of any future forecasting or matchmaking, declaring she desired a life "full of surprises." This proved to be incredibly fortunate for me, seeing as how revealing her match would bring me a life "full of devastation."

"I'm here because of my sister," Ivy finally admits, though it's clear how much it physically pains her to do so.

"Iris?" I ask, memories bubbling in my brain. Iris was a senior when we were freshman. While she didn't abuse her siren abilities during high school the way Ivy does, Iris was still adored, successful, and drop-dead gorgeous. She was student body president and gave many rousing speeches during her last year at Manchester, her words managing to reach even the most cynical of souls (mine). Iris had a stage presence that couldn't be taught; when she spoke, you listened, but not in an against-your-will, bow-before-the-queen way. Every time she spoke, it was clearly from the heart; even if she was using her siren charms to boost her appeal, there's no magic that can duplicate authenticity. I remember listening to her speak about school pride and how every person can make a difference, and as a result, I almost signed up for the environmental club. That's how good she was: I nearly participated in a school organization.

But that's not why I remember her.

It may be hard to believe, but I wasn't always the self-assured, amazing matchmaker I am now. During freshman year, I was still very much struggling with getting my powers in line, learning when I should spread the love and when to keep my mouth shut. Since everyone around me was dating and I could know every blossoming relationship was doomed to fail, I save people the heartbreak by ending things before they began. But as it turns out, ninth-grade girls aren't into hearing a total stranger reveal that their crushes are douche bags. In my effort to help, I got bullied. A lot.

On one particularly wonderful afternoon, a group of girls cornered me behind the auditorium. Things had evolved beyond the typical girl-on-girl violence of backstabbing and spreading rumors, to actual physical violence. Four floozies with razor-sharp nails were about to beat the crap out of me, when Iris walked by. She stepped in mid-punch and spoke about sisterhood and how ladies need to stick together. Miraculously, they listened and didn't bother me anymore. I never saw Iris again—her graduation came quickly after—but I never forgot her selfless act of kindness.

"Yes," Ivy confirms. "She's getting married."

"Well, mazel tov," I offer. "I know a great caterer."

"NO!" she responds with unnecessary volume. Amani, Kim, and I brace ourselves. "This wedding CANNOT happen."

"And why is that?"

"Because! Her girlfriend is not good for her, okay? You have to understand; she's making a huge mistake."

Oh great. Here we go again. Am I somehow putting out off-brand messaging? Do I need to switch from matchmaking to match*breaking*?

"What makes you think that?" Amani asks. "I mean, you're not just jealous that your sister is stealing the spotlight with her wedding planning?"

An excellent question, and definitely something I wouldn't put past Ivy. I'm not about to jump into some big family drama just because she has to play a supporting character for once.

"What?" Ivy snaps. I swear the room temperature drops ten degrees. "Are you for real? What kind of person do you think I am?"

"Well . . ." I start.

"Don't answer that. This isn't about me. Iris is too young and too beautiful to throw her life away for Brooke. My whole family is just standing by, and I've gone to every shaman and warlock I can think of. No one will help me. You are, for better or worse, my only hope."

I pause, letting the last few words hang sweetly while Ivy stews. When I don't answer, she adds an impatient, "So??"

"Hold on, I'm trying to savor this moment." I take one giant breath, exhaling slowly. "Ah, yes. I feel good about this."

"What does that mean? You'll help? Or you're just relishing my pain?"

"Both, actually."

"Ugh, you are sick. This makes me sick."

"It will cost you, you know."

"Oh, trust me, I know. I can already feel a knife slicing my pride."

I smile. "I meant dollars. But that's an acceptable payment as well." Ivy rolls her eyes. "Just bring Iris by Windy City for a reading there."

"Fine." Ivy bolts for the door, not saying good-bye or anything more. We sit in silence for a minute, letting the weirdness dissipate.

"Good Gods, are you really going to help her?" Amani eventually asks.

"Yeah, although I'm looking at it less like I'm helping Ivy, and more like I'm helping her sister. And if it turns out Iris is already with her match, it will piss Ivy off, which is a win-win if I ever saw one."

Kim laughs, releasing angelic tones that could summon woodland creatures. Sometimes I wonder if her insides are actually made of sugar. "That's going to be some session. I feel like Ivy will lose it if this doesn't go her way."

"Oh, they'll both question it, for sure," Amani adds. "A matchmaker telling a siren how to live her life? No way."

"Ivy will have to accept it. I mean, have you ever been wrong before, Amber?" Kim asks. Now there's the million-dollar question. A few months ago, I would have been offended, defending my abilities with my final breath. Matchmaking had always been an absolute, a function so central to my being that to question it would mean questioning my existence. But now I debate it daily, constantly rolling certain events and scenes in my head before I fall asleep. Have I ever led lovers astray? The possibility haunts me. I long for my past certainty, where I could brush off doubt like flour off a rolling pin. These days, the only thing I know for sure is that every time I'm with Charlie, my feelings for him shake me to the core. His companionship and affection are things I not only crave, but that make me a stronger, better version of myself. But that doesn't change what I see in his eyes. The Fates, those bastards, are taunting me with this push and pull, leaving me with riddles and forcing me to live a puzzle. Have I ever been wrong before?

Good Gods, I hope so.